SUNDOWN TOWN

A Novel

*"If history were taught in the form of stories,
it would never be forgotten."*
~ Rudyard Kipling

Kevin Corley and Douglas E. King

Best Wishes,

Kevin Corley

NOVELS BY KEVIN CORLEY

Coal mine wars. They were every bit as brutal and bloody as the American Old West. These books will take you down into the dark, dirty and dangerous coal mines with cave-ins, explosions and poisonous gases. And if you think it'll be safe on the surface, you're wrong. There'll be gunfights, bombings, and even a full scale battle with ten thousand armed coal miners fighting for the right to unionize.

SIXTEEN TONS – Italian immigrants Antonio and Angeline Vacca are set on raising their four sons to be strong union supporters. Meanwhile, quiet and secluded Joe Harrison, Antonio's hand-loading partner, chooses to become a company man after he witnesses mass brutality by some of the union members. For the next three decades, families and communities across the mining towns of America are torn apart by the unending bombings and gunfights that follow, killing too many too young.

"Kevin's words bring to life the dreams and aspirations of the men, women and children who lived our labor history... This is a part of American history that needs to be remembered." **Richard L. Trumka**, President, AFL-CIO

"*Sixteen Tons* is at its best when describing work, culture, leisure, and everyday life in close-knit Illinois mining communities...Strong women characters also add to the book, as does Corley's handling of immigration and race... His writing is fresh and engaging as the saga unfolds. Sixteen Tons is an entertaining way to learn a lot about this chapter in history." ***Labor Notes***

THROW OUT THE WATER – continues the saga of the Vacca, Eng, Harrison and Hiler families as they choose sides in the bloody Christian County Coal Mine War that took place in Illinois from 1933 to 1937.

DEDICATION

Kevin's Dedication:

For
Nolan Corley and Camille Meads

Also to:
Tim Sheard of *Hard Ball Press* for believing in me

and to
Sandy Tritt of *Inspirations for Writers* for making me a
better writer.

Doug's Dedication:

To my best friend and loving wife Pamela, retired history
teacher who is my loving history partner.

And the Springfield & Central Illinois African American
History Museum, the vehicle I've ridden as I've traveled
the roads of African American history.

Also special thanks to the following historians without whose research this book would not have been possible:

Burhorn, Eleanor, "Strike of Coal Miners at Pana, Illinois 1898-1899", (St. Louis: Dissertation, Washington University, 1949)

Meyerholz, Millie. "When Hatred and Fear Ruled-- Pana", Illinois: The 1898-99 Mine Wars", 2001

Gluck, Elsie. *John Mitchell, Miner: Labor's Bargain with the Gilded Age*. New York: John Day Co., 1929

Moreno, Paul D. *Blacks and Organized Labor: a New History*, (Baton Rouge: LSU Press, 2008) 61

Swantner, Vera. "Caught in the Crossfire"

Feurer, Rosemary. "Remember Virden! The Coal Mine Wars of 1898-1900", Teacher's Guide 2013

Hicken, Victor. "The Virden and Pana Mine Wars of 1898", *Journal of the Illinois State Historical Society* 1959

Lenstra, Noah. "The African-American Mining Experience in Illinois from 1800 to 1920." IDEALS @ Illinois University of Illinois, 2 Feb. 2009. Web. 02 May 2014

Loewen, James W. *Sundown Towns: A Hidden Dimension of American Racism*, Touchstone Press, 2005

Suppan, Heinz-Dietrich. *Pana: The Crossroads of Crisis*. Outskirts Press, Inc. 2017

SUNDOWN TOWN

A Novel

Kevin Corley and Douglas E. King

THE MAJOR CHARACTERS

While most characters are based on real men and women, many names have been altered whenever the authors chose to fictionalize them for dramatic purposes.

* Means their names have **not** been altered from the real historic characters.

AFRICAN AMERICAN STRIKEBREAKERS

* **Henry Stevens** – Called Big Henry. Sometimes spelled Stephens.
Garfield Wallace – Big Henry's mining partner.
Myrtle Jane Wallace – Garfield's wife with four sons.
Fanny May Cahill– Prostitute.
OTHERS: Swain Whitfield, Bucktooth Daniels, Quits Simpson, Sonny Joles, *Ike Alexander, *Lindsey Duncan, *Louis Hook, *Julia Dash.

WHITE & ANTI-UNION

Jeb Turner– Deputy who protects the Negro strikebreakers.
George Eubanks – The power behind the coal mine operators.
Toby Eubanks– The idle-minded 20-year old son of George Eubanks.
Howard Smithson– Owner of Springside Mine.
Frank Cogburn- The sheriff's son and Jeb Turner's best friend.
* **Samuel Brush**– Coal mine operator in Carterville, Illinois.

WHITE & PRO UNION

Tom Downs– Union leader in Pana, Illinois.
Rachel Downs- Tom's wife.
Holiday Jones- Tom Downs' right-hand man.
* **"General" Alexander Bradley**- Famous labor leader.
* **John Mitchell**- At age 28 he became UMWA national president from 1899-1909.
* **John Hunter**- Illinois UMWA president.

NEUTRALS

*Governor John Tanner- Supported the union as well as Negro rights.
Captain Gibbs- National Guard leader.
Reverend Horace James- Black leader of the Anglo-African Association.
Doctor Mills- Well-loved physician in Pana. Doctored both sides.

August, 1898

Garfield Wallace had learned reading from his great aunt, but she died before he could gain much mastery. Still, with all the confidence he could muster, he attempted to read the big sign that was tacked to the public outhouse and labeled *COLORED*.

"Wanted," he read aloud, emphasizing each syllable. "One-hundred seventy-five good colored miners."

The other black men huddled around muttered their excitement.

Garfield paused and worked silently on figuring out the next sentence. His friend Big Henry Stevens hushed the men more quickly than Garfield would've liked. He had friended Big Henry because Henry was big, an asset in the coal mine, but a hindrance when his size brought about an instant hush and therefore less time to decipher the words on the poster. He decided to improvise.

"It says here they will pay as much as three dollars seventy-five cents a day."

"How much a ton?" Big Henry asked.

If Big Henry took the job, most others would follow. Besides his formidable size, Henry Stevens had a style of leadership that normal men couldn't ignore. When Big Henry hefted a pickaxe across his shoulder, all the other men would do the same—and were quick about it, too.

"Thirty cents a ton," Garfield said, rubbing his bald head, a habit he'd had since he started losing his hair at seventeen. Excitement always brought on the head-rubbing. When he'd married Myrtle eleven years ago, he rubbed the last of his hair right off. Then when the first of four sons was born the following year, he wore a little patch of skin right off the top of his forehead. Now, the prospect of thirty cents a ton for loading coal had him rubbing his head with both hands at once.

The men were excited too, and those without a chaw in their mouths whistled. Most of them had learned mining skills while serving time in the state lock-up. Big Henry was one of the exceptions.

"Where 'bouts they paying that much? I surely want to know. I do, for a fact," Swain Whitfield asked. Swain had been a muleskinner since his slave days and now used the skill to pull coal out of the mine.

"Illinois," Garfield read, putting a whistling noise at the end of *Illinois*.

"Just don't make no sense." Big Henry shook his head. "Why would they hire colored miners? There's plenty of white folks up that way who can mine."

"I don't want to walk into no labor fight. I surely don't." Swain's head bopped up and down in agreement. "Do it say anything on there about a labor fight, Garfield? Do it?"

Garfield didn't know how to answer without more time to decipher the writing.

A clanking noise caused the miners to turn away from the poster. A chain gang of about twenty Negroes filed two abreast through the middle of the brick road toward them, the metal hobbles around their ankles making a sound that was all too familiar on the streets of Birmingham. The prisoners wore dirty and oversized striped shirts and pants. Their heads were down, as were their eyes, as they shuffled their feet in rapid synchronization. A fall on the streets would result in a severe lashing.

"Why, they got ol' Beau, they do," Swain said when an old man shuffled past them supported by a young prisoner of stout proportions. "What he do? He the most righteous man I ever knowed. I surely do say."

Garfield took advantage of the distraction to turn back to study the poster.

"They says ol' Beau looked at Missy Testerman with intent," Big Henry said. "They didn't explain what he intended."

"It must have been murder," Swain said quietly. His eyes showed white all around. He made sure no one but his friends heard him. "Ain't no man alive would look at ugly Miss Testerman with any thought except manslaughter. She one evil white gal. She surely is."

Swain was cautious when it came to such matters. Besides mule skinning, the old Negro had a talent for dice, whiskey and deflowering young girls; sins that he practiced regularly and in that very order.

When two well-dressed white men came with purpose toward the coloreds, Swain ducked quickly behind Big Henry.

"You boys coal miners?" The thinner of the two men asked. He wore breeches and high boots with a reddish collared waistcoat and a brown coat. Even with this casual outdoor outfit, he sported a tie.

Garfield had been so intent on unraveling the mysteries of the poster, he jumped a little when he heard the man speak. He immediately drooped his shoulders and lowered his head so as to avoid eye contact with the white men.

Big Henry bunched his fists and scowled at the rest of the Negroes cowering in the same manner as Garfield. He stepped past them and stood looking down into the watery, red eyes of the thin man. The white skin on the man's almost skeletal face was tight to the bone. As he looked up, Big

Henry's mouth tightened downward with an arrogant who-the-hell-do-you-think-you-are look.

"I'm Mr. Howard Smithson," the man said, emphasizing the *mister*. "I had these signs posted. The war in Cuba has drained our work force, and we need coal miners."

"You paying our colliers a decent wage for a decent day's work?" Big Henry asked without softening his deep, baritone voice.

"That's right," Smithson said. "In a little town called Pana, Illinois."

Garfield had just deciphered the name of the town as Pan-a, but this man pronounced it Pain-a.

"How those white folks up yonder goin' to treat us?" Big Henry asked.

Smithson pointed to the chain gang down the street. An elderly white woman had just hooked her umbrella around old Beau's ankle chain, tripping him. The guard flogged him while the white citizenry laughed and threw rocks at the old Negro.

"You'll be treated a lot better than you're being treated in this godforsaken country," Smithson said. "Be at the rail station Monday morning at nine o'clock. Wives and children are welcome and may be employed as rock pickers—as long as their men are in good standing."

Without another word, Smithson spat onto the sidewalk. The two white men turned and walked away.

***

That evening, Sebastian's juke joint was hopping. It was little more than a ramshackle former horse stable, but the tin roof was sound and its hard-to-find location on the edge of the lake made it an ideal gathering spot for Birmingham's colored folks. Like many other miners, Garfield brought his whole family most every Saturday night. His four boys fished or played with the other children while Garfield and his wife Myrtle drank moonshine and danced to the music from whatever musicians were sober enough to perform.

Big Henry didn't dance. Many a female had tried without success to court him, but he would have nothing of it. Some thought his indifference might be because he'd been kicked in the groin by a mule when he was a child. Truth be told, Henry Stevens' greatest pleasures were good mash whiskey, hard physical labor, and fighting. An anger burned inside that he didn't fully understand. Usually it was directed toward white men, but since he couldn't satisfy himself that way without getting lynched, he relieved his fury in other ways.

He sat at the bar waiting for the brawl that inevitably came every Saturday night a few hours or so after midnight. The bar was just a long two-by-twelve piece of lumber with three big barrels holding it a few feet above the floor. Sitting beside it made Henry feel awkward, like sitting in a grade school desk, an honor he'd never known, since his father hadn't allowed him to attend school. Maybe if he sat there long enough, someone would poke fun at him and get the row started. Win or lose, a good fistfight would always raise Big Henry's spirits when he got down in the dumps. He was sick of Birmingham. The more he thought about mining for coal in Illinois, the better it sounded. He'd heard that Northern white folks were more tolerant of coloreds.

Quits Simpson, the bartender, distracted Big Henry's thoughts by holding a bottle in front of his face. "I want you to taste some of the best squeezin's so delivered, Big Henry. Just don't go smokin' near da sheep dip whiskey."

Quits wore a fancy billycock with a feather on the side as he worked the bar. This irritated Big Henry, who thought the hat made him look like a manservant for a white plantation owner.

"Make it a double," Big Henry ordered.

Quits filled the glass two fingers high.

Henry downed the shot in a single toss. "*Whooee!*" he shouted. "Somebody definitely soured the mash." Despite the bitter taste, Henry nodded at the glass, which was immediately refilled.

"Say, how'd you get a name like *Quits*, anyway?"

Big Henry asked.

"Well, when my ma was in labor with her twelfth child, she asked the doc what she should call it. He said if he was her, he'd call it quits."

Garfield walked off the dance floor and took the stool next to Big Henry. "Like a bunch of hens on an old biddy." He pointed to his wife, who'd joined a crowd of women chastising Julia Dash for dancing too close with Sybil Hook's husband. Julia was twice Louis Hook's age, although she retained a fine figure. Suddenly the group of women turned on Sybil's husband.

"Look at ol' Hooky." Big Henry pointed and laughed at the flirtatious husband trying to dance away from the slaps of the irate women's purses. "Why, he's jumpin' 'round like a grasshopper in a hen house."

Garfield took a swallow from the glass that Quits placed in front of him, but promptly spat half of it on the floor. "Whatever boot dey poured that drink out of still has somebody's foot in it." He hocked and gave a healthy spat toward a slimy spittoon.

"You need to clean that spittoon, Quits," Garfield added.

"Wouldn't do no good," Quits said. "It'd just get dirty again. Besides, you need to clean your own soul before you criticize others."

"Is this a saloon counter you're standin' behind or a church pulpit?" Garfield asked.

"I'll be getttin' on that train to Illinois," Big Henry announced, his head swaying slightly from excess drink. "I'll not stay in a state where a colored man gets locked away so's these crackers'll have someone to fix their roads."

Big Henry had a double reason for hating white men. His mother had been a half-breed Comanche squaw until a regiment of buffalo soldiers raided her camp, leaving all of her family dead. She would have died too, except that Henry's father found her curled up under a rock, trying to get a dead baby to suckle on her dry teats. The woman was out of her head after watching the massacre, and the child wasn't even her own. Being a sergeant, Homer Stevens had the authority to give the Indian woman a chance for life. After comforting her for a few days, she accepted him as her new master. He took her with him when he mustered out and returned to his Birmingham home. She died giving birth to Henry, who entered the world at well over thirteen pounds. His father hired young mothers to take care of the boy until he was eight years old. By then, he was already big enough to go down in the coal mine. Three years later, Homer died in a rock fall and left Big Henry alone in the world.

Garfield had just been released from lockup the week Henry's father died. He took the young boy as a partner in one of the few mines that hired

Negroes. Though he was ten years older than Big Henry, they got along well and worked together for twelve years, during which time Garfield married and sired four healthy boys.

Now, Garfield nodded. "I been thinking I be doin' the same." He held up his glass. "I'll take Myrtle and the boys, too, by golly."

The two men clanked glasses together, threw the contents into their mouths and swallowed hard. They were giving their heads a furious shake when Myrtle joined them. She sat on her husband's lap. Myrtle Jane was a feisty little lady that talked more than most women and liked to give her husband as much sass as he gave her.

"Garfield Wallace," Myrtle said, "that story you told earlier wasn't as funny as the one when you kicked your mule in the butt."

"Why was that one so funny?" Garfield asked.

"It wasn't funny," Myrtle said with a giggle, "'til the mule bit you in the ass."

"He was story tellin', was he, Myrtle?" Big Henry asked, a big toothy smile on his face. He leaned back in his chair until it creaked dangerously.

"Yeah." Myrtle rubbed her husband's bald head. "He sure did tell his detestable stories to any coal miner who would listen. 'Course, he had to keep buyin' 'em rounds to stop 'em from wanderin' away."

"Ah, you're just funnin' me, gal," Garfield said, "cause you know I spotted you rubbing your rump up against Ike Alexander when we was a dancin'."

"You mad at me?" The pout on Myrtle's face displayed no denial of the accusation. She was a fine figure of a woman, even after birthing four sons. She wore her favorite narrow, gored skirt that made men and even women stare at her hourglass shape.

"Why, I'm mad enough that if I had two bullets in a gun and caught you with another man," Garfield said and paused for a hiccup, "I'd shoot *you* twice."

"You'd better hope you'd have a gun," Myrtle said, hands on hips, "'cause otherwise I'd break you into more pieces than you could sweep up with a leaf rake."

"Well," Garfield's said, his head floating drunkenly from side to side, "would you bury me, or would you not trouble yourself?"

"I suppose that if you fell down a hole," Myrtle said, "I might kick a little dirt over you."

Garfield straightened his bowtie to get his conceit back. Luckily for him, several of the musicians suddenly hit sour notes all at the same time. Everyone in the juke joint looked around to see what had caused the lapse in what was usually a faultless performance.

Big Henry wasn't yet so drunk that he failed to notice Myrtle punish her husband with a hard elbow to the chest as Garfield stared at the girl in the waist-tight red dress who had just entered the establishment. Her shoulders were scandalously bare but for two thin straps that prevented the material from slipping from her ample bosom.

Fanny May Cahill had just turned sixteen. Her pa had been trying to get her married off for two years, but her sassy disposition had ran off all her prospects. Big Henry judged by her present demeanor that her marital status was not about to change.

"Have you ever saw the likes of this weather?" Fanny said, waving a purple fan in front of her pretty face. "Why, it's hotter than a grocery store in August."

"I heard she does the naughty," Big Henry whispered as he nudged his friend with an elbow.

"I wouldn't know about that." Garfield didn't like to gossip. "But I do know that gal surly is a caution."

As Big Henry suspected, Sonny Joles was the first lady's man to try his hand with Fanny. There was something about Sonny's smile that Big Henry didn't like. It came too easy and seemed to try too hard to impress. It was said Sonny liked to wear big belt buckles, but if he did, his belly concealed them. He also liked to swing a stiff right leg. Everyone knew that beneath his baggy britches he sported either a knife or a bottle, depending on the occasion. Big Henry guessed that tonight it would be a bottle of moonshine, so he decided to goad the fat man a little.

"Sonny Joles!" Big Henry yelled, "you walk like your foot's asleep!"

"Why, I'd be," Sonny said bravely, being he was a good twenty feet from the muscular man, "I'd be boxin' your ears if you wasn't so t-tall, Big Henry Stevens."

Big Henry stood and removed his sack coat. The white and blue striped shirt beneath it was a couple of sizes too small, making the muscles in his arms and chest appear even more formidable.

"You sure is a tall drink of water, Big Fist Henry Stevens," Fanny said. "You fixin' to fight for me, Big Fist Henry?"

"Nope," Big Henry said, "I'm fixin' to fight 'cause the sun's almost up and I've been sittin' too long." With that, he folded his sack coat and turned to lay it on the bar. He had just given the fat man a good licking little more than a month ago. Henry knew that if he gave the man's slow brain enough time to recognize an advantage, he would quickly act.

A moment later, Sonny charged Big Henry and head butted him in the backside, driving him hard onto one end of the bar. That side of the heavy piece of lumber crashed to the ground, but the other end seesawed upward and caught Bucktooth Daniels under the chin with such velocity his eye teeth were driven right through his bottom lip.

Women shrieked and scattered for the door. A few of the older men grabbed their drinks and scrambled after the women. Since Sonny had accidently knocked himself unconscious with his own vicious head-butt, Big Henry grabbed Ike Alexander, who was the next biggest man in the room, and slammed a hard right into his jaw. Fights broke out indiscriminately throughout the establishment. Less competent boxers were quickly dispatched into the lake. The air was suddenly filled with bottles and chairs.

"Help me save da whiskey!" Quits shouted.

Garfield found refuge behind the bar and used a short two-by-four to help Quits block flying objects that threatened the row of bottles along the back wall.

The melee lasted for ten minutes. The fight was just waning down as the sun came up and the distant clanging of a church bell brought instant quiet to every man, woman and child in the valley.

"Lord, all-mighty," Myrtle said as she and several other women walked back into the juke joint. "Is it that time already?"

The women moved about the tavern, picking up bottles. Others swept the wooden floor. Two men raised the big piece of lumber, placed it back on the barrels, then joined the other men who were gathered around the horse trough to clean the blood off their faces.

Down at the lake, some of the older girls woke up the youngest children, who were lying in the grass, and ordered them to get themselves groomed. Garfield and Myrtle's boys didn't take to the rude awakening and began running around pulling the girls' pigtails. The women, meanwhile, patted their hair into shape and stuck long pins through decorative hats.

Big Henry was one of the few men who didn't move. With no intention to attend the preaching, he found a stout tree to lean against. He had learned the scriptures from his father and put little stock in the words of men more interested in collecting money than saving souls. Placing his jacket along one side, he rested the left cheek of his sore butt against it.

"What started all this?" Garfield shook his head. "I swear, if you put Sonny's brains in an owl's head, he'd fly backwards."

"I objected to Mr. Jole's obnoxious behavior." Big Henry moved his clenched fists in a boxing motion. "I wanted to converse, and he wanted to fight. I reckon he beat me to the punch. But a one-two combination to his nose and jaw quickly settled the matter in question."

"That's a tall tale and you knows it, Big Henry," Garfield said. "Unless you sucker punched him with the cheek of your ass when no one was a lookin'."

"That fight was just way too violent," Quits Simpson chimed in, wiping the bar with a dirty rag. "When Bucktooth got knocked in the lake, he was bit by a water snake. I didn't know which to fix first—the bite on his ass or the teeth sticking out of his chin."

"I been to dozens of cock and dog fights," Bucktooth said. He had walked toward them when he heard his name. Dripping wet, he held a kerchief against his chin. "But I ain't never seen the likes of this before. That Fanny May Cahill is sure 'nuff the most look-some-ness gal in the county, that's all there's to that, by golly."

Bucktooth wiped the water off his bowler hat. It was the pride and joy of his wardrobe. It had a rattlesnake skin wrapped around the brim. He liked to tell people it was the same snake that bit him in the upper lip when he was a child and that was why his eyeteeth grew several times longer than normal.

"You shoulda grabbed hold of that water snake while ago when he bit your ass," Quits said. "You coulda made a belt or somethin' outa his skin to go with that hat of yours."

"Ain't nobody in town got more look-some-ness than Fanny May, but her morals is plain ugly, that's a fact, fer sure," Garfield whispered to Big Henry. He rose from the ground and brushed himself off. Myrtle came out of the juke joint, took

his arm, and the two joined their four sons following the crowd along the dirt road and up the hill to
Sunday worship.

2

On August 25, the first train of colored strike-breakers were to arrive in Pana, Illinois. It was also Deputy Sheriff Jeb Turner's twenty-fifth birthday, a coincidence that he regretted, since it meant he had to spend the entire day protecting a group of Negroes he would just as soon have seen lynched.

"The two people I hate worst in the whole world are niggers and strikebreakers," his friend Frank Cogburn said. He lay his Winchester beside Jeb's and waited for the train personnel to finish their business at the Tower Hill watering tower.

"Have you ever met a colored?" Jeb asked. He pulled some tobacco fixings from his pocket and started rolling a cigarette.

"Well, I've never been formally introduced to one, if that's what you mean." Frank preferred a chaw to a smoke, and gave a long, dark spit toward a wasp hole in the ground. "But I know they's a despicable race."

"I'd imagine so." Jeb nodded. He'd once asked the teacher of his one-room school why they couldn't just send the coloreds back to Africa. Old

Mrs. Allen had patiently explained that the Negro was now the white man's burden. Because they had been kept in slavery for so long, the Africans had forgotten their survival skills. She said it was just like if you raised a wild bear in your home and then turned him loose into the woods. The bear would be dead within a week. Since the brains of the blacks were not as fully developed as the white man, it just would not be Christian to send them back to the jungles of Africa.

"But I don't begrudge their color as much as I do they's being a scab," Frank added with another spit. "Taking a job away from another man is the lowest form of scum."

"Well, your pa seems to think it's his job to keep the peace," Jeb shrugged, his eyes wide. "Plus, I be making two dollars a day—even if they's nigger scabs I'm securin'."

The two men, along with six other deputies, had arrived an hour earlier at Tower Hill by way of a big hay wagon pulled by two powerful draft horses. Frank's father, Sheriff Ira Cogburn, told them they would be riding shotgun on the train for the remainder of the journey into Pana. There was no trouble expected—unless someone had tipped off the United Mine Workers that this train was carrying the first of the Negro strikebreakers.

"This miners' union ain't gonna last much longer," Sheriff Cogburn reassured his deputies.

"They only organized a few years ago, and if the panic in '93 hadn't put so many men out of work, there'd be nothin' for unions to bitch about."

Jeb had known and respected Frank's father as long as he could remember. After his own parents died when he was fifteen, Jeb spent many days and nights at the Cogburn home. That was why, when the community divided between union and non-union, he had decided to side with the coal company. Still, he feared the sheriff might be underestimating the mine workers. Across the United States, they were now thirty thousand strong and growing.

When the engineer used the rope on the pulley to swing the water trough away from the steam engine, the sheriff signaled his deputies to board by twos onto each platform of the railcars.

Being second in command, Jeb followed the sheriff into his assigned passenger car. The first dark-skinned persons he saw were a woman and a young boy of about five years of age. It had never occurred to him the strikebreakers would bring families. The little boy smiled at him. It was a big, white, toothy smile like the ones Jeb had seen on the faces of children when they saw someone they admired. Every wooden seat of the coach was filled with men, women and children, the latter often sitting on a parent's lap. The crying of a baby came from somewhere.

Jeb was further surprised by how well-dressed and mannerly the Negroes were. He didn't know for sure what he'd expected, but they didn't look much different from white folks he'd seen on trains.

"In about ten minutes, you folks are going to need to duck down below the windows," the sheriff said in a commanding voice. "I don't want nobody raising up until I tell you to."

"What for we need do that?" a voice in the third row asked. A broad-shouldered black man stood, his head nearly touching the ceiling.

"Pana is a union town," Sheriff Cogburn said. "Folks don't take kindly to scabs around these parts."

"Ain't nobody said nothin' 'bout us comin' here to be no strikebreakers," the black man said. "We came here to mine this here coal, that's all."

"Well, someone told you wrong," Cogburn said. "You're scabs now, and if you wanna stay alive, you'll do exactly as I tell you."

A well-dressed Negro wearing a bowler hat with a rattlesnake brim stood. The fingers of his hands were interlocked but twitched rapidly against one another. "Mistuh officer, sir," Bowler hat said. "I'd like to just get on back home, if you doesn't mind, sir."

"You try to go back now and those union fellas will skin you alive." The sheriff walked back through the door and took up a spot on the front platform of the passenger car. "I'd rather stand out here than in there with those stinking darkies."

Since Cogburn had not invited him onto the platform, Jeb remained standing inside with the blacks. The two deputies in the back of the car followed his example and rested their rifle barrels against the crook of their elbows.

"What if there's shooting?" the big black man asked. "How we supposed to defend ourselves without no guns?"

"There ain't goin' to be no trouble, Big Henry," the bald man sitting across from him said. "They ain't no white men wantin' to get in trouble for shootin' defenseless colored folks. Is there, Mistuh Deputy?"

"They don't even know you're on the train," Jeb said loud enough for everyone to hear. "By the time the train stops, you'll all be within the safety of the mine yard. We've built a high stockade around it to protect you."

The one called Big Henry shook his head and growled, but his bald friend offered him encouraging words and he finally sat back down. The next several minutes passed with very little conversation in the passenger car. Jeb didn't like the look Big Henry was giving him, but he avoided the Negro's gaze as best he could. It never occurred to him the coloreds hadn't been told they were coming to Pana to be strikebreakers.

After several minutes, Sheriff Cogburn stepped back into the passenger car, nudged past Jeb and walked down the aisle. "All right, everybody," he said loudly. "Get down on the floor as low as you can."

There was a loud commotion as men and women pushed children and even babies as far under the seats as possible, then covered them with their own bodies. Big Henry was the only one who refused to follow directions. He remained straight up in his seat staring into the eyes of the sheriff.

"Damn your sorry black ass!" Cogburn shouted as he swung the stock of his rifle at Big Henry's head. "I said *get down!*"

The wood caught the big man behind his right ear and he slumped sideways into the seat. The bald man squatting next to him quickly wrapped an arm over his unconscious friend's back.

"I hope he don't wake up too soon," the woman next to him said. "Big Henry will be harder to handle than a mule on ice."

The conductor wasn't slowing the train or sounding the steam whistle as they neared the town, so Jeb followed the sheriff's example and ducked low to the window, his rifle barrel at the ready. Outside he saw the scene that had become familiar in Pana during the two months since the strike announcement. Lining the roads leading into the coal mine gates were nearly a thousand men, many of them holding picket signs.

When the strikers saw the train was not going to make its usual stop at the depot, they began shouting. Some threw picket signs at the passing cars. Others picked up rocks. Glass broke, followed by screams from some of the passengers.

Once it had rolled completely into the mine yard, the loud squeal of the brakes jerked the train to an abrupt stop. Jeb rushed out onto the platform, leapt to the ground and aimed his rifle toward the shouting that came from behind the caboose.

A hundred yards away, over a hundred company guards were in a pitched battle with strikers as they struggled to fight them back so they could shut the mine gate. Men on both sides swung clubs, and a few on the company side threatened with rifles and pistols. Wives of the picketers were also active, striking the stockade fence with sticks and shouting insults at the strikebreakers.

No sooner than the gate was shut, gun shots sounded. Jeb ducked low as he raced toward the mine tipple, and then took two steps at a time until he stood at the top, looking down into the town. From his vantage point he could see over the eight-foot high wooden stockade wall. He jumped when a gunshot splintered wood near his feet.

"They're firing at us from the opera house!" one of the deputies standing guard shouted.

Jeb aimed his rifle and joined several of the other company guards cocking their Winchesters and firing randomly toward the sides of the buildings in the distance. Being at the top of the tipple, they could see the chaos occurring throughout half the town. Women struggled to pull their children to the safety of buildings. The hundreds of strikers screaming and yelling from the streets in front of the mine would have been easy pickings, even for Jeb, who wasn't a very proficient marksman. The orders from the mine bosses, though, had been explicit. Only shoot at union men if they fire upon you. Since none of those on the streets seemed to have artillery, Jeb and the other deputies shot only toward the white puffs of smoke that were always followed a second later by a crack or a ricochet somewhere near them.

After a few minutes, the shooting from both sides slowed and then stopped. The strikebreakers and their families ducked low as they were hastily ushered from the train and into the safety of the barracks.

Only when they were all inside did Jeb take a deep breath and squat on shaky legs, his back against the wall. Lighting up a cigarette, he looked to the distant buildings he had been firing toward. Someone had painted a message on the wall of one of them.

SCABS – LOOK AROUND FOR THE NEXT 50 YEARS – WE BE THERE ONE DAY

***

The run from the train to the barracks was the most frightening experience of Myrtle Wallace's life. She carried her youngest, while the two middle boys were pulled along behind her by their firm grasp on her skirt. Garfield and their eldest son were somewhere behind, since they had helped Quits and Bucktooth carry the still unconscious Henry Stevens. Another gunshot in the distance brought screams and angry shouts from the two hundred Negroes being ushered into the building.

"You women and children have a seat on the cots!" Sheriff Cogburn shouted as the blacks entered the building. "You men go stand in the back of the room!"

There was much commotion but very little talking as the men, women and children did as they were directed. Myrtle and her boys sat on the edge of a small bed in the middle of the big room. Big Henry was carried in and laid out on a cot.

"Don't be wasting a cot on that man!" The sheriff shouted.

Big Henry was coming around. He opened his eyes and shook his big head. Garfield and Quits Simpson lifted him to his feet and guided him to the back of the room.

Myrtle was glad that Big Henry was still dazed. She feared that if he saw the deplorable conditions of the barracks, he would have started a riot. The room seemed to have once been used for storage, and there had been little effort to clean it. The floor was nothing but gravel and a little coal slack. There were no windows. The walls bore a resemblance to the inside of a poorly built barn. Small to large spaces between the boards allowed rays of sunlight into the room. The only thing that seemed organized about the place were the three neat rows of dirty cots without pillows, each with a single green army blanket tucked beneath.

"Half you men will be assigned to start work in the mine tomorrow morning," Sheriff Cogburn announced. "The other half will receive training to help guard Springside Mine. Deputy Turner will make the decision as to your assignment. If you have a mine partner you've teamed with in the past, you may request to be assigned to work together.

"Males who are at least eleven years of age will be paid seventy-five cents a day as trapper boys or fifty cents a day as rock pickers. There will be no leaving the stockade until I deem it safe, and then you are to travel in groups and stay away from all union men and activities. Anyone not following my orders will be sent home without pay and by their own means."

Big Henry was beginning to evaluate his surroundings and understand the situation. Garfield moved closer to his friend and whispered something to him.

"Men of working age will sleep in the room through that entry." The sheriff pointed his Winchester toward a double door near the men. "There is to be no fraternizing in private with females while you live in the Springside stockade. When more workers arrive, you will be the first to go live in the quarters we are fixing up near the Eubanks mine."

Myrtle gave her husband a smile and a nod. Several of the women turned toward their own men, their simple glances causing chins to rise and chests to expand. Myrtle had every intention of being among the first to move out of the deplorable building. Her youngest, Sydney, who was four years old, had been born too early. He had never caught up and was still small and prone to sickness. Her oldest sons, Dobbs, ten, and Walter, eight, were the opposite. They were already big enough to work as rock pickers. But her number three son was her greatest concern. As hard as she tried to prevent it, the six-year-old was known throughout the colored community as Ornery Billy.

The white deputies separated the Negroes into groups for a tour of the facility. Myrtle spotted her Billy crawling beneath the beds toward the front of the room where Sheriff Cogburn stood directing his men. When Cogburn moved to follow his deputies, he fell with a loud crash onto one of the cots. The room grew hush. When a white man had an unfortunate accident in Alabama, a Negro was usually held responsible.

Deputy Jeb Turner rushed to the sheriff's side.

"Your boot must've got caught in this blanket roll, Sheriff." Jeb helped his superior to his feet.

All the Negroes except Myrtle and her sons quickly exited the building.

The sheriff grabbed the blanket, threw it across the room and stormed out of the stockade building.

Jeb retrieved the blanket. He was tucking it back under the cot just as Billy tried to snake his way back toward his mother.

Jeb reached quickly and lifted the boy up by his britches.

"Why, you young upstart! What's your name, son?" Jeb asked, holding the youngster at arm's length.

"Ornery Billy," the boy said. "What's yourn?"

"Your name's really Ornery Billy?"

"Nah, Ma says Billy's my name. Ornery is just my nature. Now you gonna let me go or ain't ya?"

Jeb set Myrtle's son down, smiled at his mother and followed the others out of the building.

***

That night Bucktooth Daniels snuck out of the stockade along with Sonny Joles, Ike Alexander and Quits Simpson. The four Alabamans' escape was inspired and aided by the wife of one of the union men. Rachel Downs had been with other picketers near the gate when the strikebreakers arrived and saw them run from the train to the mine building. She noticed the Negro with the bowler hat crying as he helped three others carry a giant of a man by his arms and legs. There was something about the man's hollow-eyed look of gloom that moved her.

Later she joined a contingent of woman picketers marching up and down near the front gate screaming insults about the coal company owners and their scabs. As dusk set in, a few Negro men emerged from the building, and through the gaps in the fence began retaliating with their own shouts at the protesters. Rachel moved along the barricade watching the deputies trying to get the coloreds to go back inside. That was when she spotted the Negro in the bowler hat walking toward the outhouse that wasn't too far from where she stood.

"My husband is a union man!" the woman shouted at Bucktooth when he ventured close enough to be heard. "If you and any of the others want to leave, I can have him meet you outside the front gate at midnight."

"Yes, ma'am." Bucktooth trembled. "I surely do wants to leave."

"He'll be wearing a white shirt with a red scarf," she said. "He'll even get the United Mine Workers to pay your way home."

Just before midnight, the four colored men pried loose one of the boards that protected the compound and squeezed through. They were quickly intercepted by Tom Downs and a dozen of his union friends.

"For your own safety, we're taking you to Brugger Union Hall," Downs said.

"Is there any food there?" Quits Simpson asked. "It shore is hungry out."

Though it was late, the union hall came quickly to life when Downs and his men showed up with the four black men in tow. The one named Ike Alexander drew the most attention. Alexander was well over six-foot-tall and so muscular his suit fit like rawhide work gloves. His look was not at all like what was on the face of the teary-eyed Bucktooth Daniels and Sonny Joles. Alexander was mean and wanted everyone to know it.

"Can we eat?" Quits asked again. "It shore is hungry out."

"Of course." Downs looked at one of the other union men. "Holiday, go tell the New Grand Restaurant to prepare a meal for four."

The one called Holiday Jones gave his boss a

puzzled look, but hastened out of the building. The hall was filling with curious union miners, so Downs summoned two of his associates to join him in a conference room with the four colored men. Once they were away from the crowd, Downs invited the two white men to sit with him on one side of the big mahogany table facing the Negroes, who remained standing.

"May I ask," Downs said with a smile, "what it was that prompted you Negroes to come to Pana as strikebreakers?"

"That Mistuh Howard Smithson and another white man was the ones who brung us," Sonny Joles said. "They had a Negro named Lindsey Duncan, who told us that these here Illinois mines was hiring 'cause so many men had gone off to fight da Spanish. He swore there weren't no union trouble at all. We asked him, we surely did. Oh, that Duncan, he was a fast talker. He said that if we didn't like these here mines, they's plenty of workers needed in Pana in the furniture factory and the iron works. Yes, sir, that's what he said, all right. Ain't it so, Ike?"

"I'll kill that smart ass nigger if I see him again," Alexander said.

Quits Simpson looked up at Ike, then back to Downs. "We ain't et in two days."

**

"We gonna send the darkies back to Alabama, boss?" Holiday Jones asked an hour later. He and Tom Downs sat in wooden chairs smoking and looking through the open door to the kitchen. The four Negroes stood at a table in the cooking area of the New Grand Restaurant eating a plate of cold fried chicken and a bowl of apples and bananas.

"Nah," Tom said, "let's send 'em back to the Springside Mine. Them niggers don't want to be here, and they can persuade some of the others to leave."

Quits dropped a banana on the floor and bent over to pick it up.

"Look at those savages eat," Tom said. "I'll bet that monkey eats that banana right off the floor."

Holiday Jones wasn't sure why his boss thought the Negro wouldn't eat it, since it hadn't been peeled yet.

"See, what'd I tell you?" Tom said when Quits peeled the banana and put it in his mouth. "Pure savages."

3

The next morning, Garfield and Big Henry followed the other miners to the tipple. Each carried a big silver lunch bucket. A few of the men had their own picks and shovels. As they stood in line waiting for their turn on the cage, they donned their gray canvas miner's caps and attached their oil wick lamps to them. The iron elevator that sat at the top of a wooden stairwell made Garfield think of a hangman's gallows. Next to it was the giant wheel with a thick steel cable wound around it. The lives of over a dozen men riding the cage each way depended on the strength of that cable. If it broke, the cage could plunge over seven hundred feet to the pit bottom—certain death for the men in it.

The black man assigned to work with the white cage operator was an old fellow that Garfield knew well. Louis Hooks brought a lifetime of experience taking care of elevators, as well as the steam engine that turned the wheel. Louis liked to carry a nail between his lips, a habit he picked up after one of his molars rotted and had to be pulled. The dentist had told him to keep his teeth clean, so he picked at them with the nail at every opportunity. Louis' familiar face gave Garfield considerable comfort as he stepped into the cage and the rapid descent began.

When they reached the bottom and the boss opened the gate, the usual taste of lingering coal dust in the air caused Garfield to breathe through his nose. He had a theory that nose hairs filtered out pollutants, and he refused to allow Myrtle to trim the hairs when she gave him haircuts. He was happy to see that at least the ground was dryer than the mines in the south. Back in Alabama, miners would wade through ankle deep water all day long. Their feet resembled dried prunes during the mining season.

Garfield saw one miner standing on his toes and holding an air tester just beneath the rocky top. Methane gas was among the miner's worse fears, and it was good to see the inspection being done.

The tops were propped with oak timbers that were strategically placed throughout the mine, especially in places that rang hollow when tapped with a pick. One black man as large as Big Henry knelt in the middle of an entryway sawing a log that was as thick as his powerful looking chest. When he was done, he lifted one end of the heavy timber onto a railcar, then the other with little more effort than a mother lifting her child into bed.

Four walkways stretched out in each direction, one of which housed a series of stalls where the mules lived out their lives. The animals only saw the Earth's surface for a few weeks each summer, at which time they had to be blindfolded and slowly reintroduced to the sunlight.

The mule drivers had their own room next to the stalls. That chamber doubled as a hospital where they could lay a fallen miner—if by chance his body were recoverable and he were still breathing.

Two of the white mule drivers were crippled old miners. They each had a crutch tied to one of their thighs, replacing the lower leg that had been amputated. Three others in the room were mule drivers, although their faces were already so covered with soot Garfield couldn't predict for certain their race or ages.

The chamber in the next entryway was filled with picks, handheld drills with six-foot bits, and wide square shaped shovels the miners called number two banjos. Garfield and Big Henry picked up brass lamps designed so the flame would grow brighter if harmful gases were in the area. They lit them in the entryway, since matches were forbidden in most other parts of the mine. If a lamp went out, the holder had a long, dark walk to an approved entryway to get it relit.

All of the entryway floors had two rails laid parallel. As Garfield and Big Henry followed the pit crew boss down the slope and deeper into the mine, a rumbling sounded and the tracks shuddered beneath their feet.

A mule train of coal cars approached. The men in front of them disappeared into the walls on either side, but the indentations were all full. The train thundered closer.

"Back here!" Garfield yelled. He and Big Henry raced back and jumped into an indentation just as a mule passed, pulling several cars full of coal along the tracks and up the semi-steep grade.

Garfield made a mental note to become acquainted with where the hollowed out areas were, lest they get squeezed to death between the heavy coal cars and the unforgiving walls.

After walking a couple of miles, Garfield heard explosions ahead of them. As the dust became thicker, he followed the example of the other men and covered his nose and mouth with his bandana. This coal company blasted all day long, and shouts of, "Fire in the hole!" could be heard at any time of the workday. When they heard the warning, most miners would brace themselves against a wall and pray the explosion wouldn't bring down the top they were standing beneath. Garfield had worked once in a mine that only blasted in the evening as the men were leaving. He liked that, since by the time they began work the next morning, the dust had settled and it was much easier to breathe.

After walking a little further, they approached the pit boss. He assigned two men at a time into chambers. When it came Garfield and Big Henry's turn, they went right to work getting prepared to load the three coal cars that were already waiting in a room that was about thirty by twenty feet in size.

The two miners had worked together for years in Alabama and had a good system. Big Henry laid down his shovel and using the head of his pick began sounding the top to make certain there were no hollow areas where the ceiling might fall on them. Meanwhile Garfield checked the walls and began pulling down loose rock. Once they were certain the chamber was safe they began loading the coal cars. Big Henry loaded a few of the larger chunks by hand while Garfield used his number two banjo to shovel smaller chunks. Then before the car was completely full, Big Henry would add more large chunks to tie the coal in. When they were filled, Garfield hooked one of their pit tags on the front of each car identifying it as having been loaded by them. The goal was to make the cars so tight the coal wouldn't bounce out on its way to the surface, where the company had a check-weighman to determine the cars weight and how much the miners who loaded it would be paid. If the car contained excessive rock and sulphur, the two miners would be docked. Garfield hoped the company checkweighman would be honest, or else the entire day's hard work could result in very little money.

When the chamber was nearly empty of larger coal chunks, they had to load the final car by using their number two banjos to shovel the coal slag that was left in the room. This effort would result in very little profit for them, since most of the coal would fall through the big screen shakers used to separate the big chunks from the small. The company would sell this slag and make a profit, but despite the back-breaking work, the miners received nothing for it. Still, the mine boss wouldn't allow them to move on to the next chamber until all the coal was loaded from the previous one.

At lunchtime, the two friends sat on rocks facing each other. The hot sweat on their bodies quickly cooled, since the temperature in the mine was only about sixty degrees. Myrtle had packed both their lunch buckets. There were two spacers in each bucket that created three compartments. The bottom compartment was filled with drinking water that also kept the food cool. When it was available, Myrtle used as much ice as would fit. The next compartment held hunks of ham and cheese and an apple. The top and thinnest compartment was for a piece of pie, but since there was a shortage of food on their first day in Pana, she had placed a single piece of black licorice.

"If I knows your woman," Big Henry said as he chewed slowly on his piece of licorice, "we'll come home to a good meal tonight."

***

"I'm goin' to town," Myrtle announced to Jeb Turner as she tied her sunbonnet strings. "I'm gonna have a good meal for our men when they come home tonight."

"I can't let you do that." Jeb stepped in front of the little woman. "It ain't safe."

The conversation had started at the mine gate when Myrtle Wallace walked past two dozen armed white deputies as if they weren't even there. Most of the colored women and children gathered when they saw the confrontation.

"You sure is right." Myrtle said, her hands on hips and her head bobbing back and forth as if it were about to fall off. "It ain't safe for you if you's tries and stop me."

The colored women gave a loud, "Oooo," and stepped around the sheriff deputies to get a better view of the discussion.

"I don't think the boss man knows her very good." One of the older ladies chuckled. "When Myrtle's head starts flopping around like some limber-necked chicken, you better watch out."

Jeb sensed that if he continued arguing, he

was going to look a fool, not only in front of the Negroes, but in front of the deputies.

"You have money?" he asked.

"I's got enough." Myrtle held up a small purse. "And a few things to barter."

"Okay," Jeb said. "You and I go alone. You stay with me, and you don't talk unless I tell you to."

"Humph," the old lady whispered to her friend, "good luck with that, Mistuh Boss Man."

No sooner had Jeb and Myrtle left the stockade than he recognized that this was easily the dumbest thing he'd ever done in his life. In just a few minutes, they were strolling down the boardwalk on Locust Street. Every face turned their way. People pointed and stared. Others burst from doorways to stand outside the buildings and watch. Jeb didn't know whether to walk a few steps in front or behind her, but he knew for certain that walking beside her was out of the question. Deciding she wouldn't know where to go, he held his Winchester in both hands and led the colored woman to O'Brien's Grocery Store. He figured that the affable Irishman might be more inclined to sell to a Negro. He was wrong.

"You can just turn right around and head on out that door, deputy," the heavy set and balding O'Brien said when they walked into the store.

"Why, Frosty O'Brien," Jeb said, "I never thought I'd see the day you'd turn out a paying customer."

"Well, I normally wouldn't," O'Brien raised his chin, "except that if I was to do business with one of them colored scabies, the union folks around here would run me out of town, they would."

"You'd better think twice about that," Jeb said, "Pretty soon there's likely to be a thousand or more folks in town with the same skin color as this one, and someone's gonna make money off feeding 'em."

The store was wall-to-wall with shelves, with barely enough room in the aisles to walk. Everything a local resident could possibly need was available, from water pumps, saddles, rifles and pistols to every type of food item imaginable, including big barrels of molasses, flour, apples and sweet corn. Jeb felt a little bad that soon the coal mine owners would reopen their company store and the miners would be required to purchase all their items from them at much higher prices.

O'Brien's young wife entered from the back room. Bette was nearly twenty years younger than her husband, and if the stories Jeb had heard were true, quite a bit smarter. The store was doing twice the business in the two years since their marriage.

"Mr. Turner. How good to see you," Mrs. O'Brien said. "And who is this beautiful lady with you?"

Jeb removed his hat and slicked his hair. "This would be..." He gave Myrtle a bewildered look.

"Missus Myrtle Wallace," Myrtle said. "I's

pleased to make your acquaintance, Missus O'Brien."

"Why, she's quite charming, Mr. Turner," Mrs. O'Brien said. "I take it you are married, Missus Wallace, or are you and Mr. Turner ... ?"

"No," Myrtle said, "I's married, Missus O'Brien, and I's come to purchase food for our miners."

"I was just tellin' Jeb here that we can't be selling to no coloreds," Mr. O'Brien explained, "or we'll lose business in this town."

"Of course, you are right, Mr. O'Brien." Mrs. O'Brien started to cross her arms, but then placed one elbow on her elegant wrist and caressed her chin with slim fingers. "But don't you think that no one would be the wiser if we were to divert one of our wagons to the back of the mine yard for a quick delivery?"

"Well, I suppose not," O'Brien said. He gave a long exhale and looked at Myrtle. "How many did you say you're fixin to feed?"

"Two hundred," Myrtle said as she took a wad of bills from her purse along with a long list.

"She say I's beautiful and charming." Myrtle said fifteen minutes later as they left the store. "I likes her."

Jeb looked at Myrtle, seeing her for the first time. Before hearing Mrs. O'Brien say she was beautiful, he had just thought of her as another colored woman. His mind had somehow imagined her lips to be too fat, but now he saw they were really only slightly full and even pleasant looking. The profile of her face was well-shaped and defined, perhaps even a little petite. But her eyes were what shocked him the most. When Mrs. O'Brien had complemented her, Myrtle's eyes had shown a brown warmth that Jeb had never seen on any woman.

"Deputy." A voice behind them interrupted his thoughts. "Arrest this woman."

Jeb spun around. Half a dozen men walked out of a tavern doorway.

Tom Downs, the one making the accusation, had been in school with Jeb and Frank Cogburn, and even friendly until the recent union trouble.

"What're you talkin' about, Tom?" Jeb asked. He stepped in front of Myrtle.

"She's a whore. She tried to do business with us," Tom said, then glanced over his shoulder at his friends. "Ain't that so, boys?"

The men behind him nodded and laughed.

"Why, she only got here yesterday," Jeb argued, "and she ain't left the stockade except with me not more than an hour ago."

"That's what you say," Tom said. He stepped forward and grabbed Myrtle's arm. "What? Did she give you a freebie, Deputy?"

Myrtle pulled away from Tom. Jeb sensed she was about to push his hand off her arm, an action that could land a black woman in prison in Illinois.

So Jeb struck first, landing a glancing blow to Tom's temple that seemed to startle him more than do harm.

Tom roared like a bear and charged Jeb, knocking him into the street, and then fell on top of him. The two locked arms and rolled beneath a tethered horse as they each struggled to improve their grip on the other. The startled mare whinnied and kicked at them with its back legs.

When Jeb bit Tom's ear, the two broke apart and jumped to their feet.

"Here now! Stop that!" A voice yelled. "What's going on here?"

Recognizing that it was old Doc Mills, Jeb backed up a step and Tom did the same, although they both retained their boxer's stance.

A large crowd had formed around the men. Myrtle stood with her head and eyes looking down toward the ground. She now recognized the immense danger she was in.

"He started it!" Tom shouted.

"No, you did!" Jeb screamed back, then felt silly when he realized it was the same words he and Tom had used many times when they'd been students together in Mrs. Allen's schoolhouse.

"Now that's enough, both of you," the doctor said sternly. "For Heaven's sake, I brought the two of you into this world, now don't make me regret it."

Tom placed a hand to his head, and when it made contact with his ear gave a loud, "Ouch!"

Jeb rubbed his chest where the horse had kicked him when they rolled beneath it. He wanted to make sure Doc Mills saw he too was hurt.

"Tom, you come with me to my office, and I'll stitch up that ear," Doc said.

Tom picked up his hat, dusted it off, and started toward the doctor's office. "Jeb, you rub some horse liniment on those ribs, and if you feel anything unusual, come see me in the morning." Doc Mill turned to the crowd and waved his hand. "Now go on, all of you. Get on home!"

As the crowd dispersed, Jeb joined Myrtle back on the sidewalk. "You didn't need to hit him, you know," she said under her breath as they continued walking.

"If I hadn't, you were going to," Jeb said, then added, "and if you had, they might have lynched you right there on the spot."

"You's a good man, Deputy Turner," Myrtle said. She dropped back a step so they wouldn't be seen walking side by side.

It was the first time in his life anyone had ever accused him of being a good man.

"Nothin' I wouldn't have done for a white woman," he said quietly.

***

That evening, Garfield and Big Henry were standing at the wash house trough cleaning their faces and arms when they heard Douglas Eubanks screaming at the mine inspector. "What do you mean that escape tunnel isn't safe?" Eubanks shouted. "It's the same as it's been the last three years you approved it."

"In the past several months there has been a water buildup about halfway through the tunnel," the inspector explained, "and it's deep enough a man could drown if he falls face down in it."

"We put a plank across the water," Eubanks said, pulling at the knot in his thin necktie. He was a big man. The three-piece suit was not made for a hot day at the end of August. Sweat dripped from his moustache.

"Yes, but that area of the tunnel is much too narrow and only about four feet high," the mine inspector said. His own suit was wet with perspiration and was unraveling at the seams about the shoulders. "Those planks could hardly handle three hundred men trying to get out all at the same time."

There were several moments of silence, then Eubanks and the inspector stepped out of the building and stood a few feet from where the men were cleaning up.

"Listen, Bert," Eubanks said in a low voice,

"your office has been hassling me to pay the yearly inspection fee." He reached into his pocket and pulled a check out along with several twenty-dollar bills. "Now, why don't you tell your boss you convinced me to pay the fee, and if there's a little extra there, go buy yourself a new suit."

The inspector glanced at the money, then looked from side to side. The cash went from Eubanks' hand into the inspector's pocket so fast Garfield almost missed it.

"I assure you, Bert," Eubanks said, handing the man a cigar, "that tunnel is as safe as the roof on my children's bedroom."

Garfield followed Big Henry and the other miners back toward the barracks. He was feeling mighty secure knowing the mine had an owner who provided for the safety of his men. Still, he heard some of the other men grumbling about their white bosses. It seemed to Garfield there were two types of Negroes: those who spit in the white man's drink when he wasn't looking, and those who brought him a fresh glass without being asked. Garfield preferred to be the latter. He believed the white bosses would make his life easier if he stayed in his place. Besides, no matter which type of Negro one was, neither would ever be allowed to stand tall and look a white person in the eyes. But, then there was Big Henry, and he had to admit, sometimes his own wife, Myrtle.

When they entered the barracks, they found men, women and children talking and laughing. They sat on the cots, eating huge meals of potatoes, tomatoes, corn on the cob, black eyed peas and pickled pig's feet. Myrtle and the rest of the women were lined up along a long row of tables singing church songs as they dished out food.

To top it all off, Garfield read on the bulletin board that he and Big Henry had made almost three dollars a piece on their first day.

"We's gonna be just fine here," Garfield said as he put his arm around Myrtle's shoulders. "Just fine."

***

The next morning, Bucktooth, Ike and Quits walked into the stockade house. Quits was carrying a whiskey bottle and could barely stand. Big Henry rose from the cot where he was eating his breakfast, stomped right over to them, and stood toe to toe with Ike. Neither one of the giant men looked away or blinked. The other Negro miners crowded around the three men who had been missing for two days.

"How you boys doin'?" Garfield asked, trying to ease the tension.

"Fair to middlin', I suppose," Bucktooth said rapidly with glassy, red eyes. "We snuck out about midnight the other night looking for food. Them union fellas found us and gave us a nice dinner. They let us sleep in the livery. The next day they fed us some more, then gave us some corn liquor and talked mighty nice to us. That's the real honest truth, Big Henry."

"They said we could leave if we want." Ike said, still staring at Big Henry. "They said they'd even pay our way back to Birmingham."

"Where's Sonny Joles?" Big Henry asked. His fists were bunched but his voice was contained.

"Hell, I don't know and I don't care," Ike said. "Why, Sonny don't pay us no never mind any who."

"We was asleep last night and Sonny went outside, I reckon to the outhouse," Bucktooth explained. "He never came back in. I reckon he got on a train."

"Or was kilt and buried," Big Henry said.

"Now don't be breaking the king's X, Big Henry," Bucktooth said. "Them union fellas ain't done us no harm."

"A half dozen of our boys disappeared last night," Garfield said. "Two of 'em had wives and children. Doubt they ran off. We think they may be dead."

"It ain't no skin off my teeth. I ain't worried 'bout dying," Ike said. "Just livin' is hard enough, I reckon."

"There's way too much air in this bottle!" Quits shouted, waving a nearly empty whiskey bottle. He could barely stand.

"Here's another one, Mistuh Simpson," one of

the young men said, handing him a flask.

"Here's to those who wish us well," Quits said, holding the drink up, "and those who don't can go to—"

"Quits Simpson, you hush!" Myrtle shouted. "There's children present."

"Yes, ma'am." Quits said, shushing himself with a finger to his lips. "It's just that this hooch is good enough to make a saint swear."

"We just gonna stand here 'till snow flies?" Ike asked.

"You want some grub?" Myrtle asked, bringing in a kettle and some plates. "There won't be much but there's food to fill you."

"We told you, we done et already." Ike growled.

"Well, Myrtle's cookin' is the best food you ever slapped a lip at," Quits said as he took a seat on a cot. "I won't be deprivin' her of bein' hospitable."

"You'd best shut up 'bout eatin'," Ike said loudly, "or I'll be puttin' a bullet in your mouth for you to chew on. How'd ya like that?"

The big Adam's apple in Quits' lanky throat danced a nervous little jig. "I'd sooner not, if I had my sooners."

"Is that enough collard greens, Bucktooth?" Myrtle asked, holding out a plate of food.

"It's a great plenty, ma'am," Bucktooth said, taking the plate. "Thank ya most kindly, Missus Wallace."

"Why you larcenous old cutthroat!" Ike shouted, pointing a finger toward Lindsey Duncan, who had just walked through the door to the stockade. "You lied to us about the mine trouble."

"I ain't never done no such thing," Lindsey said. He skipped a step to the side to keep Big Henry between himself and Ike. "Don't be stirring up no ruckus now, Ike. I didn' know it myself 'til we got here."

Since Ike didn't appear sober enough to do Lindsey any harm, Big Henry picked up his dinner bucket and headed for the cage.

"Well, let's get to work then." Garfield said. "There's plenty to be did."

***

The mine didn't work the next day or the next. Then they worked for two days, then were off for a week. In the meantime, no one left the stockade. The Negroes were each provided a revolver, which they were told to carry at all times when they came out of the mine. Back in Birmingham, a dark skinned man carrying a weapon was certain to be arrested, so few of the miners were experienced marksmen.

Garfield took great pride in the thirty-two caliber Marlin revolver he was assigned. It had plenty of wear, so he spent all his free time using his pocket knife to scrape rust from it. Like most of the other miners, he had little experience firing a weapon, and was dismayed when the sheriff only gave them five cartridges and said they were not to take practice shots.

The Negroes found themselves spending more time on guard duty than mining for coal. Garfield and Big Henry were assigned to Deputy Jeb Turner's supervision on evening watch from the top of the mine tipple. The three sat together for four hours each night, staring out at the town as they watched oil lanterns in one home after another being extinguished. Conversation was minimal, so Garfield had plenty of time to practice loading and unloading his gun.

The day they were to receive their first pay, Garfield looked forward to sending Myrtle to the recently-opened company store to purchase oil for the lamps. He knew he wouldn't get a lot, but when he looked at his pay stub and saw the zero, he almost fell over.

"All I's got's a four-dollar coupon for the company store," Big Henry said. He couldn't read words, but he could recognize numbers.

Douglas Eubanks stood nearby, smoking a cigar and looking at a paper full of figures.

"Mistuh Eubanks, sir," Garfield said. "My pay-check, sir. It says I didn't make nothin'."

Eubanks turned away from Garfield and motioned to Howard Smithson to deal with him.

"You brought your wife and children with you, didn't you?" Smithson said. "Did you think the company was gonna pay for their train ticket too?"

"But sir, you said families were welcome,

Mistuh Smithson," Garfield said. "I need to get some money so's I can get some supplies to feed my family."

"Families are welcome, yes," Smithson said. "Free ride, no. Tell Missus Wallace to get what she needs at the company store, on credit."

"Wallace?" Eubanks turned around and looked at Garfield. "That's your name? You own up to that?"

"Yes, sir." Garfield lowered his head and shoulders. "I was never one to deny it, Mistuh Eubanks."

"Was your wife the one that went to town that first day?"

"Yes, sir," Garfield said, "but I beat her good. She won't be doin' that no more."

"You're a well-mannered colored man, Mr. Wallace," Eubanks said. "You own a suit?"

"Why, yes sir, Mistuh Eubanks, I's got a handsome outfit. Cuff links and all."

"Wear it tomorrow, and be at the mine gate after breakfast," Eubanks said. "Make him a company bodyguard, Smithson."

"But he's my mine partner," Big Henry protested as Eubanks turned and walked away.

"You got a son, don't you?" Smithson asked Garfield. "Why can't he be his partner?"

"Yes, sir, Mistuh Smithson," Garfield said. "I's got four sons. But the oldest one, he's shy of eleven years old."

"I'll approve his working," Smithson said. "Besides, Big Henry can do the work of two men."

"Yes, sir, Mistuh Smithson, sir," Garfield said with a little bow. "It's about time my boy worked the blister end of a shovel. Yes, sir, it is, that's for a fact."

4

Toby Eubanks was put in charge of preparing Garfield for his new position. The two were simple men with simple understandings. They found themselves getting along well enough that neither of them even wiped the jug off as they passed it back and forth during a break.

Toby had chosen the lobby of the New Grand Restaurant, mostly because he wanted the deputies who were eating lunch there to see the important assignment his father had given him. It bothered him, though, that the men frowned when he started passing the jug with Garfield. He wondered what he might have done wrong. It seemed that others, particularly his own father, always seemed to think of him as a dunce. Though Toby was from a prosperous family, he lacked much formal education. He had struggled to graduate from the fifth grade, but so had many of the other boys in the community. The problem was that his father and many of the other adults who made up his family's circle of friends had graduated clear through college. Maybe it was his lack of education that prevented his being given more responsibility in the family coal company business.

That made this opportunity to train the colored man all the more important. He would show everyone just how well he could get Garfield ready for his duties, even though the training didn't amount to much. Garfield was just supposed to stand quietly in the back of whatever room the Eubanks' told him to stand in. They would give him orders, he would do them, and then he would go back to standing.

Still, Toby enjoyed training the Negro, since it gave him a rare opportunity to be in command. He also found that he and Garfield were able to discuss the world in terms they both related to.

"You think you're an American?" Toby asked as the two sat outside on the steps to the servant's stairwell.

"Well, sure I am," Garfield said.

"I didn't know there were Americans who came from Africa."

"Well, your folks came to America 'cause they wanted to, didn't they?" Garfield said. "Mine got beat up, chained, beat up some more, put in the bottom of a boat, starved, beat some more, and then sold to an American. I'd 'spect we're American now."

"Well, yeah, that's mighty thoughty of you, for bein' a nigger. I guess you can be an American if you want, since you put it that way." Toby took a big swallow from the jug, gargled it and spat it into the street. Then he remembered something his mother had once said to him. He thought he'd try to apply it to this situation. "You know, Garfield, you remind me of the frog that wanted to be an ox. He ate hisself 'til he swelled up so big he burst into a million pieces. The moral of that story is that there's a lot to be learned from poverty, like what's necessary and what's not."

"Why's a fella have to be poor to figure that out?" Garfield asked.

"Why there's those folks who have and those who ain't," Toby explained. "God made things that way and it's always been that way. Those who are smart and knows how to make money, like my pa, deserve what they get. After all, the higher they climb, the further they have to fall. And those like you, why, you're just lucky you don't have so far to fall, don't you see? That's what these union fellas don't understand, don't you see?"

"The United Mine Workers formed about ten years ago, but they wasn't much until the panic of 1893." Garfield repeated information he'd recently learned. "But I heard they's near doubled their membership right now."

"Well, those union boys just don't understand business, Garfield," Toby continued. "The panic of '93 caused the price of coal to drop from a dollar sixty-three to eighty-two cents a ton. Competition among coal companies became fierce. Some companies cost more than others to operate because of things like the depth of the coal and the size of the seams, don't ya see? Not to mention added expenses, like if they had to ship to marketplaces far away. Why, if a company wanted to stay in the black, they had to drop wages lower than the price of coal had dropped, don't you see?"

"Why couldn't they just drop wages the same rate as the drop in the price of coal?" Garfield asked.

"Well..." Toby's mouth opened wide and his eyes rolled upward as he searched for an answer. "I suppose they could, but then there wouldn't be much room if an emergency arose, would there?"

"Oh," Garfield tilted his head. "I suppose not."

"Plus," Toby continued, "there was so many other men who needed work, what with the panic and all."

"Were those men experienced?" Garfield asked. "Experience goes a long way toward keeping a man safe down in the coal mine."

"Well, Garfield, back in them days it was a band of immigrates that scabbed. That's why my pa brought in them foreigners who had experience working mines in other countries."

"Oh, well sure," Garfield said. "That makes sense, don't it?"

"Sure it does." Toby nudged Garfield's ribs with his elbow. "Plus, my pa says them immigrates didn't always speak English so good, and that made it harder for the Mine Workers to recruit 'em into the union."

***

When Big Henry found out there was a colored barber named Herschel Pullen who had lived in Pana for several years, he decided to pay him a visit.

"Get on outta here," the Negro barber told Big Henry when he saw his massive frame in the doorway. "I'm fixin' to close up."

"It don't set right with me," Big Henry said. He strolled into the little shop and began picking up and inspecting the tools of the trade. "A colored man doin' servant work for the whites."

"A lot of coloreds is barbers." Pullen hurried to the window and pulled the curtain shut. "I don't aim to die broke."

"The way a man dies is less important than the way he lives," Big Henry said. "Why you actin' like some lowly house nigger?"

"Better than bein' a dirty scab."

Big Henry grabbed the barber by the neck and drew his fist back. Pullen didn't make a move to resist. He also showed no signs of fear.

"That halo don't quite fit, do it?" Pullen said calmly.

Big Henry released his grip and took a step back. The barber went about the business of sweeping hair off the floor as if he had not been seconds away from getting his skull fractured.

"There's a bullet in this town for every nigger scab," Pullen said as he worked.

"And earth enough for ever man who tries." Big Henry studied the old man. "How'd you come to live among all these here white folk?"

"My mammy was a escaped slave, carrin' me in her womb, years before the war betwixed the states." Pullen said as he worked. "These folks in this here town hid her and others in tunnels beneath their houses. They took care of me and my mammy when nobody else would, protectin' us from the law until Lincoln set us free. Then when the President got kilt my mammy took me to Springfield and we stood for six hours waitin' to pay our respects to that great man. I remember when we got back home she talked to me about moving to where more folks of color were at. But I didn't want to go. These Pana folks lives just got mixed up with mine, I guess."

"What about takin' a wife?"

"I found marriage to be an overrated institution."

Big Henry had never heard the idea stated that way but being a confirmed bachelor himself he couldn't argue the matter.

"We didn't come here to be scabs, you know." Big Henry got out of the barber's way by moving to an area that had already been swept.

"The United Mine Workers," Pullen shouted firmly, "are fightin' for—"

"White folks!" Big Henry interrupted, his words like a loud clap of voice thunder. "They's not fightin' for us. They's fightin' for white folk's rights."

The barber calmly used his broom to sweep some hairs off the big man's boots. Big Henry lifted them one at a time and allowed him to sweep the bottoms.

"I don't know why a simple idea like freedom and equals rights for everybody comes so slow," Pullen said without looking up from his work. "Maybe it takes a while for folks to get to know and understand people who have different ways from them. Maybe after they do gets to know them strangers, they figure out they really ain't so much different after all. I reckon all folks just wants to live free and have others respect their God given rights. I suppose that if they don't kill each other before they learn that lesson then the freedom train moves on a little further down the line."

When he left the barber shop Big Henry walked several miles in a light rain to a broad valley that housed a narrow creek. He found the Negro called Cooter on his hands and knees in a pole barn helping a weakened mare give birth. The smell of the fall rain did little to mask the odor from the manure pile in the barnyard. With trembling hands, the old Negro wrapped one end of a rope just above the hooves of two emerging legs. He gave one hard tug on the other end and the foal's head entered into the world. A loud sucking sound brought the remainder of the dead body.

"That your mare?" Big Henry asked.

"No, sir, it's ol' Doc Mills' nag," Cooter said without any indication he was startled by the sudden thundering voice from the giant standing behind him. "She too old to be birthin' but she got loose one morn' and by the time we found her she was in a motherly condition."

"She's bad hurt." Big Henry squatted next to Cooter, whose hands were bloody from the work. "Where's the sawbones? Why ain't he tendin' his own animal?"

"He's down yonder in the wash-em-up." Cooter looked for the first time at Henry. "He was up all night deliverin' another brat into the world. He trusts me. And I don't need no wet nosed nigger boy askin' me irritatin' questions. Now instead of standing there jawin', hold this poultice for me 'till the bleeding stops. It'll draw the poison."

Big Henry had seen plenty of blood in his life, but for some reason it still turned his stomach. He took his kerchief from around his neck and used it to hold the poultice against the mare's birthing canal. Meanwhile, Cooter dragged the dead foal out of the barn and rolled it into a hole that he had already prepared. By the time he finished filling the pit, Big Henry had removed the poultice and was stuffing a big chaw into his mouth.

"Cut me a plug of that tobaccy before I expire," Cooter ordered. "And I'll have one of dem nigger babies in that jar in the tack room while youse at it. All this work's gave me the weak trembles. Hurry 'bout it, boy. I ain't in the habit of givin' orders more than once."

Since the old man was busy using a hairy saddle blanket to wipe the blood off his hands, Big Henry retrieved the glass jar. It was half filled with rock candy and liquorice root.

"Why you call black licorice *nigger babies*?" Big Henry reached into the jar, then held a candy along with the tobacco out to the old man. "Ain't you got no pride in your people? You should be fightin' aside us."

Cooter accepted the treats and stuffed them both in his mouth. "I'd rather wrestle a bear cub from his mammy than tangle with the United Mine Workers."

"Them unionists see the world as nothin' but a rich man-poor man war."

Cooter ignored the comment. He worked on jawing the licorice into the tobacco.

Big Henry took a step toward the man, using

his size to add weight to his words. "Seems to me envy is just one step from hate."

The old man knelt back down and dipped a cloth in the bucket. He cooled the mare's face and neck as he chewed fast and hard on the tobacco. After a few moments, he rose and looked at Big Henry as if he were surprised he hadn't left. He gave a long spat into the slop bucket. "Why don't you go back where you came from?" he growled.

Big Henry swiped at the sweat on his forehead with an oversized hand. "You talk like you're half white."

"I kilt me one of them mulattos once." Cooter chuckled. "Somebody else shot him, but I finalized him." He shook his head with a smile. "He always appreciated a fancy hat, I recall. Now he's got a marble one on his head."

"You keep rilin' me and you'll be wearing a cross on *your* head." Big Henry's voice was a clap of thunder that turned quickly into a distant rumble. "Oh, this is as pointless as a rabbit tryin' to explain speed to a snail. You're scum for stickin' with these whites against your own. Now go sit over yonder in the dark where you belong."

"One man's whoop is another man's holler." Cooter shouted as the young giant turned and walked away. "You mind that crick bottom. You hear? I might be shooting me some squirrels befores you get clear of them thickets. You hear me, you damned scab?"

Big Henry was in a surly mood twenty minutes later when he approached the main road into Pana. Being called a scab by two of his own riled him to the point of violence, that is if he could find someone to be violent with.

The immaculately dressed black man he saw standing outside an old smoke house made him mad enough that he gave an aggravated spit. The problem was a cool, heavy breeze from the north had suddenly come up blowing the spittle back onto his shirt. When he lowered his head and brushed at the black ooze, another strong gust lifted his miner's cap and carried it into the nearby timber.

"Damn!" Big Henry wasn't inclined to swearing but believed that nature was provoking his bad behavior.

"Never spit into the wind, Mr. Stevens." The man put a hand onto his own head and squashed his bowler to keep it from also blowing off. His eyes were magnified by thick eye glasses.

"Who you?" Big Henry ignored his lost cap and walked to within inches of the man. He shouted above the wind that had quickly turned into a howl. "How you knows me?"

"Rev. Horace James, at your service." James said with a slight bow. "I heard you've been calling on Mr. Pullen, and not for a haircut."

"What that your business?" Big Henry allowed

his head to bobble on his neck. "Nigger, why you dressed rich as churnin' cream, anyhow?"

"I'm prouder of who I am than what I am."

"Yea, and if'n a bull gived milk he'd be a cow."

"Well right now I feel like a longhorn steer in summer lightening." James turned and looked up into the darkening sky as he talked. "Please don't hold my education against me."

"I ain't had no schoolin'," Big Henry bellowed proudly, "only livin'

A sudden swirl of wind caught the smaller man off guard. After stumbling a few steps, he ducked down and spread his legs wide to keep his balance. On the road toward town dust and debris was swirling in an ever-increasing circle.

"Could we step into this smokery to converse?" Rev. James shouted, both hands now firmly grasping the brim of his hat. "While you are anchored rather securely I fear that in a storm such as this I am little better than a tumbleweed blowing in the wind."

Despite his contempt for the bespectacled man, Big Henry's instinct was to protect the weak. He took the reverend's arm and guided him to the narrow smokehouse. The wind made opening the door a struggle, even for the young giant. Once they were inside, it banged shut with a force that shook the old building. From the ceiling where the flue had once been, narrow streaks of sun rays brought forth the only light to the windowless room. Outside, the wind continued to intensify, causing the building to shake.

"Are we safe in here?" James asked.

"Not if that tornado touches." Big Henry felt his superiority over the man return. He had been momentarily frazzled by the reverend's big words and fancy talk.

"What tornado?" James' eyeglasses were fogged, but with the dim lighting he made no attempt to wipe them clean. He did however place his hands on his ears.

"The one that just made your ears pop." Big Henry replied matter of factly. "Hear that train? It ain't no train at all."

James' eyes were a ghostly fog and seemed even larger than when his glasses had been clean. Big Henry couldn't help himself from goading the man by jumping a little each time the building seemed like it would collapse from the wind. For several long moments the train-like sound roared before the storm finally passed.

When the terrible noise ended, Rev. James bolted through the door and breathing heavy rushed into the clearing. He immediately removed his glasses and wiped them clear on his shirt sleeve. Two nearby trees were blown over, their stubs leaving jagged crown-like projections where they had stood. In the distance, a dark funnel rose above the treeline and then up into the dark clouds, only to disappear as if by magic. A flash of silvery lightning against those clouds was followed seconds later by a loud clap of thunder that made Rev. James jump once more.

"Now what was you saying 'bout education, Preacher?" Big Henry said calmly.

James loosened his perfectly knotted bow tie then extracted a gold timepiece from his watch pocket. He took several deep breaths as he flipped it open and checked the time. It only took him a few seconds to regain his composure, a feat that both disappointed and marveled Big Henry.

"If our race is to ever achieve equality we must not allow the reminders of our slave days to endure." James closed his watch and tucked it away.

"You ain't gonna win against no white folk by dressin' like a daisy and usin' purty words," Big Henry said. "You'd best man-up if you want to be treated equal."

"Big Henry, I just returned from Carterville, Illinois where men of our skin pigmentation joined the United Mine Workers of America. Like you, they had been recruited to be strikebreakers. However, because leaders from both sides were able to sit down and negotiate, both white and black miners are now standing side by side to bring better wages and working conditions to the coal mines."

"Is they livin' side by side with them white folks, too?"

"Well, no, they have a community of houses that were built by the UMW."

"Bet them black folks houses is somethin' to see." Big Henry laughed. "They built houses for slaves too, didn't they? My pa grew up in one. Lost two of his toes when he was a babe. Chewed off by rats."

"Big Henry, our people were hundreds of years in slavery. We are not going to solve all our problems over night, and definitely not by violence. Maybe not even in our lifetime. But hopefully our children and grandchildren will have it better."

"Preacher, my mother was a Comanche. Indians been fightin' white men for hundreds of years."

"And how has that worked out for them?"

Big Henry had run out of words.

"Let me try to talk to the UMW leaders and see what they offer." The little man reached as high as his arms would stretch and touched the young giant's shoulder. "Henry, why won't you just listen to what the union men have to say?"

Big Henry brushed aside the preacher's hand. Being called a scab by two of his own had put him in a foul mood but then to be offered advice from a dandy who carried a gold timepiece was more than he could abide. Without another word he turned and walked toward town.

5

Since Big Henry didn't like or trust white people, when Jeb Turner told him to follow him to the top of the mine tipple, the big miner kept his hand close to the gun tucked in the front of his belt. For some reason, the whites thought of Big Henry as the leader of the Negroes. That was an assumption he both regretted and took pride in. He knew it was because of his size and strength, but sometimes he didn't want the responsibility of making decisions for the other coloreds.

He had been on his own since he was eleven and his father died in the mine. Big Henry had been standing just a few feet away when the three-foot long slab of rock dropped off the mine top and crushed his father's skull. He was leaning over his father's body when several other miners came running into the chamber. No one seemed to know what to say or do. After several moments, Henry hefted his father's body into a mine car and started pushing it up the slope. Without a word, the other men helped. By the time they exited the mine, over a hundred black miners had joined the impromptu funeral procession. Henry never waited to be given instructions after that. When something needed doing he simply did it and others always seemed to follow.

"They're fixin' to send colored deputies into town," Jeb told him when they were alone.

"I know that," Big Henry said. "Why you bring me all the way up here to tell me somethin' I already knowed?"

"It's a set up," Jeb said. "The mine operators are hoping you'll be ambushed so the governor will send the National Guard to Pana to protect the mines."

"So, what's wrong with that?" Big Henry asked. "The soldiers would make sure us coloreds could work, wouldn't they?" Big Henry almost laughed when the white man's mouth popped open.

"Why you so surprised?" Big Henry said. "You think colored folks ain't used to the white man sending him off to die? My grandpa was killed during the War Between the States, fightin' for the 54th Massachusetts. You never heard of the 54th Massachusetts in your history books, have you? No, sir, you wouldn't, 'cause they was colored boys who thought they was fightin' for freedom for blacks."

"Negroes *were* freed," Jeb said.

"Oh, yeah?" Big Henry said. "You ever been in the South? Why don't you come on down, we'll go vote together?"

Jeb shook his head.

"Besides," Big Henry said, holding up a thirty-two caliber Marlin, "I got a gun. The boss man don't want us to get kilt."

"Have you checked it to see if it will fire?"

Big Henry looked at Jeb's eyes. He cocked the revolver, aimed into the sky and pulled the trigger. A dull click sound came from the weapon.

"That gun was made in 1875 and probably hasn't been fired in ten years," Jeb said. "Come with me."

He led the big man back down the mine tipple to a secured room in the rear of the main building. After telling the guard to take a coffee break, Jeb unlocked the padlock and, opening the door, walked inside. Big Henry followed. When Jeb lit the lamp, it was the big Negroe's turn to open his mouth in awe. The room was filled with hundreds of rifles, pistols and boxes of ammunition.

Jeb picked up a thirty-eight caliber Colt and handed it to Big Henry. "It doesn't have as much stopping power as the Colts our soldiers in Cuba are using, but it's a good weapon." He found a box of bullets and held it out to the miner.

"Why you doin' this?" Big Henry asked. He stuffed the ammunition inside his shirt.

"Seems to me the times requires it," Jeb said and moved back to the door. "We don't have enough miners to get any of you boys kilt."

Big Henry tested the balance of the weapon in his hand. "The times requires it." He repeated the white man's words as if he were also testing them. Tucking the gun beneath his belt, he followed Jeb Turner through the doorway.

***

"What did you do, Preacher?" Tom Downs asked. "Ride through the Buckeye and Rosemond townships yelling, 'The niggers are coming?'"

Rev. Clarence Morton had just loped into Pana with over one hundred well-armed farmers on horseback or in surreys. Tom was starting to feel his rank diminishing. Hundreds of union coal miners from all around central Illinois had already poured into Pana that week. Saloons had started running out of whiskey and wagons had to be quickly dispatched to bring more of the liquid courage into town. Tom Downs had his hands full trying to get the new arrivals to understand that he was the man in charge of the strike, a feat that wasn't easy when dealing with strangers.

To make matters worse, General Bradley, the leader of the previous year's strike, had arrived by train and unceremoniously assumed command. Tom kept reminding everyone that Alexander Bradley wasn't really a general at all. He had only received the title because he organized a "stomping strike march" on Washington DC back in '94. The man had a flamboyance that Tom despised. The "general" wore a light blue suit with pointy toed shoes and flourished a silver-handled cane like a British dandy. To make matters worse, Bradley liked to tell everyone that he had begun working in an Illinois coal mine when he was only nine years old. Having never stepped foot in a coal mine, it was an accomplishment that Tom couldn't claim.

The arrogant Bradley showing up was bad enough, but now a preacher, of all things, had a large contingent of men following him. Though he was among the six union leaders standing on the train station platform, Tom was starting to feel insignificant.

"Well, I don't know how you got 'em," General Bradley said, "but a lot of those boys don't look real excited to be here."

"They'll defend themselves all right," the reverend said, "when they start getting' shot at by darkies. They'll be warriors, by golly, they will."

"We need to hide these warriors," Tom said, with a playful emphasis on the title the preacher had given them, "or them scabs might see they're outnumbered and not come out to fight at all."

"Put 'em in the warehouse next to the hotel," Bradley said with a wave of his hand.

"Aren't we goin' to charge the stockade?" Tom asked.

"You're pretty anxious to get kilt, ain't ya?" Bradley extracted a big plug of tobacco with his fingers, flicked it into the grass, then wiped his hands on his trousers.

"We'll never have a better opportunity. The stockade is undermanned right now." Tom resented the audacious question. "Sheriff Cogburn deputized the niggers and sent them out to patrol the town. We've got boys following them around giving them hell, but sooner or later them darkies'll be goin' back to the mine yard. We need to decide what we're going to do before Eubanks and the Smithsons get to the mine."

"That's right, General," Rev. Morton agreed. "The mine owners will be coming out of the hotel soon, and if they get inside the stockade, they'll never surrender those dark-complected Spaniards."

Tom wished he had thought to call the Negroes dark-complected Spaniards. It was a good name, since there was a war going on in Cuba and everyone hated the Spanish.

"Then we don't let them get to the mine yard," Bradley said with conviction. He turned to the tallest member of the leadership. "Can you still whistle real loud, Holiday?"

The miner known as Holiday Jones put two fingers to his mouth and gave a shrill blast so loud those nearby covered their ears.

"When you men hear that whistle, come running with your boys," General Bradley said. "We'll take Eubanks and the Smithsons hostage, march them up to the mine gates and demand the niggers be put on the noon train out of here."

"What'll we do if they say no?" Holiday asked.

"Then we lynch the damned capitalists!" Rev. Morton shouted.

***

Tom Downs walked along Locust Street a step ahead of Holiday Jones. The boardwalk was eerily empty for that time of the morning. Gunshots sounded in the distance to the west, and a moment later more came from the north. He smiled, knowing that every one of the local union men knew the shots were a result of his orders to keep the patrolling Negroes busy.

When they were across the street from the hotel, he rolled a cigarette and invited Holiday to do the same. Holiday's hands were shaking a little as he poured a spot of tobacco onto a roll of paper.

"Just relax, old timer," Tom said, bracing the palms of his own trembling hands against his stomach as he began rolling his own.

When Holiday was done with his cigarette, he raised the paper to lick it shut. "I hope I have a whistle left in me."

That bothered Tom more than a possible shooting. He had never learned to whistle himself, a deficiency he'd always regretted. If Holiday failed to perform, he wasn't sure how to handle the situation.

Before he could come up with an alternative plan, he saw David Smithson and his nephew Howard emerge from the door of the hotel. The men were immaculately dressed in three-piece suits and with what Tom considered to be ostentatiously colorful bow ties.

A moment later, Tom's left ear went deaf when Holiday let loose of a whistle that would have put any steam engine to shame. A second whistle from an alley across the road brought the streets to instant life. From the warehouse to the south emerged over two hundred men, most of which carried Winchesters. A few of them fired shots into the air.

The two Smithson men immediately ran away from the mob but were cut off when another even larger crowd turned onto the street in front of them. Then from the hotel side came Rev. Morton's warriors carrying shot guns and squirrel rifles, and from the rail depot emerged several hundred more union men. More shots were fired into the air. Tom raced into the fracas, grabbed a rope from one of the strikers, and while other men held the captors, he ripped their bow ties off them and tied a slip knot around the necks of the two mine operators.

Feeling he had regained command of the mob, Tom began pulling the Smithsons toward the railroad station so they would be in direct sight of the Springside Coal Mine.

"Where's Eubanks?" General Bradley bellowed above the shouts. "Go find Eubanks!"

Several hundred men scattered, most of them miners who had worked for Eubanks and hated him. Tom noticed that more than a few men departing were the farmers Rev. Morton had recruited. He suspected they would be high-tailing it for home as soon as they could sneak around the buildings to retrieve their mounts.

"Hey there!" A voice yelled. "What's going on here?"

Tom didn't need to look to see who it was. He had heard that voice in his dreams ever since the day Dr. Mills had broken up the fight between him and Jeb Turner by talking to them like they were school boys. That experience had provided plenty of opportunity for Tom to think of things he should have said that day.

"This here's a union activity, Doc!" Tom shouted, with hoarse conviction, then added the line he thought would bring a chuckle from the men. "It ain't no medical emergency."

To Tom's disappointment, none of the men

responded to his wit, due to the attack that immediately took place when two of the out-of-town union men began pummeling the doctor with their fists. As a half dozen local men came to the doctor's defense, Tom yanked on the rope and continued to lead the captives on toward the train station.

***

Myrtle Wallace had insisted Garfield wear his Sunday best, a nagging that her husband very much appreciated when he found himself standing just inside the door to an elegant restaurant. He thought he must look fine in his single-breasted frock coat that his wife had stayed up most of the night stitching.

He noted that Douglas Eubanks' striped flannel coat had patch pockets and brass buttons. His son Toby had on a navy blue blazer, although his waistcoat didn't quite match it. They were eating a fine breakfast. Their napkins were in their laps instead of tucked under their chin. They ate one bite at a time and even swallowed before speaking. Toby found a moment to acknowledge Garfield's good behavior by giving him a little smile and a nod. Garfield was pleased but avoided a smile of his own. Instead he used the aristocratic sideways nod that Toby had taught him.

Garfield had seen southern manservants and the fancy lives they led. He imagined that if he could learn the social graces, he might be able to gain such a position with the Eubanks family. Maybe Myrtle would even get hired on as a chamber maid or a cook. He thought that when his sons got a little older they would look fine dressed in knickerbockers and driving a fancy carriage.

Garfield was lost in these revelations when he heard the first gunshots of the morning. While the sharp pops startled him, the Eubanks' didn't even look up from their plates. After a second round of shots, Douglas Eubanks turned toward him.

"Go see what that's all about," Eubanks said, then returned to his sausage and eggs.

Garfield went out onto the street. It was unusually empty. Just as he started to turn back into the restaurant, he heard shouting. Running to the end of the block, he peered carefully around the last building. When he saw the two Smithsons being pulled down the street by a rope around their necks and surrounded by hundreds of men, he ran as fast as he could back into the restaurant.

"They's kidnapped the Smithson bosses!" Garfield shouted. "Looks like they's fixin' to hang 'em!"

"How many?" Douglas Eubanks asked, jumping to his feet.

"Looks like thousands." Garfield said truthfully.

"What we gonna do, Pa?" Toby asked. The son

seemed frozen in his chair. "They'll hang us sure."

"They must be ransoming the Smithsons to demand the niggers get sent away," Eubanks said. He turned back to Garfield. "Can you get us to the Springside Mine?"

"That's the direction that mobs a heading," Garfield said. "I could get you to *your* mine though, and then we could take the tunnel to the Springside mine."

"Pa, that tunnel ain't safe," Toby said.

"Sure it is, Mistuh Toby," Garfield said reassuringly. "Your Pa told the mine inspector it was safe just a few days ago. Now, we'd best get out the back way if we's not gonna get you Mistuhs caught."

Using clotheslines full of clothes as cover, Garfield led the two men down alleys and through backyards whenever possible. At one point, he spotted Big Henry and about a dozen other coloreds being chased by white men, but they were too far away to ask them for assistance. When the three men reached the mine yard, Eubanks shouted for the guards to open the gates.

Once they were inside, Garfield found the mine yard woefully unprotected with far too few deputies. When Eubanks announced their intention to use the escape tunnel to get to the Springside Mine, the mine boss held up the palm of his hand.

"Sir," he said, "that tunnel ain't safe for man nor beast."

"That just ain't so, Mistuh Boss," Garfield said. "Mistuh Eubanks told us it was safe. Now, worrin' ain't never helped nobody, do it?"

When Garfield saw Mr. Eubanks close his eyes and shake his head, he was sure the mine operator was impressed with his supporting him on the tunnel issue. Garfield was becoming more and more confident that his handling of the situation was about to gain him favors. After all, navigating the Eubanks' through town and to the mine gate had been no easy feat. He felt a powerful surge of self-importance as he led the father and son to the cage.

"Cut the rope!" Garfield yelled at Louis Hooks once the men were on board. The cage operator rang the bell and the elevator dropped rapidly. Garfield sensed that the Eubanks' had not had much experience going down into their own coal mine, since Toby clung to the stabilizing bar in the middle of the cage as if it were his mother's teat.

A little over seven hundred feet later, the descent of the cage slowed and the darkness transformed into the dim lighting that Garfield Wallace was accustomed to. At the pit bottom, he pushed the cage gate open and stepped onto the gravely ground.

"Pa, what's happening?"

"Shut up, Toby," Eubanks said.

"Don't worry, Mistuh Toby," Garfield said. "Your

eyes will get used to it in a minute." Garfield found an oil lamp hanging on the wall, lit it. and turned it up to full brightness.

"How do you know which way to go?" Toby asked.

"Feel the breeze?" Garfield told him. "Miners can tell which way we're going from the flow of air. Big fans circulates air from both ends. The warm air come from below and the cool air from above. We's gonna walk toward the warm air for about half a mile. When you start feeling cool air on your face it means we're half way there."

"Get moving, then," Eubanks ordered.

Watching the lamp, Garfield led the way. He thought about telling the bosses what it would mean if the lamp changed its brightness, but decided the young Eubanks might be better off not knowing.

The three men walked for ten minutes in silence, making slow progress. Both father and son stumbled a lot and emitted sounds that made Garfield uneasy. He feared he might take a wrong turn and need to double back, an event that sometimes occurred even with the most seasoned miners. He prayed that wouldn't happen. Such a mistake might hurt his chances of obtaining a cushy job with the mine owner.

Finally, they reached the very narrow and low-ceilinged area the mine inspector had just a few days before argued was not acceptable. Garfield breathed a little easier, but the mine bosses swore and moaned until they came into a wider chamber about one hundred yards later.

"I feel cool air!" Toby Eubanks suddenly yelled. He and his father rushed past Garfield and hurried toward a dim light glowing in the distance.

"Stop, Mistuh Eubanks!" Garfield shouted. "Stop, Mistuh Toby!"

Garfield tried to get the lamp to shine its light toward the direction the two were running so they could see why he was warning them. The sound of feet slipping on wet lumber followed by two loud splashes was all it took to bring an end to Garfield Wallace's dream of being a sophisticated manservant.

***

"Fire this nigger!" Douglas Eubanks shouted the moment the cage reached the surface. He and his son were still dripping wet.

Jeb Turner took a mortified Garfield's arm and led him back toward the cage.

"Go back to the Eubanks Mine and don't say a word to anyone about what happened," Jeb whispered to him. "I doubt he'll remember anything about you in a few days. Just keep your head down and spend as much time mining as they'll let you."

Garfield nodded his appreciation and returned quietly to the cage.

"Where's the nigger deputies?" Eubanks yelled when he saw the stockade walls lined with white men.

"Why, you sent them into town to draw the strikers into a fight," Toby said.

"So, why aren't they fighting?" Eubanks demanded.

"I'd expect they're fightin' for their lives, Mr. Eubanks," Sheriff Cogburn said. "You told them to split up into groups and go purge the town."

"You, there!" Eubanks shouted at a white deputy. "Give me your clothes."

"Mr. Eubanks, my clothes is filthy," the deputy said. "Why, that colored fella that brought you's got a better suit than what I've got on."

Jeb backed up a step, hoping the mine owner wouldn't be reminded of the miner he had just fired.

"I ain't wearing no nigger clothes." Eubanks removed his own wet shirt and threw it at the man. "Now give me your shirt."

***

Big Henry and his men weren't fighting for their lives, they were fighting for their pride. It seemed that every street or alley they went down they were being bombarded by a barrage of rocks. Occasionally, a gunshot rang out and some dirt would be kicked up at their feet, but none of his men were ever hit.

They spotted mostly young boys causing the problem, but one time as the men spread out below a two-story building, several tubs of waste water was dumped on them. Female laughter and sexually explicit swear words came from above. One of the blacks who was most affected by the soaking fired a couple of rounds into one of the windows.

When Big Henry peeped around a corner and saw hundreds of white men gathered near the railroad tracks, he turned and ordered his men to hightail it back to the Eubanks Mine. Arriving at the gate, they were quickly ushered inside and ordered by the head deputy to take the escape tunnel to the Springside Mine. The cage was at the bottom, so they had to wait several minutes for it to be brought up. When it arrived, a perspiring and out of breath Garfield opened the cage door.

***

Jeb thought there was something about lynching that seemed to really rile the colored folks. When they saw Howard Smithson standing atop the wagon on his tip toes with a rope around his neck, the Negroes were so incensed they couldn't be controlled. They were ready to rush out of the stockade and attack the lynch mob. Neither Eubanks nor the sheriff and his deputies seemed able to stop them.

The sheriff waved his arms, running in front of the crowd.

"We won't tolerate no lynchin'," Ike Alexander shouted. "Even if it is a white man. We seen 'nough of that down South. Besides, them union boys lied to us the minute we came in town. Said they'd pay for us to go back to 'Bama, and then they turned around and sent us right back into the mine. You gave us guns. Now we's fixin to use 'em."

Ike was a fighter and not afraid of dying. Without Big Henry around to make rational decisions, the men seemed willing to follow Ike to their deaths.

Jeb sucked in a deep breath. He recognized their frustration. The guns they carried seemed to give them a sense of power and an ability to do something about their situation. He could think of nothing that would stop them.

Then a tiny White woman, her gray hair in a tight bun, stepped in front of the mine gate. She held up the palm of one hand and brought over a hundred blacks to an almost instant quiet.

"That's my son out there with a rope around his neck," Mrs. Smithson said. "I'll not see my child die today."

There was much grumbling among the blacks. When it grew louder and the anger began to return, Jeb thought the strikebreakers were about to rush past the old lady and through the gate.

"That'll be enough!" Myrtle Wallace shouted. She stomped across the mine yard from where the women and children had gathered to watch the proceedings and stood shoulder to shoulder with Mrs. Smithson. "I'm a mother, too, and I'll not see this woman lose her child because you men are too stupid and bloodthirsty to think straight."

The Negro men shook their heads and started getting loud again. Jeb was shocked to see Myrtle run up and grab the shotgun out of Ike Alexander's hands, then aim it at the mob. She rushed to return to Mrs. Smithson's side.

"These here coloreds don't understand maternity, Missus Smithson, but they sure as hell understand buckshot." Myrtle cocked both barrels. "Now you boys need to calm down and think with what little brains God gave you."

"There's a half-dozen union boys walking toward the gate!" one of the deputies shouted from the walkway near the top of the stockade fence.

"Well, let 'em in!" Eubanks yelled.

Only one of the union men walked into the mine yard. He handed Eubanks a note, then took a step back and stood at attention, his face perspiring profusely.

Eubanks read the letter aloud: "Mr. Sheriff, please bring all deputies and Negroes from Springside Mine with you and come with this committee at once."

The blacks again began talking loudly. Eubanks didn't hesitate. He took a pen from his breast pocket, turned the paper over and quickly scribbled his reply.

The union messenger didn't even glance at the paper. He turned and walked as fast as he could out of the stockade.

When the union committee returned, General Bradley held up the paper to the striking miners. "It says," Bradley shouted, hushing the crowd, "release the Smithsons immediately and we will talk!"

Tom Downs threw his arms in the air and rallied the miners into a roar that he was sure could be heard for miles. Just then the whistle from the noon train sounded. There was a flurry of activity as the union men realized that if they didn't get behind the tracks, they would be left between the arriving train and within rifle range of the stockade.

"Let's lay the Smithsons on the track and let the train run over 'em!" one of the strikers shouted when all the union men were on the town side of the tracks. "Then it will be an accident."

There was a roar of approval, and Holiday Jones

used a skinning knife to cut the rope just above Howard Smithson's neck. The captive gasped as he rolled his head trying to loosen the noose.

"No! That's too good for 'em!" Tom shouted. He pushed Holiday aside. "Hang 'em and leave their bodies there for the nigger scabs to look at."

Another roar of approval. By the time Holiday found a new rope and had Howard again suspended from the tree, the train had pulled into the station and blocked the view of the lynching from the Springside Mine.

"Get those passengers off that train and get it moving!" Rev. Morton yelled to the conductor.

"Want I should hang 'em then?" Holiday shouted.

Morton didn't answer. He was watching a handsome and well-dressed man step out of the passenger car. The preacher lowered his head, took his hat off. "Oh shit," he whispered.

Tom Downs was one of the few men close enough to hear Morton's expletive. For a moment, he was tempted to give the rope a hard tug in the hopes it would break Smithson's neck. Before he could act, though, he heard the well-dressed man yell, "Get that rope off that man!"

"Now there's a dandy if ever there was one." Holiday said quietly.

Though appearing to be under thirty years of age, the man had a commanding presence that brought the eight hundred strikers to near silence. Holiday cut the rope for a second time, and Smithson again dropped to his knees. He repeated his head shaking and gasping.

The stranger from the train walked over to the wagon and jumped up into the back of it next to Smithson. He held out his hand to Holiday, who handed over his knife. After the man cut the rope that bound the prisoner's hands, he turned and faced the mob while Smithson was roughly pulled off the wagon.

"A lot of you men know me, but for those who don't, my name is John Mitchell, and I'm the vice-president of the United Mine Workers of America."

There was a flurry of conversation, and a few more of Rev. Morton's warriors turned and headed for home. When the crowd became silent again, Mitchell continued.

"In case you think I don't understand the plight of the colliers, I will tell you that I started working in the coal mines sixteen years ago when I was twelve years old." Mitchell paused for the words to take effect. "I've suffered injuries and loss of friends and family, just as most all of you have. Now we are on the verge of a great victory. One that can lay the foundation for better wages and work conditions not only in Pana, Illinois, but across the entire United States.

"You men all know what happened almost exactly one year ago in Lattimer, Pennsylvania. We lost nineteen union boys that day, shot in the back by the sheriff and his deputies. From what I hear, this Christian County sheriff would like nothing more than an excuse to do the same to you men. I want you to remember there is nothing so pleasing to the coal mine owner as the sound of his own voice echoing through the empty heads of an ignorant workforce.

"Well, I know you men are not ignorant. At this very moment, we are working through the governor's office, the state legislature, and the court system to see to it that we win this strike and get you men the victory that the UMW so desperately needs."

Mitchell pointed down to the ground in front of the wagon where the Smithsons stood with their faces lowered.

"Mr. Smithson!" Mitchell shouted loud enough that it could be heard by all those nearby, "will you give me your word that you will meet with the United Mine Workers tomorrow morning and discuss the terms of these miners' contracts?"

There was a long silence in which Howard Smithson tried to speak but his throat seemed still raw from the effects of the hangman's noose. Finally, his uncle raised his head and spoke loudly enough that everyone could hear.

"We will!" he shouted.

The cheers that followed were even heard by Big Henry and his men as they exited the cage into the Springside Mine tipple.

***

Standing in the open mine gate with hand over mouth, Mrs. Smithson watched the train pull slowly out of the depot and resume its north-ward run. She had heard the cheers and prayed it was not the moment her son had died. When the caboose had passed out of the station, she saw the backs of hundreds of men as they walked toward town. It took her a moment to spot the two men who were walking slowly across the open field toward Springside Mine. When she saw it was her son and brother-in-law, she dropped to her knees and began crying. Myrtle Wallace fell to her knees beside her, and with arms around the mother, cried with her.

The following morning, neither David nor Howard Smithson showed up for the scheduled meeting with the United Mine Workers.

6

After his parents passed in '88, Jeb had sold
their few possessions and took a room in Ma
Pendergast's Boarding House. He had struggled
for a few years, but now his job as Chief Deputy
paid him as much money as he needed. Ma's cooking was a pleasure he'd never before experienced,
his own mother had never displayed much of a
culinary talent. Ma Pendergast also allowed liquor
on her premises, something most other boarding
houses didn't. That was because Ma enjoyed her
Elderberry wine.

His third floor bedroom was small, but on a
corner so its two windows usually provided a
breeze in the summer. In the winter, he shared an
open fireplace that was between his room and the
one next door. That adjoining room was typically
used by traveling salesmen and therefore often
vacant. He had come to think of the responsibility
for the fire during cold nights as his own.

Since the strike began a few months before, Jeb
hadn't spent much time at the boarding house. He
was being paid two dollars for each twelve-hour

day, but if he was stationed at the mine yards, which he usually was, he received four dollars a day. Jeb found himself saving plenty of money because he ate with the Negroes and sometimes picked up a few dollars shooting dice with them.

It was a good life. In fact, Jeb was counting his blessings one evening when Ma Pendergast knocked on his bedroom door. Without opening it, she told him he had a guest waiting in the parlor. Before he could inquire who it was, the elderly lady was easing herself back down the steps. Jeb threw his shirt back on and gave his wavy hair a quick brushing. When he entered the parlor, he immediately cussed himself for being unarmed. Tom Downs was lounging comfortably on the davenport. Tom made no attempt to rise and greet his old schoolmate. He did however point to a bottle of scotch on the coffee table, which Jeb immediately made good use of.

"How are you, Jeb?"

"Tolerable."

"I'll get right to the point," Tom said. "You are on the wrong side of history."

"How you figure?" Jeb said, downing a shot.

"The United Mine Workers are going to win this war against the capitalists."

"You fixin to shoot 'em, Tom?" Jeb asked. "I see you're carryin' your pa's silver-handled Smith and Wesson. Didn't he used to tell us that Wyatt Earp hisself gave him that weapon?"

"No, Earp gave Pa a starting pistol for the horse races," Tom said, then after a brief hesitation, revised the story. "Well, actually Pa stole it. But Earp knew he was stealin' it, so I guess Earp let him have it all the same. That's not what I came here to talk to you about. The UMW wants to put you on their payroll as a security guard. They'll pay you four dollars a day."

"Ah." Jeb placed extra sarcasm in his voice. "And as a security guard you would, of course, want me to kill our good friend Frank Cogburn and his pa, the one who always took you and me fishing and hunting when we was kids?"

"Well, what about the friends you'll be killing if you stay working for the coal company?" Tom asked, his voice deepening slightly. Rising quickly from the davenport, his hands trembled as he pretended to inspect a coffee table filled with Pendergast family memorabilia.

"I ain't kilt nobody yet." Jeb raised his chin and looked down at Tom. "Have you?"

"That badge don't give you no right to tell me who I can hate." Tom's eyes turned toward the fireplace mantel. He leaned an elbow on it.

"It will if you do something about it," Jeb said, pouring himself another drink. "That would just be wrong, Tom."

"Well, Deputy, sometimes the right amount of

wrong can be beneficial."

"We've had quite a few Negro miners go missing lately," Jeb added.

"They're probably dead in those coal mines." Tom didn't take his eyes off the photographs on the mantel. "I heard they're losing a man a day down there due to the fact they ain't skilled miners."

Jeb was glad Tom wasn't looking at him. He wasn't certain he could hide the glimmer of doubt in his own eyes. He'd heard Big Henry and Garfield complaining that many of the Negroes didn't know what they were doing. About twenty injured strikebreakers couldn't work. He wondered if it could be true that accidents in the mine might account for some of the coloreds who had disappeared.

"The union needs to win this thing, Jeb." Tom turned back toward him. "If they don't, it may be generations before laborers get another opportunity."

"You sound like your pa," Jeb said. "That's why I didn't like goin' fishing with him. He'd never shut up, preachin' union to the fish even after they were on the stringer."

"I ain't my pa."

Jeb shouldn't have brought up his father. Part of the reason for Tom's flamboyance was to compensate for his embarrassment over his father's suicide. Since they'd both lost their parents before adulthood, there was a silent understanding between the two former friends.

"The union will never quit," Tom said.

"And the coal companies ain't never been beat," Jeb said. "What'll you do if those two traits stay the same for both of 'em?"

The hollow area around Tom's eyes appeared dark. He had the glazed-over stare that Jeb had seen in men who believed deeply in their cause.

"Why ain't you talkin' to the coloreds about joinin' the union?" Jeb added.

"Because there's more to it than just that," Tom said. "We have to let the coal companies know they can't be bringin' scabs from other states without consequences. Otherwise, they'll just bring dagoes or chinks next."

"Why would they bring Italians?" Jeb asked. "They's white folks."

"Them wops is only half-white," Tom said. "My pa called them spaghetti snappers, black Italians. That's why they can't be unionized. They's savages. Yes, sir, Johnny Bulls make the best union men. England, Scotland and Ireland is where unions originated 'cause they's smarter there."

Jeb had to think about that. His own parents had never talked about other folks based on their skin color or where they came from. He seemed to have remembered once though, when he was very young, his mother's sister Mary was visiting from Virginia. Aunt Mary had been using a lot of words Jeb had never heard of to describe groups of people. Then one day his aunt had used the word *nigger* and his mother asked her to not talk that way in front of the children. Jeb thought it strange that he was only just now remembering that incident.

"Ira Cogburn darn near raised me after my parents died," Jeb said. "He don't cotton to such ruckus. He says we got along fine before the union came."

"Oh yeah?" Tom said. "Ask those niggers getting crushed to death by rock falls in the coal mine that you're protecting."

"This is a pointless conversation." Jeb turned toward the stairs then added one last comment over his shoulder. "You're getting' a might reckless with your hate, Tom."

The next afternoon Jeb was standing near the cage when the dead bodies of two colored coal miners were brought up.

***

Because of the rift in the community between union and non-union supporters, the coal company decided to run a school within the Springside stockade. The white children of the deputies as well as Negro boys and girls were allowed to attend. Though they sat on different sides of the classroom, when they went outside, they shared recess together.

One afternoon, four boys held their shoeless feet in the center of a circle. Three of the pairs of feet were white and one black. Butch Shallabarger pointed at them one at a time as he said each word.

"Eeny meeny miny moe," Butch said, "catch a nigger by the toe—"

"Hey, that ain't right!" Walter Wallace shouted. "It's catch a *tiger* by the toe."

"*Tiger*?" Butch yelled back. "That's stupid. Tigers ain't got toes. They got claws."

Walter couldn't argue with that, but Ornery Billy was standing nearby and took offense. Butch was a big boy even for thirteen years of age. Until the Negroes arrived, he had worked the rock picking crew for two years and even gone down in the mine to help his father on a few occasions. His father had chosen to stay with the coal company and was serving as a deputy, so Butch's mother insisted he go back to school and complete the fifth grade.

Butch spent enough time playing in the coal slag pile that when he blew his nose, coal dust came out on his white kerchief. In fact, it had turned not only black, but highly explosive. Since he never washed it, the cloth had become even more hazardous, a fact that became almost lethal when Ornery Billy got the idea to set Butch's britches on fire. The incident probably would've never happened had Butch tucked his kerchief well enough into his back pocket after recess one day. But that fuse hanging down his backside and the availability of an oil burning lamp were just too convenient for Billy.

The explosion was minor compared to some of the fireworks the boys often set off, but the surprise of it occurring during a math test startled everyone. Girls shrieked. The teacher flipped the chair she sat in backwards onto the floor. Even the boys jumped out of their desks and ran for the exit. Having no idea he was being followed by red flames streaking from his backside, Butch also ran out the door. He still had no idea he was on fire until one of the Negro women who happened by carrying a bucketful of dirty dishwater saw him and doused the flames.

Billy was lucky that no one but his brother Walter had seen him light a piece of kindling on the oil lamp and crawl with it to behind Butch's seat in the back row of the class. Walter usually liked to tell on Ornery Billy, but this time he kept quiet. He remembered that it was not only a tiger and a nigger that hollered when they got caught by the toe.

***

A few nights later, Big Henry was on guard duty with Jeb. They were at the top of the tipple enjoying a smoke and pleasant conversation when Myrtle came stomping up the steps.

"Oh, Lordy, Lordy!" Big Henry said. "I knows that look."

"A white girl at school looked in the outhouse and saw Billy peeing," Myrtle told Big Henry. "Then she ran into the classroom and told everyone that he had a big wee-wee, and Billy shouted that his wee-wee wasn't big and started pulling down his trousers to show the class. That youngin' won't listen to me, and his pa is still spending all his time hiding in the mine from Mistuh Eubanks. But he listens to you, Big Henry. He needs a man to talk to."

"Yes, ma'am," Big Henry said. "I'll go do it directly."

"You'd better." Muttering to herself, Myrtle started back down the long flight of stairs. "I swear that Ornery Billy has spent half his life causing mischief—and the other half coverin' up for what mischief he already done."

"What do I tell him?" Big Henry asked Jeb when she reached the bottom flight. "I ain't hardly never talked to a child before."

"I guess it's time to teach pride," Jeb said. "If he's confident enough, maybe he won't care if folks say things like that."

The next day Myrtle again took the long march up the steps during their watch.

"What's wrong now?" Big Henry said. "I talked to the boy this mornin'."

"And what, pray tell, did you tell that youngin'?" Myrtle shouted.

"I told him the truth," Big Henry said. "Why? What happened now?"

"Well, today when Mary Ellen teased him that he had a big wee-wee, that boy stood right up in class and said, 'Yes, I do, and it is splendid indeed'. Did you tell him to say that?"

Big Henry shrugged while Jeb turned his head and coughed.

"You better straighten that boy out, Big Henry," Myrtle shouted, "or don't you never bring me your clothes for washin' again!" She turned, her every step down the stairwell a clap of thunder.

Big Henry hung his head. "It backfired on me, didn' it, Mr. Jeb? What'll I do now?"

"I guess," Jeb put a hand on the big man's shoulder, "it's time to teach humility."

7

Tom Downs had chosen to hide his own face with a kerchief in the style of western banditos, but most of the other men wore hoods with peep holes cut in them. He had to admit that they did look scarier than he did, but he feared the men wouldn't recognize him as the leader if he wore a hood like everyone else. And besides, his wife Rachel didn't sew very well anyway.

It had been two weeks since John Mitchell arrived in Pana and halted the lynch party with the Smithsons as the guests of honor. Mitchell had promised action, but thus far, the only action had been that another hundred Negro strikebreakers had arrived. The mines were now operating at near capacity. Since the mine owners were more belligerent than ever toward the United Mine Workers, Tom decided to step matters up.

They had spent an hour hauling heavy rail ties to the tracks to make a blockade, but the train stopped a hundred yards short. Maybe that was why the conductor and engineer had time to gain their composure before the masked men made it to the train. They didn't look very surprised when two hundred men stepped out of the wooded area with their heads covered and started walking toward them. The two railroad men sat on the steps of the big engine smoking cigarettes when Tom led the mob up to the train.

"They's in the second and third passenger cars." The engineer pointed over his shoulder indifferently.

"Who's in the first car?" Tom asked.

"Why, the white folks, of course," the engineer said.

Tom resented the sarcasm, but he had no choice but to ignore it. He ordered half the men to go to the left while he led the rest to the right. Approaching the second car, he saw dozens of black faces looking through the windows at the masked men. From inside the coach, he heard a few screams and then shouting, followed by silence.

"You niggers are not wanted in these parts," Tom yelled. "You won't be harmed if you do as I say. Now pick up your belongings and walk slowly outside. Line up along the train."

"Get your guns up and cover them boys," one of the men in a hood shouted.

"I'm giving the orders around here, Holiday."

"Oh, sorry, Tom."

The blacks came off both ends of the passenger cars carrying duffle bags and valises. They were almost all men, a few women and two little boys.

"Where's the rest of your kinfolk?" Tom asked

an old colored man who kept coughing.

"We was told there might be trouble," the woman standing beside him said, "so most men didn't bring any family."

She clung to the arm of the old man who now hacked up blood. Her head was lowered and hidden by her tall hat that was filled with ribbons, feathers and bows.

"He your father?" one of the masked men asked. "What's wrong with him?"

"He my man," the woman said, looking up at the men. "He got pneumonia, I'd 'magine."

The beauty of the Negro woman's face surprised even Tom, although she didn't look much more than a child. On closer inspection, though, he noted that beneath her Navy suit and white blouse she seemed to have ample bumps. The old man started vomiting.

"Take your man into the woods to be sick!" Tom yelled as he and all the masked men backed away.

When the two disappeared into the timber, he walked between the blacks and his armed men. He liked it that most of them kept their eyes to the ground as if he were some sort of Caesar.

"Well, you scabs ain't coming into Pana," Tom said. "Start marching back toward that town you just passed, and we'll put you on the next train going east."

There was no disagreement from the strikebreakers, and the procession began a slow shuffle along the railroad tracks. The women struggled to carry bags that were too big for long distance. The two hundred masked men walked on either side, sometimes tripping or poking the men and women as if they were cattle. The union men who were lame or less physically fit took the nearby dirt road with the carriages and mounts. After about a mile Holiday came running up to Tom.

"We forgot that sick nigger and the girl," he said.

"Well, Hell's bells, Holiday," Tom stomped his foot as he shouted, "take some men and go back and get 'em."

Holiday motioned, and a half-dozen men followed him to the road, mounted horses and trotted back along the railroad tracks.

When the convoy of Negroes reached the little town of Tower Hill, they were told by the station manager that the next train east wouldn't be arriving for another three hours. Tom decided there was no need to keep all the men there, especially since half the four hundred people who lived in the village had come out of their homes to watch the action. He kept fifty reliable men and sent the remainder on back to Pana.

***

Jeb knew something was afoot when he saw the

union men ride back into town. Several of them tied up their horses on the hitching posts and headed straight to the Tipple Tavern. He decided to have a drink himself and see if he could find out what was going on.

The saloon was filled with the sound of deep voices talking in short sentences. Gravely coughs often culminated in dark spats into the silver spittoons that stood next to each column in the room. Jeb ordered a short one, and was downing it when he overheard one of the men ask, "Where's old Holiday Jones?"

"Oh, he and some of the boys had to go back and see about a couple of the scabs who were lagging," his friend answered. "It was an old man and a purty little nigger gal. I think some of the boys were planning a little party with her."

Jeb left the tavern quickly, rented an Appaloosa pony at the stable and whipped the gelding into a hard gallop east along the railroad tracks. He had not been told there would be a trainload of Negroes arriving that day, but since John Mitchell had come to town the UMW had been pretty quiet. The strikers had done little more than picket and throw rocks at the two trains that had recently brought strikebreakers in. Perhaps the mine operators didn't see the need to pay for deputies on the trains as they had previously.

The Appaloosa had once been a cart horse and

never learned to neck rein properly with a rider on his back. Jeb hated pulling one rein off to the side every time he wanted to change directions. Besides that, the animal breathed heavily when moving at more than a trot, and his galloping gait was about as comfortable as riding a wheelbarrow down a rocky hill. Still, Jeb got two miles out of the horse before it began to tire.

A group of men gathered in a grassy glen.

Jeb reined in hard, the Appaloosa kicking up dust with his hoofs. The men sat on tree branches, drinking and smoking. Beneath a nearby oak, an elderly colored man lay on his back. He appeared to be sleeping, though he was breathing hard. Jeb trotted his animal into the camp.

Holiday Jones stood up quickly when the deputy rode in. "What you doing here, Jeb?" He shifted his weight back and forth from one leg to another.

"You boys must be up to no good, Holiday," Jeb said as he dismounted. "You're as nervous as a long tailed cat in a room full of rockin' chairs."

"I hardly never drink alcohol this early, Jeb," Holiday said, his eyebrows forming a choirboy slant. "My judgment may not be too keen at the moment, that's for sure. Let the liquor light up a bunch of scallywags like us, and you never know what'll happen."

Just then a boy no older than fifteen walked out from behind a tree carrying a bottle. He was teetering with half-closed eyes. The youngster tripped over a saddle, fell, and landed hard on the ground. No one made a move to check on him.

"Where's the colored gal, Holiday?" Jeb asked.

Holiday pointed over his shoulder, and a miner named Cyrus Cheney, who'd been propped against a poplar, jumped to his feet. "What in tarnation is this?" Cheney shouted, then staggered toward Jeb. "Why, you young scudder, get moving. This ain't none of your business."

"You move again," Jeb said, pulling his pistol, "and you'll be leavin' meat and marrow all over that tree."

Cheney stepped back a few steps and stared at the deputy.

"Bring me the girl, boys," Jeb ordered. "And Holiday, you can lay that old fella over your mount. I'll leave the horse at the livery."

Holiday did as he was told. Two boys who could still walk went into the woods. They returned a few minutes later with the girl. Jeb glanced at her. He thought she didn't look or act like she'd been in much distress.

"I'm Deputy Jebediah Turner. I'm taking you and the old man to town."

"Well, I'm Fanny May Cahill," the girl said, a look of amusement on her face, "and I reckon I'll just let you."

"I'm also puttin' you boys afoot." Jeb loosened

the tether line that held several horses. With a firm grasp on the reins of the Appaloosa—as well as Holiday's mare—he fired two shots into the air. The spooked horses galloped back toward Pana.

"You could at least let us saddle 'em so's we won't have to carry all that tack into town," Cheney growled.

"Sorry, boys." Jeb shrugged. "I sure didn't think of that. If I cross someone with a wagon, I'll be sure to send 'em your way."

Jeb tucked his pistol back in his belt. Taking the reins of the Appaloosa, he brought it round for the girl to mount. As she was putting her left foot up into the stirrup, the horse gave a forward kick with its rear leg and she leapt out of the way.

Cheney used the moment to his advantage by jumping onto Jeb's back, knocking him to the ground. The two rolled in the grass. Just as Jeb thought he had leverage to throw the man off, one of the other boys rammed him with a head-butt to the stomach, then punched him several times in the face. The black girl wound her arms around Cheney, scratching at his face and eyes.

Jeb popped the second attacker in the nose, and the man ran back into the woods. A moment later, Cheney scurried the same direction.

Jeb lifted the girl by the waist and threw her onto the Appaloosa. He grabbed the reins of Holiday's horse. Walking ahead of the animals, he led them both away from the melee. A mile and a half later, he stopped at Ora Langford's farm pond. The Appaloosa seemed wind broke so he let the animals water. Jeb pulled the old man off Holiday's mount and laid him gently in the grass. He was still unconscious but breathing steadily.

Strategically deposited all around the farm pond were granite-like rocks as big as cows. Old Ora had dug them up out on Williamsburg Hill, then spent countless man hours and money to have them transported and placed around his farm. He had then selected and planted various trees and shrubbery that would give the two-acre pond an Eden-like appearance. This ambiance was made even more perfect by the rocky stream that slid off a steep hill and gurgled quietly into the pond.

Jeb knelt beside the creek. He washed the dirt and blood from his face and arms. Removing his shirt, he was dabbing water on the spots of blood when he heard a splash behind him. When he looked, he spotted Fanny Cahill's dress and shoes hanging on one of the bushes. Rising and walking around the vegetation, he saw she was doing the backstroke toward the center of the little lake. Bright green lily pads surrounded the shoreline. The reflection of the blue, clear sky shone on the water. The fact that she could swim more gracefully than anyone he'd ever seen wasn't as startling as the fact that she was butt naked.

The only reason he wasn't totally shocked was that he had seen many naked girls in photographs and even caught fleeting glimpses of some of the whore's bodies that he occasionally dallied with at a local brothel. He had also courted a girl for several months a few years before, and on one memorable evening had seen her backside exposed as she hurried from the covers of the bed to her privacy screen.

Despite these experiences, seeing this colored girl so boldly skinny-dipping made blood rush to his face. He decided to ignore her by sitting down in the grass, taking off his boots, and clearing the pebbles poking into his feet. As he was giving his toes a good cracking and putting his boots back on, Fanny was now on her stomach, frog-kicking back to shore. He continued to look down at his feet and began rearranging his britches as if it was the most important part of his day. Jeb knew about peripheral vision as well as how to use it. When the colored girl arrived in shallow water, he perceived her rise slowly. She remained standing longer than needed to allow the water to drip her dry in the afternoon sun. He sensed she was daring him to look at her.

"How's your jaw?" she asked.

"It's some better than it was." He rubbed his cheek but kept his head toward his feet.

"Wouldn't hurt you to take a swim yourself, you

know. You smell mighty horsey," Fanny giggled as she walked out of the water and stood in the grass. When Jeb remained silent she added, "You ain't been givin' me any more conversation than a hog grunt. So you got no carnal interest in naked women, Jebediah?"

"Not colored ones especially, no." Jeb was able to keep his eyes focused on his trousers he was tucking neatly into the top of his boots.

"Well, tell me how we different than white women."

Jeb decided to feign disinterest and looked up at her. He figured that the sunshine must be playing tricks, because her skin was so dark and shiny and clean it glistened. Her profile was enhanced in that her arms were raised as she ran her hands through her hair. The next thing he noticed was how tiny her waist was compared to her chest and hips. He thought he could probably touch his thumbs and fingers together if he were to put his hands around it. Her shoulders, arms and legs, though, were full and healthy-looking. Most unusual were the perfectly shaped mounds of her rear end that stood out like two little black globes.

"Not different," Jeb said, looking away again. "Just . . . different, that's all."

"I don' know why you be so persnickety about your fleshly pleasures." Fanny put her dress back on. "Even proper white men down south don' mind a dalliance with a colored gal now and again."

"It ain't proper. God made folks of color so's we wouldn't fornicate outside our races." Jeb then decided an insult might dissuade her from conversation. "I guess it's true what they say about colored women being whores."

Fanny quickly stepped toward Jeb and slapped him hard in the face. It was an action he hadn't expected. He rose slowly to his feet, struggling to maintain a stone-face.

"What choice do you think we have?" Fanny demanded. "Being pretty ain't a blessing for colored gals like it be for your lily-white ladies. Men, mostly white men, been havin' me since I was eight years old. You think I enjoy having fat, sweaty, stinky old men huffin' and pantin' on top of me? Leavin' their slime inside me that won' come clean even when I scrub my privates 'til I bled? Why, I was of child and lost babes two times before I was twelve. Then I wasn' taken to seed no more. So the other womenfolk told me it was a woman's place to endure, and I needed to make white men pay if they wanted wanton pleasure, 'cause no nigger men would never want nothing to do with me. So I started tellin' men they could have me like a wet fish or they could pay me good and I make them scream halleluiah two or three times before I send them home to their missies.

"Why, I got so good, a coal mine man would pay

a day wages to have me. Storekeeps pay twice that, and bankers pay me whatever I asked. Sometimes twenty dollars or more. I got to where I knowed that if a man was sad, he pay me more, and if he happy, he pay me more, and if he drunk, he pay me even more, and if he don', I steal whatever in his pockets when he asleep or puking."

"Why you telling me all this?" Jeb asked. "I ain't gonna pay you nothing."

"You don' have to pay me, Jebediah Turner." Fanny stepped forward to where he could feel her hot breath on his face. "You gets me for free."

"Why is that?"

"'Cause then you'll want me to stay safe when we goes to town." She ran a finger around his ear. "That ol' man won' help me if I need it, but you will."

"I don't copulate outside my race."

Fanny again slapped him hard on the face. "You don' talk that way to a lady."

Jeb was ready this time and hit her back, although not nearly as hard. "You don't strike a white man in these parts. Otherwise, you might hang, even if you is a girl."

Instead of getting angry, Fanny looked at him with a lustful intent Jeb had never seen before.

"Oh, I goin' be likin' you, Jebediah Turner," she said. "And before we through, you goin' like me too."

***

That night, Jeb paid a visit to a brothel, but for the first time in his life, his plumbing froze.

"Why, Jeb, honey," Ella Russell said, "your worm won't come out and play."

Jeb shoved her off him, stood, and pulled up his britches. When he descended the steps into the tavern, he had to push his way through the shoulder to shoulder drunks and barmaids that were jam-packed in the smoke-filled room. Once outside in the fresh air, he took a deep breath and leaned for a moment against a lamp post. The street was empty except for a few sheriff's deputies standing at each corner cradling a Winchester in one arm while smoking or drinking coffee with their free hand.

"Lust is the ruination of a man," his father had told him. It was the evening his mother had cold cocked his pa with a fry pan. "My advice to you is if you must indulge in the flesh, pay for what you need, then just walk away. Otherwise, you'll be paying for a dry cow for the rest of your life."

He walked toward the mine tipple; a crescent moon hung above it. His father's counseling had come the week before he died. Jeb never had a chance to tell his pa the advice had come too late. The fifteen-year-old boy had already fallen deeply in love with pretty Rachel Dobbins.

Halfway to the mine gate, he regretted he hadn't purchased a bottle of whiskey to help drown the indecent thoughts he was having of Fanny May Cahill. Though it was a mild evening, he felt a heat that bordered on fever. The devil was toying with him, of that, he was certain. He had invited Satan into his heart the moment he had raised his eyes toward the Negress. The thing that confused him most was not the lust he felt for her. It was the humanness of her story. For some reason he couldn't comprehend, he wanted her, not just from lust, but also to protect her. She was a child who'd been taken by evil men and could do little more than succumb to the life they created for her.

He shrugged off the feeling, a protective instinct similar to what he had once felt for a crippled colt. Then he remembered: he eventually had to shoot the horse.

8

Over the next two weeks, many more blacks arrived by trains, which were again protected by gunmen hired by the coal companies. The number of blacks living in Pana quickly surged to more than eight hundred, although sometimes it seemed there were as many fleeing the town as arriving. The filthy conditions inside the stockade and the cooler days of the Illinois fall did not sit well with the mining families from Alabama. Sickness became so common, the big cot room was divided off with the healthier women and children sleeping away from those less fortunate.

Jeb was busy keeping the Negroes safe from union strikers, a task that became much more complicated when some of those with families were moved to a newly renovated building just outside the Eubanks Mine. It was quickly dubbed the Alabama Hotel by the coal company, but the pro-union people in Pana called it the Alabama Coon House. Still, Myrtle insisted that the Wallace family be among the first to leave the stockade.

The Alabama Hotel was a camelback, shotgun

apartment building with a second floor at the end of the elongated structure. The long, narrow hallway was on the side like on a train with coach compartments. The families were more crowded than they were in the big stockade around the mine yard, but it was cleaner despite the red tar-paper covering the holes in the roof.

"Why is this called a shotgun building, Mama?" little Sydney asked.

"Because if the doors are open at both ends, a shotgun blast will go clean through the hallway and out the other side—right into the backyard."

"Wow!" the four boys said in unison. Their mother immediately regretted telling them the definition. She worried her Billy might test the theory.

The family of six was given a room barely big enough for one large and one small feather bed. The four boys fit well enough in the bigger bed by sleeping width-wise. On the rare occasions Garfield wasn't staying down in the mine hiding from Eubanks he slept in the little bed with his back to the wall and his arms and legs wrapped around his wife. The room had a narrow, horizontal window high enough that Garfield had to stand on a chair to open and close it. The high down-stairs ceilings allowed the heat to rise and keep the lower areas cooler, although hot days were getting fewer.

Myrtle considered them lucky to be down-stairs where the boys could go out back into the courtyard to relieve themselves. Otherwise, they would've had to stand in line to use the toilet room at the end of the hallway.

Beneath the upstairs camel hump was a low-ceil-inged cafeteria where the women cooked meals on a row of ovens and served their families at wooden tables and chairs. The walled-in courtyard out back made a fine gathering place in good weather.

Since Negroes were now allowed to travel into town, the city passed an ordinance stating that between sundown and sunup, coloreds were to go directly to their destinations and were not allowed to loiter on the streets. Neither were the Negroes allowed in most places of business, a nuisance that thirsty men couldn't abide.

Jeb and two of his fellow deputies were sum-moned to the Sunrise Tavern late one Saturday night. The occasion that caused the ruckus was a popular miner's birthday. With only two taverns in town that accepted company coupons, the black miners migrated to the one closest to the Eubanks mine gate. The owner, Horace "Hardrock" Cowan, had sent for deputies the moment he saw two dozen Negro men and women enter his establish-ment. He had made the mistake of serving the strikebreakers in the past because business had been slow. Hardrock was not very well liked in town. He'd come to Illinois not two years before to scab for the coal mines, a fact that hadn't been forgotten by those native to Pana.

Although he hadn't forbidden Negroes, allowing so many at one time was more than he'd bargained for. Therefore, when Deputy Turner and his men entered the tavern, Hardrock raced to the door to meet him.

"You gotta get these people outta here, Jeb," Hardrock pleaded. "Ain't no decent white folk gonna ever want nothin' to do with me."

"Hell, Hardrock," Jeb said, "no one wants nothing to do with you now."

"Yeah, but—"

Hardrock's plea was interrupted by Fanny Cahill walking through the door with an elderly Negro suitor on either arm. Jeb didn't know why Fanny had to wear dresses that set so low on her shoulders. The back of his neck burned, and he hoped it wouldn't be noticeable in the dimly lit room. He'd been successful in battling thoughts of the pretty colored girl—at least for a few hours of the day. Now her inopportune appearance was sure to set him back in his attempt at self-restraint.

"Excuse me, Deputy Turner," Fanny said, nudging her way into the rapidly filling room, "these nigras-rich gentlemen promised to purchase me a drink."

"You see, Jeb?" Hardrock grabbed the collar on

the deputy's jacket. "These coloreds even bring their womenfolk into the tavern. Why, it ain't decent."

"Why, Mistuh Hardrock?" Fanny asked. "You ain't fixin to evict these folks and their honest money, is ya?"

"Ohhh." Hardrock rubbed the top of his head so hard his well-greased hair stood straight up. "I don't know what to do."

"You got some rooms upstairs, ain't ya?" Fanny reached up and patted the proprietor's hair back into place, then put her head next to his and whispered something that Jeb couldn't hear. He thought he saw a flick of the girl's tongue doing a quick circle inside Hardrock's ear hole.

From that moment on, the Sunrise was considered a colored tavern. Fanny took up residence in one of the upstairs rooms. The back steps from the alleyway became one of the most used stairwells in town, especially by white men.

Meanwhile, the white prostitutes in town began to lose their most prosperous customers.

"Men are just naturally attracted to strange," Ella Russell, Jeb's favorite sporting girl, told him one night during a visit to her brothel. She had confided to Jeb that her clientele had indeed changed. While many of her white customers had migrated to the Sunrise, she was now bombarded by Negro miners who would pay several days' wages for a romp with her.

It bothered Jeb that she didn't seem to be complaining. He had come to personally understand what *attracted to strange* meant. Ella's skin was as white as soap. Quite the opposite of the shiny, dark chocolate smoothness of Fanny Cahill. Still, he wasn't sure he liked the idea of sharing Ella's pleasures with a colored man. He considered taking his business to a widow lady he occasionally dallied with.

"That saloon ain't decent, and we need to shut it down," Jeb told Sheriff Cogburn a few nights later.

"It's a pretty sorry affair, that's for sure," Cogburn agreed. "But, at least we know where the coloreds are, and they ain't getting' in trouble with the white folks."

"Well," Jeb said slowly, "they got a fat, old black lady with no teeth called Buffalo Butts, and a young, light-skin gal named Sissy who's not even fourteen. They's sportin' gals, I hear."

"Not to mention Fanny Cahill," Cogburn said with a smile. "That place sours you to no end, don't it, Deputy?"

Jeb didn't comment. The story of his rescue of the pretty colored girl after the train incident had caused him considerable embarrassment.

"Why, old Buffalo Butts got more men goin' upstairs to see her than the younger whore or even Fanny," a young deputy named Mert Whitmer said. He had just turned seventeen. "Why you suppose they prefer to see the fat lady?"

"Ain't nothin' like a fat woman for hard winterin'," Cogburn answered with a grin.

Mert lit a cigarette and stepped outside to ponder the sheriff's answer.

***

Jeb was in an intemperate mood that evening when he walked the long way around to get to the Springside Mine. He'd taken to avoiding the street in front of the Sunrise Tavern. He couldn't stop himself from looking up at the window to Fanny's room. Either her silhouette or that of one of her clients would set his imagination on fire.

He entered the mine yard and approached the steps to the steeple tower. Voices sounded from the back of the stairwell. He would have assumed it was just a couple of deputies tipping a bottle, but then he heard a stifled cry. He circled around to the back, where several large shadows gathered around a smaller one.

"Why, she ain't even got no fuzz on her muff."

Jeb recognized the voice as belonging to a white deputy named One-Eyed Sherman. The man's hands were up a little black girl's dress.

"Well, her melons are full," one of his friends said. The man grabbed her face and put a sweaty kiss on her mouth.

"You men get away from that girl and get back to your posts!" Jeb shouted when he saw One-Eye unbutton his trousers.

"What for you giving *us* orders?" One-Eye growled. "We're on the night shift. This here's our break time."

"Then get to your bunks," Jeb ordered. "There may be action tonight, and we don't need you boys falling asleep on duty."

"Well, this here will only take a few minutes, general," One-Eye said, emphasizing the title he'd tagged him with.

Jeb pulled his pistol and aimed it at the three men.

"Get away from her," Jeb shouted, "or I'll be filling your head with daylight."

"Why, you're taking this pretty serious there, general," One-Eye said. "You one of them nigger lovers?"

"You rape that girl," Jeb said, "and these coloreds will have your hides."

"She won't tell nobody." One-Eye put a hand tightly on the girl's throat. "Will you, pretty gal?"

The girl shook her head, the tears in her eyes dropping onto One-Eye's coal stained hand.

"Get your filthy paw off that girl," Jeb demanded, cocking his gun. "Or I'll shoot your good eye right out of your head."

The other two men let go of the girl and backed away. When One-Eye saw he was being abandoned, he released his grip on the girl. She gasped and immediately put both hands around her neck to rub the blood back into it.

"Get on home to your mama, child," Jeb ordered. The girl pulled down her skirt and ran toward the stockade building.

"If I hear of you boys doing this type of thing again," Jeb said, holstering his sidearm. "I'll tell Big Henry myself."

That night, Jeb sat alone at the top of the mine tipple watching for signs of trouble from the Opera House. It was just after sunup when he saw a little black boy slowly climbing the stairs toward him. Black children often played on the steps of the tipple and were tolerated by the deputies because there was nowhere else for them to play. It also gave the guards amusement watching them. It was unusual though, that this boy was here so early in the morning and alone. Jeb watched him as he put his right foot, then his left foot on each step as he climbed toward him. When the boy turned onto the final landing, he saw he was only about five years old. He had a coffee cup in one hand and a piece of paper in the other. Without looking Jeb in the eyes, the boy set the cup down and the paper next to it.

"My sister said to give you this," he said. He turned and began descending by sitting and scooting down one step at a time.

When the boy reached the second landing Jeb picked up the piece of paper and looked at it. It was a pencil drawing of a little girl all darkened in except for her mouth and big round eyes. A big man with an eye patch was standing over her. The man had horns on his head and a pitch fork in one hand. Next to them was a man holding a gun. That man had a halo on his head.

9

"I heard you been fightin' my husband again," Rachel Downs said to Jeb when she saw him standing in front of the telegraph office.

"That surprise ya?" Jeb asked.

"Why should it? You and Frank Cogburn been beatin' up on Tom since you was old enough to walk."

"Now that ain't so," Jeb objected. "We never needed to team up against Tom. Either one of us could handle him by our loneself."

"Not everytime," Rachel reminded him.

Jeb knew it was true. It was a sore subject, though. Jeb had been undefeated against the lankier Tom until the year they turned sixteen. That was when Tom decided he wanted Rachel more than Jeb did. She had been the prettiest girl in Pana. Looking at her now in her white dress with puffed elbow-length sleeves and ribbon bows, her long eyelashes and petite features beneath her feathery hat, Jeb had to admit she was still a beauty.

"I always wondered something." Jeb changed the subject. "Why's Tom call you Palomino?"

"When he met me he said my hairs as purty blond as a Palomino pony standin' in an evenin' sun."

For a moment Jeb felt more jealous of Tom's ability with words than he did at his possession of the prettiest girl in the county. The image in his head of Rachel standing naked in an evening sun faded into a similar pose of Fanny May Cahill; one he was familiar with since it came to mind so often.

"They say you saved an old man and a Negro woman," Rachel said as if reading his mind. "I'm glad."

"She's a whore now." Jeb looked down at his boots.

"Fiddlesticks. I might've been a sportin' gal myself if Tom hadn't won that fight," Rachel said.

Jeb doubted that, although he recalled that Rachel had spent time with about every boy in town until she got with Tom.

"He didn't win that fight." Jeb preferred to talk fighting rather than love making. "I tripped over your umbrella, and Tom sucker-punched me with that ax handle."

"Well, anyway," Rachel said, "I'm still glad you saved the black woman."

"What did Tom say about it?"

"You know Tom hates scabs," Rachel said. "He blames them for his parents dyin'."

"A lot of folks lost their jobs because of scabs," Jeb said. "But they didn't kill theyself like Tom's pa did."

"It weren't just losin' his job that done him in," Rachel lamented. "Tom's pa was just fed up with tryin' to get miners to understand they'd never have nothin' unless they united against the coal company. Ever' time he'd get the colliers to understand what he was sayin', the operators would bring in foreigners who couldn't speak English. A bunch of the miners he'd worked so hard to unite would get new jobs or move away. Then he'd have to start all over again. He just got tired, I guess."

Jeb wasn't sure what to say. He was making a good living protecting the mine owners and the colored strikebreakers. Truth be told, he didn't have much affection for the operators, but he was developing a healthy respect for the Negroes. Men like Big Henry and Garfield Wallace were as honest, loyal and hard-working as any white men he'd ever known. Still, he wondered why they tolerated the abuse in wages and working conditions from the company.

"Did you really want Tom to win that fight?" he asked.

"How do you think my umbrella got betwixed your feet?" Rachel said as she turned and walked away.

***

Garfield had stayed out of Eubanks' sight for several weeks by virtually living down in the coal mine. Then one day, the mine owner walked right up to him and told him to go get the mine boss. Garfield felt sure he'd been recognized and was about to be escorted from the stockade. As he hurried through the mine yard, he wondered if they would allow him to retrieve his wife and boys and take them with him. When he finally located the boss man and returned with him, Eubanks ordered him back to work with barely a glance.

"I've been listenin' to the sound of rocks creaking down in the mine for so long," Garfield told his wife that afternoon when he came up out of the mine, "I've forgot what the voice of a woman can sound like."

"Mine's the sound of a heart breakin' for loneliness." Myrtle kissed him hard on the mouth.

The next day Garfield enjoyed his newfound freedom by visiting downtown Pana. The miners had been warned to travel in groups. Since most of the men only had company coupons with which they'd been paid, they could spend it only at Eubanks Company Store or two of the town's saloons. While the other miners chose the Sunrise Tavern, Garfield felt obliged to visit the O'Brien store where his wife had purchased food on their first day in town.

In the store, Garfield walked right up to the counter and gave Mrs. O'Brien a toothy smile. "I'm Garfield Wallace, Missus O'Brien," Garfield said. "My missy said you was the nicest and prettiest gal in town. I just want to thank you for helpin' us out that first day we come to Pana."

The door to the store opened and three scruffy looking men walked in and stood behind Garfield. Mrs. O'Brien turned quickly away from him.

"This nigger bothering you, Mrs. O'Brien?" one of the men asked.

"Well," Mrs. O'Brien said, taking out her fan and waving it in front of her face, "I never had a colored speak to me so informally."

"What did he say, ma'am?" the man asked.

"Why, he said that I was pretty."

Mrs. O'Brien's husband entered the room, and she rushed into his arms.

The next thing Garfield knew, he was being pulled out of the store by the three men. Almost immediately, a dozen more white men and women were on the scene. Garfield put his head and eyes to the ground. He knew the manner of behavior that would be expected of him if he was going to avoid a beating.

"What's going on here?" a man asked as he pushed his way through the crowd.

"Glad you're here, Downs," the man said. "This

nigger got fresh with Missus O'Brien. These black sons-of-bitches take our jobs, and now they think they can treat themselves to our women. We oughta throw his sorry black ass in the hoosegow."

"You got a wife and kids here, nigger?" Tom asked. "Maybe we should treat them the way you treat our women."

"No sir," Garfield lied, "I come alone."

"Well, the way I see it," Tom said, "we have to make a decision here. I don't think anyone would object to us hanging a nigger for molesting a white woman—or we could just put you on the next train goin' south. Why, we'll even pay your way, boy. Now, which'll it be?"

"I suppose I'd best be getting home to Alabama, sir," Garfield said.

"Well, I suppose you're right," Tom said. "Take him to the railroad station."

The crowd grew larger each block, and by the time they rounded the last corner to the depot, there were close to one hundred observers. That was when Big Henry and four other Negroes stepped in front of the procession. Big Henry was the only one who looked straight into the eyes of Tom Downs and the other white men.

"Let him go," Big Henry said.

"Why, we ain't holdin' him at all," Tom said. "You see our hands on the boy? He said he wanted to go back to Alabama. Now, that's a wise choice, and we citizens of Pana are fixin' to pay his way. If you boys is smart, you'll be joinin' him."

"Come stand over here, Garfield." Big Henry turned his eyes back to Tom. "If he wants to go home, it will be us who walks him to the train station."

Garfield started to move. Tom stopped him with an extended arm.

"Now, we ain't gonna have you boys intimidating this poor man into stayin' if he don't want to." Tom pulled a pistol from inside his jacket.

Big Henry pulled a knife, and one of the other blacks found a good-sized rock on the road that he raised into a throwing position. The other strikebreakers held their ground, but continued to keep their eyes down.

Tom jabbed the pistol into Garfield's back and pushed him toward the jailhouse. The crowd followed. Big Henry didn't budge, but his allies backed away. A half dozen men were suddenly on Big Henry. One used a rifle butt to knock his knife out of his hands.

"Forget the other nigger," Tom shouted. "This one's the leader! Take him to jail!"

Big Henry was so strong and struggled so mightily, not enough union men could get close enough to lock a grip on him. One man got flipped over onto his back, and two others were knocked unconscious when he rammed their heads together.

Even when he was brought to the ground, Big Henry found ways to kick and bite.

"Take him to Eubanks' store then!" Tom shouted when they made little progress moving the young giant. "We'll get some rope and tie him up."

"Go get the sheriff," Garfield told one of his friends.

As the man ran off, a group of blacks came out of the Sunrise Tavern and joined their fellow strike-breakers watching Big Henry being dragged into the store. Buffalo Butts Bertha pushed her way to the front of the group, followed by Fanny Cahill. Fanny stumbled and fell forward into the crowd of United Mine Workers. They quickly shoved her back away from them. She and Bertha balled their hands into fists and stepped back toward them. A toothless snarl from Buffalo Butts gave the union men hesitation.

"You think a nigger whore can whoop a white man in a fight?" The man standing in the lead position sneered.

"We don't need to beat you, Holiday Jones." Fanny held a fist in front of his eyes. Though the man had led the gang rape of her on her first day in town, he was now a loyal paying customer. "All we gotta do is leave a mark on your face!" Fanny shouted. "That'll do your reputation more harm than anything you can do to us."

The prospect of a bloody nose from a prostitute caused the union men to take a step back. Both blacks and whites shouted insults at one another as the leaders on both sides contemplated strategies. Garfield, who had inadvertently begun the chaos, was for trying to exchange himself for Big Henry.

"They done threw you back like you was an ol' carp," Ike Alexander scoffed at his suggestion. "You's just small fish next to Henry Stevens."

By the time Sheriff Cogburn arrived with Jeb Turner, there were dozens of blacks on one side of the store door facing the growing number of whites on the other. The two officers pushed their way between the crowds and marched into the store. A badly beaten Big Henry was lying hogtied with his stomach on the store floor, his hands and legs behind his back. Two men were getting ready to slip a pole beneath the ropes and carry him to the jail.

"Untie that man!" the sheriff shouted.

"We're just helping you, sheriff," Tom said. "This nigger tried to attack us with a knife."

"The way I heard it, you were holding a gun," Jeb said.

"What do you want him charged with?" Sheriff Cogburn asked.

"Why, assaultin' a white man, of course," Tom shouted.

"All right, then," the sheriff said. "How do you plead, Big Henry?"

With a gag in his mouth, Big Henry was only able to make an angry growl.

"Fine," Cogburn said. "The defendant pleads guilty. I fine him four dollars. Deputy Turner, see if he has four dollars in his pockets."

"That's bullshit, Cogburn!" Tom shouted.

"He's got a coupon for four dollars at the company store, sheriff," Jeb said, holding up a piece of paper.

"Big Henry," Cogburn said as Jeb began cutting the ropes off him, "I order you to remain in the confines of the mine yard until further notice. Now get on out of here."

Big Henry stood tall and rubbed the blood back into his powerful arms. He ignored the streaks of dark crimson running from his mouth and nose. When he stepped forward to leave the store, the union men gave only enough room so they'd have an excuse to shove him with their shoulders.

Once the big Negro was outside, the union men stepped in front of Jeb and the sheriff so they couldn't follow. Tom was standing next to Big Henry when several dozen blacks pushed their way toward them. Some of them carried clubs and knives, and a few had Winchesters and pistols. Garfield Wallace was in the lead. He quickly recognized that his best friend was having a stubborn fit that would most likely be his last.

"Just turn right around and get back to the

mine," Tom said, waving his gun at the Negroes.

"That's our intention, Mistuh Downs," Garfield said. "We just come to collect Big Henry."

Tom recognized that the blacks were outnumbered three to one. He walked straight up to Garfield and swung his pistol butt down hard on his head. "Get 'em, boys!"

Big Henry grabbed Garfield before he could fall, and backed immediately into the protection of the black miners. He had no idea from where the first gunshots came, but he was aware that dozens more followed, and a billowing white cloud encompassed him from behind. A moment later other Negroes were being carried or assisted as they rushed to get to the mine gate.

By the time Jeb and Sheriff Cogburn were able to get through the crowd, the shooting had stopped. Men were running for either their homes or to get into positions in buildings where they could fire at the mine tipple. It was from those vantage points that sporadic firing returned.

"Get deputies to go around and close every business, especially the taverns!" Cogburn yelled. "In an hour from now, I don't want anyone on the streets!"

Jeb ran toward the city jail.

***

The next morning, state warrants were issued for all Negroes involved in the riot. Governor John Tanner sat in his Executive Mansion office reading the Pana Daily Palladium newspaper to the National Guard captain who stood facing him.

"It says here," Tanner said, paraphrasing the story, "that the riot started when a black fired a Winchester into the crowd of whites. In the next several minutes, over one hundred shots were fired and five of the coloreds were wounded."

"You think anyone is dumb enough to believe that a Negro fired the first shot into a crowd of white people and didn't hit anyone?" Tanner asked. "That makes no sense at all. With over one hundred shots fired, no whites were even hit, but five blacks got wounded."

"I guess colored folk ain't very good shots," Captain Gibbs said with a shrug. Having been awakened from a sound sleep a few hours before and told to board a special train for Springfield, his eyes were barely open.

Governor Tanner set the newspaper down and ran his fingers through his thick moustache. "It sounds like if the county sheriff would've done his job and locked up the Negro with the knife, none of this would have happened."

"Why do you think he didn't?" Gibbs asked.

"The sheriff has two hundred deputies guarding the coal mines," Tanner said. "He's probably on the take from the mine owners. This isn't the only coal company that would like to see the National Guard sent in to protect their scab labor. Virden and Carterville mines are also refusing to pay the agreed upon wage scale."

"Why?"

"They say it's because it costs them more to have the coal shipped to Chicago than the mining towns that are closer," Tanner said. "I think it has more to do with the fact that they don't want the United Mine Workers to be telling them what to do."

"Listen to the paper's description of the black that had the knife," Tanner said. Putting his reading glasses low on his nose, he read, "Henry Stevens is as hard as iron and his muscles stand out like whip cords. His biceps are as large as the calf of an ordinary man's leg. He stands about six feet, two inches tall and he weighs in the neighborhood of two-hundred pounds."

"So how do you want the Guard to handle the situation?" Gibbs asked.

Tanner stood and began pacing in front of the long conference table. "When Altgeld was governor, he was faced with the ninety-four Pullman strike. He refused to use the state militia, so President Cleveland sent in federal troops. That made Altgeld look bad, so later when the coal miners went on strike, he sent in the state militia nine separate times to protect the mine operators."

"That oughta have shown those miners who the bosses are," Gibbs said. "Why not do that this time?"

"Votes," Tanner said in a low whisper. "And Cora."

"What was that, sir?" Gibbs asked, leaning forward.

"Nothing," Tanner said. "I want you to keep the peace and protect the coal company property. But you are not there to help the coal company run their operations with labor that has been imported from other states. You are to report to the sheriff, but you will answer to me. Is that understood? We are not there to protect the Negro miners from Alabama at the expense of the good bona-fide citizens of Pana."

"Sounds a little complicated," Gibbs said.

"Start by disarming the citizenry," Tanner said. "Keep me informed of your progress, but keep in mind that I'm also dealing with similar situations in Virden and Carterville. If you're successful, I may not need to send troops to those places."

"What if they don't give up their weapons, sir?"

"Then I fear," Tanner said and glanced at his wife Cora's photograph on his desk, "there will be blood running in the streets of Pana."

***

That afternoon, the National Guard arrived in

Pana on the three-thirty train. Captain Gibbs was shocked to see nearly a thousand people, including many picketers, cheering them when they disembarked. Tom Downs was the first to shake Gibbs's hand and offer his soldiers quarters in the Opera House and City Hall.

"No, thank you anyway," Gibbs told him. "I'd rather my men not be that close to your saloons. Too much temptation, you know? I think we'll settle in your ball park. That will place us centrally between your downtown and the mine yards."

Just then the crowd made a loud "awing" sound. Moving as one they rushed closer to a flatbed car where soldiers had pulled a tarp off two big Gatling guns. Young boys pushed their way to the front of the spectators, all the while pointing and shouting their enthusiasm. When the guns and all the equipment were loaded on wagons, the guardsmen formed rank. With all the pomp of an Independence Day parade, they marched the short distance to the ball park. For the next several hours, men, women and children enjoyed watching the soldiers put up tents, stack rifles in tripods, and build camp fires. Later that evening, another troop arrived. By the time the sun began to set and the most curious of the local youngsters were called home, there were ten officers and one-hundred-seventy-five enlisted men prepared to protect the town of Pana.

Having thwarted Tom Downs' attempt to manipulate the soldiers to the union's cause, Captain Gibbs stood in his tent that evening doing the same with the coal company spokesman.

"This is my town and your men are under my jurisdiction," Sheriff Cogburn said, his jaw quivering slightly.

"The governor has given me strict orders," Gibbs said. "I am not to assist with the protection of out of state workers to the coal mine."

"The last trainload of workers were sent packing by two hundred masked gunmen at the Tower Hill station," Cogburn reminded him.

"Then we will guard the Tower Hill station," Gibbs said. "But that's all."

***

The next day, Jeb accompanied Sheriff Cogburn to the office in Eubanks' home to give the mine owner the bad news. The big brick mansion was located in what had become known to the wealthy as Quality Hill. It was called Snob Hill by everyone else. The only time Jeb had ever been in that neighborhood previously had been during the Panic of '93. He and some of the other young men had been hired to make deliveries and do odd jobs around their houses while the wealthy residents mourned their losses. Now he and the sheriff trotted past the immaculately mowed lawns and beautiful shrubbery. Jeb recalled that it was a far sight prettier now than it had been in the year after the panic when the rich folks couldn't even afford cheap labor.

They were ushered into the house by a manservant. While they waited in the grand foyer to be announced, the sheriff began googling over the lavish furniture and décor. Jeb on the other hand chose to nose around and see if he could identify any areas that might lead down to the legendary tunnel that it was rumored connected the homes of the various company owners. Speculation around town was that the tunnels had been built in case any of the homes were besieged by irate strikers who might pose a threat to the lives of the capitalists.

Ten minutes later the visitors were ushered into the study, where Douglas Eubanks sat behind a great oak desk.

"That Gibbs is an ass," Eubanks said after hearing the sheriff relate his conversation with the National Guard captain.

The sheriff had taken the only chair facing the mine owner's huge desk, so Jeb stood back by the door. He felt a little awkward, since even Eubanks' feeble-minded son Toby had a chair, though it was small and located in the corner of the room behind where his father sat in the biggest leather chair Jeb had ever seen.

"Another train with the niggers is due in town tomorrow at noon," Cogburn said.

"If Gibbs would have only agreed to let the militia escort the train past the picketers and into the mine yard," Eubanks declared, slamming his hand on his desk.

"Pa," Toby uttered, leaning forward in his chair. When his father glared over his shoulder at his son, Toby reclined again and chewed on one of his thumbnails.

"Maybe we should try to sneak the coloreds in at night," the sheriff suggested. "Maybe in a boxcar."

"Pa," Toby said again, this time pulling on the sleeve of his father's suit jacket.

"What is it, Tobias?" Douglas Eubanks shouted at his son.

"I'll bet them soldiers would come runnin' if they heard gunshots." Toby snickered. "Wouldn't that be a good joke on them soldier boys, Pa? To see them come a runnin' and then we just stand there and laugh at 'em?"

"Just shut up, Toby," Eubanks said with a wave of his hand. "Let us think."

Toby cowered back down toward his chair in the corner where he returned to chewing on a thumbnail.

"Maybe Toby has something there," Jeb said.

Sheriff Cogburn turned in his chair so he could

see his deputy. Father and son Eubanks raised their heads and tilted them sideways at the same time. They both stared at Jeb with one side of their lip cocked slightly upward.

"Those soldier boys would sure come a runnin' if they heard gunshots," Jeb said with a smile, "wouldn't they, Toby?"

***

At eleven forty-five the next morning, a long series of gunshots sounded from a building located somewhere between the rail station and the Eubanks Mine. Hundreds of strikers standing in front of the mine gates dropped their picket signs and dove for cover in nearby buildings. The streets emptied in a noisy, yet well-practiced manner. Over one hundred National Guardsmen in the park grabbed their rifles from the tripods, formed rank and marched double time onto Locust Street. Once in position near where the shots had been fired, Captain Gibbs ordered his men to form a perimeter defensive position.

Following the sound of bayonets being fixed on the rifles, there came an eerie silence. A few dogs barked. A few chickens clucked. Cows mooed in the distance. The soldiers held their guns at the ready. Then the whistle from the noon train sounded. Still no one moved—not the people in the buildings nor the soldiers on the street.

The train pulled past the depot, steam hissing and billowing in soft clouds from the braking system. The men, women and children that departed the first passenger car were halfway through the mine gates before someone in an upper-story window noticed their skin color.

"Niggers!" an old woman shouted.

Union men rushed out of the buildings, but were instantly halted by confused soldiers who instinctively stepped in front of them. By the time Captain Gibbs realized that he had been duped, the train was emptied of its passengers and was chugging slowly out of the town.

"Damn those scallywags!" Gibbs shouted. then for some unfathomable reason drew his sword and pointed it at the mine gate. "We've been snookered!"

Jeb thought it a little sad that Toby never received any credit for coming up with the idea of tricking the guardsmen into protecting the arrival of the strikebreakers. For that matter, he didn't receive any credit, either.

The blame was what mattered. The United Mine Workers and newspapers all over the nation quickly ran with stories that Governor Tanner had sent the National Guard to help the coal operators. After that day, Captain Gibbs and his soldiers were booed and hissed everywhere they went in Pana.

10

Fanny hadn't accepted a client all evening. She ignored the knocks on the door. Instead, she just lay in her bed with the room locked and the lights out. The working hours for her profession were nearly past when she finally forced herself to get up and go downstairs.

Only a few Negroes were still in the tavern. Most had nearly drunk themselves into unconsciousness. She walked past them and toward a table in the back corner where Big Henry sat alone, pouring shots of whiskey from a bottle. She craved a friendly shoulder and plopped down in one of the chairs next to him.

"You know, Big Fist Henry, I ain't never seen you drink nothin' but whiskey."

"After I get done with security guardin'," he said, "my only wet comes from a bottle."

"You stand watch with Garfield and that *white deputy*, don't ya?" She didn't want to say Jeb Turner's name, but the thought of him brought mist to her eyes. The next second, tears ran along her cheek and into his glass of whiskey.

"Here," he handed her a handkerchief. "I don't particularly care for watered down rotgut. Woman, why you weeping?"

"Oh, my brain is leakin' all sorts of notions." When he didn't say anything, she went on. "What we doin' here, Big Henry? Why can't Negras ever have a place of our own?"

"Well, I'd 'spect it's kinda like with the Indians. Ever time people of color build something worth anythin', there's always white folks ready to take it away from 'em."

"I hate white folk." Fanny's eyes turned fiery.

"Even after Mistuh Jeb saved you?"

"That white boy didn't pay me no never mind."

"Well, maybe he didn't get a real good look at ya."

"Sir, he seen me as naked as I was on my first birthday. He didn't do nothin' more'n glance at me."

"I reckon that shows he gots a piece of the Lord in his heart." Big Henry gulped down another shot. "Maybe you shoulda showed him your soul instead of your flesh."

"I showed him that too." Fanny sighed, remembering she had shared her troubled past. "He see me as nothin' but a nigger whore."

Their conversation was interrupted when Quits Simpson raised his head from a pool of spilled beer at a nearby table. "Where's a nigger whore?" he said through half-closed eyes. "I's got two more dollars, and I wants me some tail."

Big Henry stood and walked over to Quits' table. He gently pushed the drunk's head back down on the table and held it a few seconds until he fell asleep again. He turned to Fanny. "Let's take a walk."

When the two were outside on the empty boardwalk, she took his arm and they strolled behind a stable. The back of the barn looked out onto open fields. They walked to the end of a corral that held half a dozen horses. A red sorrel mare clopped lazily to the fence so Fanny could rub her mane. Above them, a cloudless, moon-bright sky filled with shiny stars arched from one horizon to the other. In the distance, timbered hills dotted here and there between harvested farmland and occasional patches of prairie grass.

Big Henry rested his massive forearms on the top of the wooden fence.

Fanny felt the warmth of his body and moved closer. They stood that way for several blissful moments. Stroking gently under the mare's mouth, Fanny rested her head on Big Henry's chest, though he wouldn't put his arm around her. He was one of the few men in town who didn't partake of her pleasures. She felt comfortable with him.

"See that star up there?" Big Henry pointed.

"The north star," Fanny said a little harshly. "Why is it that ever nigger always point to that star when someone gets down in the dumps?"

"My pa called it the hope star," Big Henry said as though looking hard enough would bring them the experiences of their ancestors. "He said our people hoped it would lead them out of slavery and to somewhere in this world where there's good. No one wants to live through such terrible goin' ons, Fanny May. We gots no control over the times we livin' in. All we can do is somethin' about the times to come."

"I don't want to be a whore no more, Big Henry."

"Then don't be."

"How? Ain't no man, black nor white, will take me, and don't nobody want to hire a retired sportin' gal."

"You try prayin'?"

"If there's a God, he sure won't listen to the likes of me." Fanny gave the mares' head a gentle push, and she wandered back over to the other horses. She leaned back against the fence.

"Sin is sin," Big Henry assured her. "God don't rank sins. He sent Jesus to forgive us 'cause he knows ain't none of us perfect."

"I went to a tent meeting once." Fanny chewed her lip, then looked out at the animals. "The preacher took all my money, then stuck his head inside my skirt. I's pretty sure he weren't lookin' for no loose change."

"I tend to avoid them tent evil-angelists myself." Big Henry nodded. "I'd 'spect the most impotanest thing is you tell God your sins and ask for forgivenness."

"Can't I do that right now?" Fanny felt a glimmer of hope.

"I think you're supposed to confess to a human," Henry answered after a moment of thought. "Thata way God knows you's serious enough to stand being embarrassed."

"Well, can I confess my sins to you?" She moved away from the fence and looked straight up into his face. "I'd be plum embarrassed to tell you some of them thin's I done."

"Well." Henry hesitated again. "I remember the Good Book says somethin' about whoever has ears let him hear. But you might wanna find somebody with a little less bad on God's books than I's gots."

"I heared there's a church in town," Fanny said, her eyes opening wide, "where a holy man sets behind a curtain and listens to your sins."

"That might work. Say, I 'member somethin'. I think it would be okay if I share with you a blessin' that a preachin' man give me when my pa died." Big Henry placed the palm of his hand on Fanny's forehead, closed his eyes and said, "May your heart be raised to the kingdom of heaven more than all thy brethren."

He gave her face a little shove and Fanny fell backwards into the dew wet grass.

She jumped back to her feet. "Is that how it's supposed to work?"

"Yep, that's exactly what happened when he blessed me."

"I'm boundin' to you, Big Henry." Fanny took his arm and pulled him back toward the saloon. "I'd best be getting to that church early in the morn' if'n I want to shed some of them sins of mine by suppertime."

***

Fanny didn't work for three days. Instead, she went each morning, afternoon and evening to the church and knelt in front of a statue of Jesus on the cross. She had plenty of money saved in a hiding place, but her previous experience with holy men had taught her to not bring more than a nickel at a time. Her instinct proved correct, in that the man who called himself a Father was quick to abscond with the coin each time he saw her kneeling at the altar.

By the end of the third day, her prayers were coming easier, making her feel that the Holy Spirit was doing a good job taking hold of her soul. She told the Father everything and tried to not leave out a single detail. Between each trip to the church, she searched her memory for any sins she may have forgotten. Having a newly recalled sin almost everytime, it got to where the priest would head to the confessional as soon as she entered. Once, after a particularly long and detailed session, the Father was drenched in sweat when he emerged from behind the curtain.

Fanny liked the church. It smelled good from all the candles burning and was quiet even when there were several other people in it. They always entered solemnly and knelt like she did. Some of them made the gesture across their face and chest she had seen other folks do—not so much in Alabama but quite a few in Pana.

Each time she stood to leave, the priest would tell her, "Your faith has saved you; go in peace."

"I feel truly obligin' to you," Fanny would always say. She wasn't sure what else to say to a man dressed in a robe. On this day, she was feeling real nice so she told him, "That's real gentle of you, Father."

The moon, barely visible this cloudy night, was getting on toward midnight. Since her religious conversion, Fanny had taken to walking up to her room by the outside stairwell rather than through the busy tavern. Once, she had to wait half an hour for Bucktooth Simmons to grow frustrated enough to leave before she could get home. Bucktooth liked to whittle. It was his custom to sit on her outside steps and whittle little sculptures of horses. When he got one finished, he would offer it to Fanny with the hopes she'd give him a discount on her services.

"I ain't no art collector, Bucktooth," she told him in the days before she became a Christian. "These legs only spread for hard cash."

Fanny was reminded of these harsh words as she neared her building. She made a mental note to add them to her next confession. Since it was such a dark night, she hurried up the steps with key in hand. Feeling for the hole in the door lock, she peered into the shadows along the narrow balcony.

"I sure do wish I had a piece of that black ass," a voice said from the far end of the balcony.

"If wishes were horses, beggars would ride," Fanny answered. She quickly worked the lock, then added. "I have seen the Lord, and I ain't no sportin' gal no more."

She was inside and almost had the door closed when it came crashing against her shoulder. Two National Guard soldiers threw her on the bed. One of them slammed the door closed behind him so hard a picture on the wall crashed to the floor. The other man grabbed the back of her coat, nearly separating her shoulders as he pulled it off.

"Don't tear the dress." Fanny shouted. She had been through enough situations like this to know not to fight it unless she had an advantage. "I'll take it off."

"Don't worry, missy." The taller of the two tossed two dollars on her dresser."We intend to pay for your service."

Just then the back door swung open. The soldiers snapped to attention. A uniformed man Fanny recognized as being a major entered. She gave a sigh of relief.

"You men were told there was to be no fraternizing with the locals," the officer stated firmly.

"Yes, Major Samuels. We're sorry, sir," both soldiers said at once.

Samuels' cold stare at the guardsmen turned toward Fanny. "You're the whore all my men have been talking about."

"Not no more, Major. I's retired." Fanny rose from the bed. The top of her dress had been pulled down, exposing one of her breasts. She spun away from the men and covered herself. When she turned back around, Samuels eyes were lit up like two full moons. She knew the change in his face was not a good thing. *Lord*, she thought, *please give this man the strength to overcome.*

"You men will, of course, be disciplined when we return to camp." Samuels gave a snarly smile. "As for this nigger whore, I think it good she also receive a consequence. Therefore, as you were, men."

"Pardon, sir?" the tall soldier asked.

"You paid for this harlot's services." Samuels picked up a short broom that was leaning in a corner. Twirling it like a baton, he sat in a chair by the window and crossed his legs. "Now mount her like the bitch she is."

The soldiers didn't move.

"Do as I say, soldier." Samuels emphasized each word, then continued calmly, "and perhaps I will forget about this incident entirely."

Though the two soldiers appeared dumb-founded, Fanny understood what the major wanted. She had experience with men who would pay to watch. Unbuttoning her dress, she let it drop to the floor. Then, completely nude, she lay stomach down across the edge of the bed.

When both men were finished, Fanny retrieved a blanket to cover herself. She felt the major's eyes still on her, but the two soldiers had rebuttoned their trousers. With red faces, they stood at attention, facing the outside door.

"If I find out you've told anyone about this incident, I will have you court-martialed," Samuels said. "Now get back to camp and let the other men know that no one is to ever visit the nigger whores in this town again."

The guardsmen hurried out of the room, slamming the door behind them.

"Why didn't you fight more?" Samuels asked. He

remained sitting in the chair twirling the broom. "I prefer a bitch to struggle." He leapt to his feet, grabbed her by the hair, pulled her head back, and put his nose an inch from hers.

"When a fella takes to bustin' a nut," Fanny said, a hiss in her words, "there ain't nobody can stop 'em."

Samuels pushed in on one of his nostrils and blew a wade of snot out the other onto her mouth.

When she awoke the next morning, Fanny was naked and sprawled out on her stomach on the wood floor. Her entire body was so sore she didn't try to move. After several minutes of not knowing how she got there or why her face felt numb, the memory of Samuels' evil laugh and the cruel beating he gave her returned. She tried to roll over, but a throbbing pain from the back of her neck to her thighs was so intense she nearly lost consciousness. With a loud groan, she returned to her stomach. Once recovered again, she noticed a piece of paper lying next to her on the floor. It was bent so that the writing on it showed. *SWEEP UP WHEN YOU LEAVE.*

The realization of the message's meaning came to her, and the incredible pain on her backside became even more intense. Unable to lower her stiff and aching head, Fanny looked over to the long, vertical mirror on the wall. She screamed from the effort, but she managed to roll into a position on her side where she could see the reflection of the horrible welts that had formed across her entire back and legs all the way down to her knees. Then she spotted the broom nearby. Reaching out, she grasped the bristles of the brush and dragged it toward her face. The handle was coated with dark, dried blood. Disgusted, she pushed it away from her.

"That's what I get for praying," Fanny gasped before rolling again onto her stomach and returning into unconsciousness.

11

Tom Downs was getting famous. His management of the Tower Hill rejection of colored strikebreakers earned him the praise of both General Bradley and John Mitchell, who had just become the interim national president of the UMWA.

"We're bringing union men from all over the state to stop Negro scabs from coming into Virden," Bradley told Tom. "We want you to bring twenty of your best men."

"Marksmen?" Tom asked.

"No," Bradley answered. "Smart men. We want boys who can keep their heads and follow orders. John Hunter turned back the first wave of scabs with a minimum of force, a lot like you did at Tower Hill. Peaceful persuasion, he calls it, and since he's the president of the Illinois UMW we need to follow his lead."

Tom figured Bradley didn't quite realize the type of persuasion he and his masked men had actually used, but he decided to keep that information to himself. After the previous week's trainload of scabs arrived in Pana under the protection of the National Guard, the frustrations among the strikers increased dramatically. Many had begun carrying weapons again, although they usually tucked them discreetly beneath their fall clothing.

"And another thing," Bradley added, "keep in mind that the coal company would like to start a gunfight. They want to force the governor to send the guard into Virden like he did here."

Tom was glad that Bradley didn't know that it was his own cold-cocking of one of the black men that started the ruckus in Pana. Still, he had to admit that peaceful persuasions had worked at other locations in Illinois. Two carloads of black strike-breakers were recently sidetracked at Galesburg, and fourteen other Negroes were taken off a train near Minonk. It had become such a common practice that any Negro traveling through central Illinois was under suspicion of being a scab. Even innocent blacks learned to duck down in the passenger cars whenever they passed through towns.

The train ride to Virden got off to a bad start when four Negroes were allowed seats in the passenger car with the Pana men. When Tom questioned the conductor, he was told there wasn't a colored car available.

"No boxcars either?" Tom asked.

"Separate but equal, the law says," the conductor said referring to the 1896 Supreme Court decision *Plessy vs. Ferguson.* "I'm not needin' to be sued."

"We's United Mine Workers just like you's," one of the Negros said. "We don't like corporate greed or scabs, no matter their color."

Tom had heard that Negroes had been brought from Tennessee to be strikebreakers at the Carterville, Illinois, coal mines. He couldn't fathom why the United Mine Workers had recruited them to join their ranks. Despite the fact that violence had been averted by the integration, the idea of white men working alongside blacks repulsed him.

"I heard they built a fort around the Virden Mine." Tom turned to Holiday Jones. He didn't want to acknowledge any type of conversation with the Negroes.

"I saw the famous stockade at Virden as I came up from St. Louis," Holiday said. "It's not in any sense a formidable-looking affair. In fact, I feel a well-intentioned donkey could demolish it in about an hour. That's because none of the local carpenters would go against the union and take the job. They had to bring in some boys who weren't real handy with a hammer."

"Well, if the coal company manages to get the scab train into the stockade like they did in Pana, they'll have the high ground advantage," Tom said.

"That don't make no never mind," Holiday said. "Bradley told us not to bring guns, didn't he?"

Tom smiled. He opened his coat a little to show off the forty-four caliber Colt tucked beneath one side of his suspenders. The other two men sitting in the seats across from him briefly opened their coats to display their own side arms.

"Heaven help us," an eavesdropping Negro said.

"Union men, indeed," Tom said loud enough to be heard throughout the car.

The colored man turned his face back toward the window.

The conductor gave one final shout of "All aboard!" He then stepped off the platform and, making certain the tracks were clear, gave the highball sign to the engineer. A moment later, two short blasts from the train's engine signaled they were moving out.

The passengers felt a slight lurch. Then came the rhythmic cadence of the great iron wheels turning slowly and then increasingly faster.

For a reason he couldn't understand, Tom's heartbeat seemed to keep pace with the sound of the pistons that drove the wheels. He wiped at the sweat on his brow, then glanced around to make certain the other men hadn't seen his apprehension.

The battle for unionization that his father had fought for and that had finally driven him to suicide seemed to be coming to a head. He pulled his hat down over his eyes, sat back in the seat, and tried to imagine a world where men didn't need to fight for the right to make a decent wage.

***

Swain Whitfeld began to question his decision to go to Virden, Illinois, and work the coal mines the moment a dozen heavily armed white men boarded the train in St. Louis. The five passenger cars were already filled with colored miners and their families who had come up from Birmingham. Now, with a half dozen detectives at the entrance of each coach, women and children had to sit on the miners' laps or squeeze into the aisle.

What made Swain most uncomfortable, though, was the fact that each detective was armed with what appeared to be a shiny new Winchester rifle. At least he thought they were new, since he could see grease in the barrels of the guns that were closest to him.

"I sure do wish I'd have come up here when Big Henry came. I most surely do," Swain told Luke Johns.

"Why?" Luke asked. "Some of those boys who came back to Birmingham said they was livin' in the worst kind of squalor they ever saw in Pana."

"Yeah," Swain said, "but at least they had Big Henry to watch after 'em. Yes, they did."

"That's true," Luke said.

The next hour of the train journey was nearly quiet except for the constant clanking of the iron wheels on the tracks. Though they appeared to be hardened men, several of the detectives looked anxious and perspired more than they should, considering it was a cool October day.

Finally, the white men started checking their weapons and propping the windows open. The women tucked their children under the seats even before one of the detectives shouted, "All right, all you coloreds get down as low as you can!"

Since Swain hadn't brought his wife and young ones along, and Luke had a half-dozen children, Swain covered the two oldest with his own body. He thought that in other circumstances he would have comforted them by softly saying their names, but on this occasion, he was at a complete loss as to which of the six children he was atop.

Chancing a glance out the window, Swain saw signs a town was approaching. He had once worked a prison gandy dancer gang and knew something about the protocol for when a train approached a city's outer limits. But on this occasion, the engineer neither blew the whistle nor was there the screeching sound of brakes applying. Swain was terrified. He tried to squeeze himself beneath the children, but they had such powerful grips on the seat legs, he couldn't budge them.

As the rays of the sun caused the shadows from the buildings to dance in and out, he heard loud shouting from outside. Then hard objects hit the side of the passenger car. The angry bellows became a constant roar that rumbled through Swain's chest, making it feel like his lungs were on fire. That was when he realized he had been holding his breath. He panted fast and heavy into the ear of one of the children.

The screams around the passenger car never slowed, and even became louder. It seemed the picketers were coming right in through the windows.

At last came the screeching of the train's brakes and the loud thumping of the rail cars as their bumpers crashed together, pulled apart and crashed together again and again. The final bump and complete stop of the train was followed immediately by a single gun shot.

A roar of gunfire followed, almost totally blocking out the screams all around him. Glass sprayed from the windows and bounced off the back of his coat. Pinch-like stings burned his neck and the top of his head. He reached to adjust his hat for protection, but it wasn't there, and when he brought his hand back around, it was red and sticky with blood. The gunfire slowed for just a moment, then returned just as fiercly as before. When he dared to glance up, pieces of metal ricocheted around the room and holes appeared like magic through the side of the wall. Then his head took a sideways jolt and everything went black.

***

When his train pulled into Virden that morning, Tom had been dismayed to see hundreds of picketers standing along either side of the railroad tracks. Ever since he had talked to Bradley, he had imagined he would be given a high command befitting his successes in Pana. When he stepped onto the station platform there was not only no one to greet him, but he had to figure out on his own where to take the twenty men he commanded. After careful deliberation, he decided he would need to let his Pana constituents think he'd already conferred with General Bradley on their role. He positioned his men as close to the mine gates as he could and told them to be watching for his instructions.

A cloudy grey sky offered just enough rain to be an irritant to the strikers. Several wagons and buggies had been pulled close enough to the tracks to provide some shelter during the occasional downpours. While UMW leaders had given instructions that no weapons were to be visible there were plenty of shotguns and squirrel rifles kept handy in the wagons for hunting of the local game. Dozens of campfires were used mostly to keep the coffee pots warm or to heat up a pan of beans should the regular union meals be delayed.

These were provided for and attended by a women's auxiliary group that had been formed to keep the picketers comfortable. The auxiliary women would often take up the picket signs themselves to give the men breaks during the day.

The stockade appeared better constructed than Holiday had described. The high towers looked well-fortified, with several company guards looking down into the rail station. Two sets of tracks forked away from one another to the north, and the one leading into the mine yard had a solid swinging gate that would open when a coal train arrived.

Tom remembered that when the first train full of strikebreakers had arrived in Pana, the union men had battled and lost in their effort to keep the mine gate open after the train entered the stockade. Sensing that the leaders of the Virden strike had made no plan for this contingency, Tom decided to take the initiative himself.

"You boys," he said to four men in his command who had not taken the opportunity to light cigarettes, "go bring some of those rail ties over here." He looked up at the guard towers. "When they bring the ties around, the rest of you sit on them."

"Sit on them?" Holiday asked. "Why, we'd look silly with all the other picketers standing."

"Remember how we couldn't keep the mine gates open at Pana?" Tom asked.

Holiday looked up at the guard towers for a moment, then clapped his hand on Tom's back. "Hot diggity! I think you got it, Tom."

Two hours later, excited shouts sounded from picketers farther down the railroad tracks. White smoke puffing in the distance announced the arrival of the northbound train, although the usual double blast of the whistle was conspicuously absent.

"All right, boys!" Tom yelled above the shouts of hundreds of picketers. "You know what to do. But wait until the caboose is passing the gate."

As was expected, the train entered the town at a forty-mile-an-hour clip, showing no intention of stopping at the depot. Picketers were ready with rocks, logs and whatever else they could find to throw at the passing passenger cars. Behind Tom and his men, the mine gate swung open with several hundred armed company men on either side to hold back the angry protesters. A few picketers started to rush forward, but they quickly jumped out of the way when the monstrous black engine approached the mine yard, its tooth-like cow-catcher sweeping along the tracks with determined and murderous intent.

The mob was so thick, one union man was accidently bumped into the side of the moving train. He screamed as the beard and skin on one side of his face was scraped clean, right down to the cheekbone. When the red caboose approached the mine yard, the Pana men quickly hefted the heavy railroad ties and, pushing forward along the sides of the train, jammed them at the bottom of the gate. Hundreds of union picketers rushed forward, screaming and shouting, only to be met at the entrance in a vicious collision with the security guards. Clubs, fists and rifle butts swung with sickening cracks against men's faces and ribs, but the men farther back on both sides continued to push forward, piling on top of those who were unfortunate enough to be there first.

After several seconds, some of the union men squeezed their way along the gates and into the open mine yard. Tom was one of them. Just as he looked up into the nearest watchtower, he heard a single gunshot followed almost immediately by dozens more. He pulled his revolver. With little aim he began shooting in the direction of the company guards.

Sporadic firing followed the first long and thunderous hail of gunshots. It was during those first few moments that most of those killed or wounded were hit. Men from both sides had immediately ran for cover, leaving dozens of the dead and wounded in the field.

Tom found a safe spot, hunkering down behind a wagon that was inside the mine gate. Since he'd already used up his entire pocketful of bullets, he had no choice but to lay quietly and listen to the shooting and the cries of agony from the wounded who were pleading for help. The acrid smell of gun smoke lingered like an angry blue fog in the air. Tom found himself trembling uncontrollably. Having never seen anything like this, he was afraid for his life. When he calmed a little, he dared a glance between the spokes of the wagon wheels. Some men were lying still on the ground, others were writhing in pain. One man was crawling, leaving a trail of blood in the dirt behind him.

Then the train made a hissing sound as the steam built up in the boiler. It began to move forward with the familiar chugging sound of the big pistons working forward and backward to turn the heavy wheels.

Tom had a sudden fear that maybe he had been hit and didn't feel it. He sat up and began touching his legs and arms, searching for blood. He had a moment of panic when he felt a wetness on his pant leg, but then realized it was a few drops of his own pee.

Suddenly a hand touched his shoulder. When he looked up, he saw the glazed eyes of a man with a bloody hole in his neck. The man coughed and spit up blood that spewed onto Tom's pant legs.

"Help!" the man gasped. He dropped onto his knees, but continued the pleading stare.

Tom pulled off his thin necktie and wrapped it

once around the man's neck. When he saw that blood was still flowing freely, he stood and pulled off his own coat, then ripped a piece of his white dress shirt near the bottom. A bullet immediately splintered the wood next to him, so he ducked back down again. Placing the shirt beneath the necktie, he put pressure on the wounds on both sides of the man's neck and tightened the cloth as much as he dared without choking him.

Then Tom made a decision. He lifted the wounded man onto his shoulder and stood. He had planned on making a run for the mine gate, but when he felt the immense weight of the man, he decided to walk calmly and hope the snipers let him pass.

He felt as if he were in a dream as he walked across the yard, stepping over and around dead and wounded, the weight of the wounded man and his own fear making his knees tremble. One gunshot was fired, but the bullet only kicked up dirt near his feet, so he just kept walking.

Once through the gate, Holiday and two of the other Pana men came running toward him and helped with the wounded man. When Tom stepped into the train station depot, he was surrounded by miners shaking his hand and slapping him on the back.

"You saved that nigger's life!" cried one of the miners.

"He ain't no nigger," Tom said, a little bewildered. "He's a union man."

Tom looked over to where the man he had rescued was being laid out on a desk for examination by a doctor. His mouth dropped when he realized the man's skin was as black as coal.

***

When Swain awoke, it took him a moment to figure out he was laid out on the aisle floor of the passenger train. He raised his hand to an ache near his left ear and found that his head was bandaged. The car was in chaos, with men and women talking loudly as they struggled to move about the crowded room. Children were sitting on the backs of the seats, some crying, others in shock. They watched their parents trying to help the wounded.

No one tried to stop Swain when he sat up and then pulled himself into a seat next to Luke Johns' oldest daughter. She was about eight years old. Her name was Molly. He smiled at her, but she quickly turned her head and looked out the shattered window where hundreds of white people stood looking into the passenger car.

"Are we in Springfield, child?" Swain asked.

Molly gave a single nod of her head.

His head ached when he moved it, but he just had to look around the passenger car. He watched as Luke laid his wife out on the floor in the spot that Swain had vacated. She had blood on her stomach and was clutching one of Luke's hands while he cried and patted her head with his other. The floor space was filled with wounded, as were most of the seats. Those who could stand were busy taking care of those who couldn't.

"Why can't we get off the train?" Swain asked Molly. "I surely do want to know."

"They won't let us," Molly said without turning her head from the window.

A well-dressed white man stepped through the door. He wore a double-breasted waistcoat, a shawl collar under his sack coat, and gray trousers. His square-toed shoes had felt spats.

"Look at them fancy spatterdashes," Swain said. "I'll bet his shoes don't get dirty."

"My name is John Hunter, and I'm the Illinois President of the United Mine Workers of America."

Two of the white company detectives that Swain hadn't seen near the front jumped to their feet. One of them struck Hunter in the head with his rifle stock. The detectives pushed him back onto the landing and then tossed him roughly onto the ground. Twenty minutes later, two Springfield police officers entered the car followed by Hunter. His head was covered by a blood-soaked bandage. This time the two detectives stayed in their seats.

"You folks have been lied to by the Chicago-

Virden Coal Company," Hunter said. "The coal miners in several Illinois mines are on strike because their mine owners also lied to them. The operators signed an agreement to pay the miners forty cents a ton, but the companies we are striking reneged on the deal. Now they have promised you boys thirty cents a ton, but when you get your first pay, you'll find it to be only twenty-five cents a ton. They will also deduct from your check for just about everything they can come up with and pay you in script that will only be good at the company store. In other words, they plan to force you into a feudalistic dependence that will keep you perpetually in debt to them."

Swain wasn't sure he understood everything Hunter said, but he knew it wasn't good.

"Now," Hunter continued, "those of you who want to go home to Birmingham can get out of this stinky, filthy car right now, and you'll be on a train south within a few days. Your trip home will be paid for by the United Mine Workers."

"We needs a sawbones, Mistuh Hunter," Luke said. He was still clutching his wounded wife's hand.

"We can't find any doctors willing to come onto the train," Hunter said. "If you need medical attention, you'll have to come with me now."

Luke gave Swain an apologetic look, then lifted his wife into his arms. "She's the onliest reason

I'm doin' this. Heft them belongings, children."

Since he'd been the one who convinced Luke to come to Illinois, Swain didn't think his friend would appreciate his company. That was only part of the reason he didn't want to go home, though. The real reason was that a few nights before, Swain's own wife had caught him kissing her little sister. He tried to tell her that it only happened because he'd gotten hold of some bad moonshine, but she wouldn't hear it. She chased him out of the house with a rusty meat cleaver and told him not to come back.

To make matters worse, her sister had refused to come north with him because she wanted to finish eighth grade first. That was why he had talked Luke into bringing his family. But now with Luke's wife gut shot, he was back to not having anyone to cook for him, mend his clothes, or fill his dinner bucket each day.

He watched as several other blacks picked up their belongings and followed Luke and his family from the railroad car. When they were gone, Swain began studying those who had stayed in hopes of finding a woman who might darn his socks. He figured he could pack his own lunch box, but he had never learned how to care for his garments.

***

Back at Virden, Tom Downs found himself in the position of labor hero. His mistaken reference to the black man he rescued as being a union man was acknowledged throughout the ranks as an outstanding statement that would unite the various races and ethnic groups. Tom's red-faced embarrassment by the compliments was real. Truth be told, he had been so distraught during the battle, he truly hadn't noticed the color of the man's skin. In fact, now that he thought about it, it was no wonder his mind somehow got confused. It was probably because he was so used to seeing so many black-faced white men walking home from the coal mine.

He used his newfound leadership status to oversee the transportation of the dead and wounded to the nearby homes of good union men. Doctors were found for the two dozen wounded and morticians for the eight dead. When he returned to the depot, he found Bradley discussing the gunfight with newspaper reporters.

"The UMW," Bradley was saying, "was attempting a peaceful solution to the illegal importation of out-of-state strikebreakers to work mines that were being legally picketed.

"Why, our boys had practically no weapons on them. When the detectives started mowing down our union men with their brand new Winchester rifles, our boys retrieved a few of their own hunting guns and used them for self-defense. Dozens of Thiel detectives had been placed in the colored's passenger cars during the stop in St. Louis, and the coal company brought in marksmen from as far away as Chicago to kill our boys."

"Do you know how many union men you lost?" a reporter asked.

"As of right now, we count eight dead and several dozen wounded," Bradley said.

"Was the fact that the strikebreakers were colored men a factor in your grievance?" a different reporter asked.

Bradley spotted Tom, reached out, and pulled him into the center of the room. "Do you know what this brave young man said when the black man he saved was called a nigger? Why, he said," Bradley puffed his chest, "'He ain't no nigger. He's a union man!'"

When the reporters moved on to interview other men, Tom followed along with Bradley and the rest of the leaders. A few moments later, a messenger came running up to them. "General," the out-of-breath man said, "some of our men are attacking the company store. The storekeep is holed up inside. Our boys want to destroy the store as revenge for our dead."

Bradley turned to Tom. "Take one hundred men and find out what's going on. And, Downs, don't let our boys be the reason for any more violence."

Rushing outside, Tom found his Pana men sitting on the rail ties, this time smoking, drinking and bragging about how they had used the lumber to prop open the gates. He ordered them to bring all the men gathered there and come with him.

It only took a few minutes to get to the nearby company store, a long, flat roofed building with several colonial style windows, one from which emerged the double barrel of a shotgun. Dozens of United Mine Workers had surrounded the store and were throwing rocks at it.

"Get some torches!" one of the attackers shouted. "We'll fire the building!"

When a shotgun blast came from inside, the union men ducked for cover, then regrouped in preparation for an assault. Assuming the storekeep was reloading, Tom bolted toward the building, followed by his peacemakers, many of whom were still carrying whiskey bottles.

"You, Pana men!" Tom shouted toward Holiday. "Block that charge."

Holiday found a tree stump to set his liquor on, then hurried his men to take up a position in front of the main door. Tom took the rest of the men around the side of the building, hoping to secure the rear entrance. Just as he arrived, the back door was broken down by revenge-seeking union men who rushed inside, weapons first. They immediately began ransacking the store, searching for the storekeep who had fired on them.

Loud shouts from above caused Tom to back away from the building and look up. A man scrambled along the roof top carrying a shotgun. A nearby union man on the ground raised his rifle, but Tom knocked the gun out of his hands before he could fire.

Others appeared on the roof. The storekeep ran and took a flying leap into the glass skylight.

Tom raced into the building.

The storekeep landed on the wooden floor with a loud thud. He was clearly unconscious, and his left leg and foot were at a right angle to the rest of the limb.

Irate coal miners were about to fire the store.

"Holiday!" Tom yelled.

The Pana men rushed into the building and began disarming the out of control mob. "Escort our comrades back to the picket line."

A dozen armed men were left to guard the building. When he reported back to the train depot, Tom once again received congratulations and pats on the back.

But the accolades were cut short by the unexpected arrival of a south-bound train.

"The National Guard is coming!" a miner shouted. "They'll be tryin' to take our weapons."

Men ran toward wagons and threw their guns into them. Teamsters quickly hitched the horses and whipped them to a gallop just as the train pulled into the station.

The remainder of the afternoon saw guardsmen searching for and confiscating what weapons they could find from both the union men and the coal company deputies. There was little fuss from either contingent, especially after the Guard unloaded two Gatling guns and set them up in front of the Virden Opera House.

That evening, the Pana men again took up picketing around the railroad ties placed as close to the mine entrance as the Guardsmen would allow. Torches and camp fires lined either side of the tracks for as far down the rail line as they could see. The soldiers made their domination of the situation known by stationing men at strategic locations and marching noisily about the streets.

"When we tell the folks about this back home," Holiday shouted as the Pana men toasted Tom on his successes, "they'll be runnin' you for mayor."

"I don't want to be no mansy pansy mayor." Tom held his celebratory cigar above his head. "Make me sheriff, though, and I'll run them dark-complected Spaniards out of town."

"Here, here!" the men shouted.

Tom stood. This time when he raised his hand above his head, he held his tin cup. "But, tonight, we need to toast our comrades who gave their lives today."

The Pana men grew solemn. They also stood. The images of the dead and wounded haunted each of their thoughts. They raised their own beverages above their heads toward the moon-bright night—and allowed the demonic spirit of revenge to enter their hearts.

***

Swain Whitfield and the other blacks who refused to leave were held in the five passenger cars in Springfield for three days. Locals, both white and black, walked around the train and stared at them like they were animals in the zoo. A few times a day, church people handed food and water to them through the windows. Toilet buckets were set up in the back of each coach, and a few coats hung from the ceiling for privacy. The smell of the buckets—in combination with the smell of unwashed bodies—became almost unbearable.

There were always at least two armed guards at the exits making sure they didn't run off. Hunter or one of his union representatives appeared often and asked if any of them wanted to take advantage of the free ride back to Birmingham. Those that remained by the third day were a stubborn lot and determined to get the jobs in the coal mines that had been promised them.

Hunter again arrived, this time accompanied by

several Negroes who had already chosen to take advantage of the UMW's free ride home. Luke Johns was among them. Hunter allowed each man he had brought testify that they were being well taken care of. Luke went first.

"They's treatin' us real fine, they surely is," Luke said, then hastily walked down the aisle and sat in the seat next to Swain. While the others gave more lengthy testimonials, Luke lowered his head and whispered, "We gonna jump off the train when it stop in St. Louis," Luke told him. "Ain't none of us wantin' to go back down South. They says there's jobs in St. Louis."

"How they treatin' you?" Swain asked.

One of Hunter's men walked down the aisle and stood next to their seat.

Luke sat quietly until all the speeches were finished and Hunter offered one last appeal. "If you turn down this opportunity to leave this morning," he said, "the United Mine Workers is not prepared to make you another offer. You will be on your own."

As he was getting up to leave with the others, Luke let a small piece of paper drop from his pocket. Once they were gone, Swain retrieved it. He summoned one of the wives who could read.

"It's from something called the Illinois State Register and dated October 13, 1898," the woman said.

"That was two days ago," an eavesdropping miner said.

Those remaining in the passenger car huddled around her as the woman slowly read one word at a time.

A PITIABLE AND SHAMEFUL SPECTACLE

Shivering and hungry in the third story of what is known as Allen's Hall are huddled together about 106 negroes, men, women and children, practically prisoners of war, and in danger of their lives if they should attempt to assert their liberty. They are without anything to eat, and after today will be without a roof to shelter them, and are in danger of their lives if they get far from the hall. ...

Yesterday, mine workers officials served notice that they would neither protect nor provide for the Negroes after 6 o'clock, and soon afterward it began to be whispered about town that several of the Negroes, who were with a former load that was taken from the train several days ago, would be lynched. An angry crowd, requiring the efforts of the police to restrain, surged about the door of the hall throughout the greater part of the day, threatening mob violence.

Two Negroes slipped out of the hall, apparently intending to hop a train south, but they were captured by strike sympathizers. One "was kicked well nigh into insensibility" before they were returned to Allen's Hall.

"Seems like ever thing that happens is either the work of the Lord or some trickery of the devil," the woman who had done the reading said.

"We's better off here than at that union place," Swain said. "That sure is a fact, yes, sir."

"Well, I ain't goin' back to 'Bama either, I can tell you that," one of the miners said.

Everyone was in agreement that no conditions in Illinois could be as bad as had been in Alabama, where they would be forced to work on road gangs or down in the mines as prison labor.

Before the sun went down the third day, a steady rain began. It's sweet smell partially masked the odor from the toilets. For a reason he couldn't understand, the familiarity of the fall shower raised Swain's spirits and gave him hope. If the coal company operators found out how stubbornly he and the others had stuck it out, he was sure they would be taken care of.

Then a new man walked into the passenger car. "I represent the Chicago-Virden Coal Mine," the man said. "Go home. We will no longer protect you or provide for you. We decided we don't want you no more."

With that, he turned and walked out, followed by the security guards. The Negro strikebreakers sat stunned. They were now unprotected and had no way of paying their way back to Birmingham or even St. Louis. To Swain Whitfield, that left only one option. He would take his chances on Pana, Illinois, and the broad shoulders of Big Henry Stevens.

12

"The National Guard is to prevent any more of those damned out-of-state strikebreakers from arriving at any mine in Illinois," Governor Tanner told Captain Gibbs in the loudest, non-shouting voice he could muster. "If another rail car comes to Illinois carrying strikebreakers, it is to be shot to pieces with Gatling guns."

"Yes, sir," Captain Gibbs said. The governor's voice was so commanding he caught himself standing at attention, and then tried to look nonchalant as he spread into an at-ease stance. "No Negroes will be brought into Pana while I'm in charge."

"The Illinois newspapers are mostly behind me," Tanner said, flipping his cigar ashes onto the big mahogany conference table filled with newspapers. "But those scallywag papers out east are on the side of the Negroes. They say they have the right to work. They see it as a racial issue. Look at this *Baltimore Sun* headline, 'WAS THE CIVIL WAR IN VAIN?'

"And look, the damned *Boston Transcript* even says that I encouraged the union violence." Tanner caught himself and tried to lower his voice. "Simply because I won't interfere with the strike. Hell, the Secretary of War even wants me to protect the coal companies. He offered me national troops if the Illinois National Guard is insufficient."

"We will get the job done the way you want us to, sir." Gibbs shuffled from one foot to the other. "If the coloreds refuse to retreat when told to do so, I will order my men to fire. If I have to lose every man under my command, no Negro shall land at Pana."

"I know I have no legal authority to prevent the arrival of strikebreakers," Tanner said in an even lower voice, shaking his head. With his cigar puffing like a steam engine, he paced rapidly. "I'm simply doing the will of the people. The country must face the fact that government intervention to allow corporations to import strikebreakers is a violation of human rights."

"I agree, sir," Gibbs said. "Now, about Virden, sir."

"Yes, Virden." Tanner chewed vigorously on his stogie. "I only agreed to send troops to Virden with the understanding the coal company not open the mines with scab labor. Send half the troops you have in Pana to reinforce Virden, but they are not to do anything to help one side or the other. You understand?"

"Yes, sir."

"Now tell them to send the newspaper men in for a statement."

Gibbs walked to the door. When he opened it, he had to step aside quickly so he wouldn't be knocked over by the rush of a dozen reporters all shouting questions at once.

"Governor, the mine operators say that your lack of action to send the Guard into Virden is the reason for the violence!" a reporter shouted in a baritone voice that drowned out his rivals. "Is blood on your hands?"

"No, sir, it is not," Tanner said. "I have been warning the mine operators for months that any attempt to import strikebreakers from other states would make them criminally and morally responsible for violence. In fact, I intend to work for legislation that will make it illegal to bring imported strikebreakers into the state."

"Governor, a victory by the workers in Virden would be an un-paralleled victory in labor history," the reporter said. "What about the property rights of the coal company?"

"Huh?" Tanner coughed. "What about the property rights of the miners? The laboring man's only property is the right to labor, which is as dear to him as the capitalist's millions, and he has the same right to carry arms in defense of his property as the capitalist has to protect his millions."

"Governor, isn't your decision to send the Guard

to Virden a slap in the face of Negro rights?"

"Negro rights?" Tanner's facial muscles twitched as he spoke. "Young man, did you know that I was the only governor to allow colored troops and colored officers to fight in Cuba? Now, this is the first time in the history of Illinois or of the nation that the military power of the law, during an industrial contest, has been exercised in defense of the rights of American labor. I am proud of both those firsts."

That evening, Tanner lay in bed in the Governor's Executive Mansion reading more of the newspaper accounts of his Virden decision.

Suddenly, the paper was ripped from his hands. It floated to the floor where it joined a dozen others.

"Oh, Cora." Tanner scowled.

Cora English had been a wealthy sophisticate when she married Governor-elect Tanner. That had been less than two years ago, and only eleven days before he took office as Illinois' twenty-first governor. Her dazzling beauty had brought many a suitor, but her heart was won by the man who wooed her with his passion for social justice and equality for all. The two lovers had spent countless hours sharing their ideals. That was why when he stood tall against everyone from his own political party, even the President of the United States, he knew he was not standing alone.

"True freedom and equality will only come when the humblest and weakest human being has the same civil and social rights as the rich and powerful." Cora had repeated these words to him at least once a week since he was elected governor.

"I fear I will not live to see a world such as that," Tanner told his wife.

"But history will remember you for what you have done," Cora whispered in his ear. "History will prove you right, my love."

The lovers embraced and, for at least a few moments, were able to escape the horrors of a troubled world and enjoy the sweet amnesia of marital bliss.

***

"We won!" Tom Downs shouted as he led the Pana men off the train. "We just received word that no out-of-state scabs will be working the Virden mines!"

The hundreds of picketers at the Pana rail station cheered. Each of the twenty returning men were hefted onto miner's shoulders and paraded to the front of the Opera House. Dozens more men, women and children came at a rush when they heard the shouting. The street was almost immediately shoulder to shoulder.

The twenty were let down on the boardwalk,

where they clustered around Tom, gently pushing him to the front.

"SPEECH! SPEECH!" the crowd chanted.

"My words are for the mine operators!" Tom shouted, pointing off toward the Eubanks Coal Mine a block away, where dozens of deputies lined up along the gate to watch. He made certain that his words echoed his dead father's voice. "For years you have hired who you pleased, fired who you pleased and did anything you damned well pleased. Your miners were kept in a constant state of poverty by your greed and your damned company store!"

Tom paused. He was learning how to build anticipation in a crowd. "Your day is over!" he shouted.

The crowd erupted in a long period of applause and shouts. Finally, Tom held up his hands for them to quiet.

"I am personally going to make sure this town will never experience such as we just saw in Virden, Illinois." Tom paused again, and then shouted as loud as he could. "I hereby announce my candidacy for sheriff of Christian County!"

As the cheering again erupted and he was hoisted on United Mine Worker shoulders for an impromptu parade around the town, Tom wished he'd had the foresight to request a band be present.

"They gave the UMW district president a wooden gavel after the gunfight in Virden," Holiday Jones said later while he sat with Tom and Rachel eating at a potluck the union women had prepared. "It was carved right from a post that one of the company thugs fell on when he got shot and kilt."

Tom didn't say anything. He'd heard about the gavel, but it was a sore subject with him. Hunter hadn't even been in Virden during the gunfight. Despite the fact that the name Tom Downs was on the lips of every citizen of Christian County, he still would've liked to have been given a gavel.

***

Her bruises were beginning to heal, but Fanny was still obsessed with her desire for revenge on Major Samuels. Still, the horror of that terrible night and the hatred she felt for the soldier was not nearly as great as what she felt for the black man who sashayed arrogantly into the commissary at Springside Mine. Fanny Cahill was the one person not happy to see Swain Whitfield.

Dozens of miners gathered around the tables while Swain told his story of the Virden gunfight, getting wounded, and being held prisoner on the train for three days.

"Then that coal company told us to go on home, they didn't want us no more. Yes, sir, without so much as a bye-your-leave." Swain looked at Jeb Turner, who was the only white man in the room.

"Can I get work in this here mine?"

"Is he a hard worker?" Jeb asked the miners.

"I weren't raised lazy," Swain answered before anyone could speak. He snorted through his nose and gave a spit. Then turned his head toward the other miners.

"Well, he's fer sure a take-your-time kind of guy," Quits answered when no one else spoke up. "And, above ground, he takes for the shade, but below he generally finishes what he starts."

Jeb looked at Big Henry, who said, "Well, he does have a talent with mules. I suppose since he walked here from Springfield, he deserves a shot."

"Report on Monday," Jeb told Swain, then turned and left the room.

"Let's have a drink and swap a lie or three!" Quits Simpson shouted as the room full of miners took turns slapping the newcomer on the back.

Fanny thought she could guess why Swain chose to walk fifty miles to Pana rather than return home to his wife and children. She had been avoiding the man since she was a young child. Though many other men quickly followed, it had been Swain Whitfield who had introduced her to the world of the flesh. Seeing him being treated as a hero was almost more than Fanny could bear. She moved to a table in the back corner of the room and sank into a chair. One of her young admirers rushed up behind her.

"Would you let go of my chair so I can sit down!" Fanny shouted.

"I was fixin' to be a gentleman and push it forward for you." The young man blushed.

"Well, you can't push it forward," Fanny scolded him, "the table's right there."

"Why, I declare!" Swain said. "Is that Fanny May Cahill I see? I knows I do."

"Sure is," Quits Simpson answered. "She's as sweet as honey, ain't she?"

"Yeah," Swain agreed loudly so everyone could hear. "Like honey poured over thunder, I surely say." He walked over to Fanny and rubbed his hip against her chair. "Hey, baby," he said. "What kinda wedding should we have? I'd like to know."

"A double wedding," Fanny said. "You marry someone else and so will I." She hurried out of the busy room and stomped back toward the Sunrise Tavern, thinking of ways to kill Swain Whitfield with every step.

13

"It takes just the right amount of chicory and egg shell to make a good pot of java," Big Henry said as Garfield handed Jeb a cup of hot coffee. The three men had developed the habit of standing guard together at the top of the mine tipple each evening. Their conversations had become free and easy as their bond developed.

"Is it strong enough for you, Mistuh Jeb?" Garfield asked. Jeb and Henry liked their coffee strong. but Garfield preferred to sneak a spoonful of blackstrap molasses into his when it was available.

"Strong enough? Why the spoon I tried to stir it with is standing up like a wedding dick," Jeb said with a cough. When neither Big Henry nor Garfield responded to his wit he changed the subject. "Why do you love coal mining so much, Big Henry?"

"Well," Big Henry said. "I don't know about why white folks like it, but myself, I like not having a boss staring over my shoulder all the time. I've seen bosses down South followin' coloreds around the fields with a whip. I reckon bosses don't follow me around in the mine 'cause they's scared of fallin' rock or gas explosions."

"What about you, Mr. Jeb?" Garfield asked. "Is deputyin' your dream?"

"Oh, no," Jeb said. "If I had my druthers, I'd be travelin', seein' the other side of a river or hill for the first time, walkin' through a forest after a mornin' rain. Yes, sir, if I had to work underground, I'd just as soon dig for gold or silver. I sure didn't know the whole of coal minin' 'til I seen you fellas doin' it."

"Why, that's silly, Mistuh Jeb," Big Henry said. "Which is more important to survive on? A pound of coal or a ton of gold or silver? You gonna keep warm with gold? You gonna run a train with silver? What good do gold or silver really do for anybody except look nice?"

"Gold is like a pretty gal who can't cook or sew," Garfield agreed, "that's a fact fer sure."

"Kinda like Fanny Cahill, I'd imagine." The words were out of Jeb's mouth before he thought about them. The look of amusement Big Henry gave him made him so fidgety he spilled some of his coffee.

"Myrtle says there's a powerful sad in that gal's eyes," Garfield said.

"She be as wild as a cat in a canary cage." Big Henry nodded as he continued his all-knowing smile at the white man. "A woman like that can make her man mad, happy and sad all at the same time."

"She ain't much of a do-gooder," Garfield struggled to be agreeable. "That's fer sure."

"Did you see the way she look at Ol' Swain when he walked into the stockade?" Big Henry said, finally looking away from Jeb. "She just don' cotton to him one bit."

"Did I ever tell you about the milk cow we had when I was a boy?" Jeb began a lie to change the subject. "She could give more milk than any cow in the country, but one day she fell down into the silo."

"How'd you get her out?" Garfield asked.

"Well, sir," Jeb said and smiled, "I just jumped down there with her and milked her 'til she floated right out."

"Reminds me of the day I caught Ol' Grandpa," Big Henry said while Garfield pondered on Jeb's milk cow story. "I fought that ol' catfish for two full days 'til my cane pole broke. So, I lassoed him with my saddle rope. I just had him pulled up on the bank when it started rainin'. Oh, it was the hardest rain I ever seen. The raindrops was as big as buckets and just as heavy. Ol Grandpa was still a fightin' when I threw that rope over a high tree limb, tied the other end to the saddle horn and had ol' Ruthie, my ox, pull that fish til he hanged off the ground. He was longer than ol' Ruthie and weighed near as much."

"As much as an ox?" Garfield gasped. "You sure it weren't no whale?"

"No, sir, it was definite a catfish, fer sure. I grabbed my shotgun and was just getting' ready to put a blast into Ol Grandpa's head when one of them big raindrops came down and smacked me right in the top o' my noggin. I was so dazed I couldn't move, but I saw that fish flop his tail up and whack that rope so hard it snapped like a twig. Ol' Grandpa flipped around and knocked that big tree right to the ground. Then with another flip, he went head first back into the water.

Garfield leaned forward, taking in every word of Big Henry's story.

"Well, sir," Big Henry continued. "Just right then I heard a flashflood stormin' through the valley toward me. I was so dazed I was just fixin' to lay there and drown. I looked over toward the big wave that Ol' Grandpa made when he hit the water and just as the wave broke the shore, I saw his giant head bob up above the surface. His round eyes looked like two full moons. He was a starin' at me. Now, I've heard folks say a fish ain't got no feelin's, but I swear that big critter knew I was in trouble."

"What'd he do?" Garfield slid further up to the edge of his seat.

"I saw him draw in a mouthful of water. Why, it drawed in there like a waterfall into a crick. Then that catfish did something I'd never seen before. Why, he spit a long stream of water that arched like a rainbow right into my face. Well that shook me right back into wakefulness. I jumped on ol' Ruthie's back and rode her to the top of that draw just as the flashflood hit."

"Did you ever see ol' Grandpa again?" Garfield asked.

"No, I sure didn't, but I heard a story that a few years later some folks saw him swallow an alligator."

"Oh, now I know you's storyin'," Garfield said. "That last fact just don' prove out. An alligator could eat his way right out of a catfish. Ain't that right, Mistuh Jeb?"

***

"Deputies ain't gonna be allowed to protect anymore Africans while they're being brought into Pana," Tom Downs told Holiday Jones. "The gunfight at Virden ruined Sheriff Osborn's tenacity. He's afraid I'll beat him in the election."

"Hell, I think he don't want to be sheriff no more," Holiday said. "I heard he's told people he can't wait to get rid of the headache."

Tom didn't want to hear such talk. He was

smelling blood and believed the victory in Virden had changed the momentum back to the UMW. Now was the time for a blow that would resonate through every coal operation in Illinois.

"Anyway," Tom continued quickly, "I found out from Major Smauels the company is fixin' to sneak some niggers in on a boxcar."

"Well, hell, that makes it easy," Holiday said "We'll just stop every train comin' into the county and search 'em."

"I got a better idea," Tom said. "Only a few people even know they's comin' in, don't they? So, who's gonna miss a few darkies if they disappear?"

"Why do you hate scabs so much, Tom?" Holiday asked.

"My father lost his job a few years back because of the scabs being brought in," Tom said. "It broke his spirit. He told his partner he was fed up with life. A few minutes later, he went alone into a mine chamber, put a stick of dynamite under his chin and blew his own head off. My mother died of broken heart a year later. Scabs are greedy, selfish bastards that don't deserve to live."

"Then let's send 'em to hell," Holiday said, "where they belong."

***

The two big Gatling guns the National Guard

had brought into Pana were too burdensome to keep out in the open, so they were secured in a warehouse on the edge of town. Because of the problem with transporting them and the fact that over half of the Guard had been sent to keep the peace at Virden, Tom's men had even less problem than they'd anticipated borrowing one of the weapons.

The rendezvous place the ambushers chose was several miles east of the village of Tower Hill and was fairly isolated. While Williamsburg Hill was a fine place for hunting game, as well as morel mushrooms in the spring, the heavily timbered soil offered little else. The owners of the few scattered houses in the area were well known to the Pana men, so finding ways to get the residents to be absent from their homes was fairly easy.

"Place the gun between those two oak trees facing the clearing," Tom told Holiday. The twenty men he commanded had been his comrades at the Virden gunfight. They knew what was about to happen. They trusted him the same as he trusted them. "Then hide the gun from the clearing with some loose brush."

Four of the men had Gatling gun experience from the recent war with Spain. They were familiar with the M1893 model and its six barrel fire power. It would take all four of them working together to maintain the six to seven hundred rounds per minute rate of fire. They went to work, backing the horses that pulled the armored field carriage up to the designated trees. Tom directed the rest of the men to block the tracks, this time with a heavy wagon full of thick, twenty-foot logs. He had learned from his previous experience that it was much simpler if they made for an easier removal of the barricade. This time he also positioned three men a couple of hundred yards down the tracks so they could give instructions to the train conductor if he showed signs of wanting to stop too soon. Since this Gatling gun model did not swivel like the newer ones, the location of the stop was a much greater factor than it had been before.

Major Samuels had told Tom that the blacks would be in the only boxcar that had the sliding doors completely shut. It was the job of the men standing along the tracks on either side of the train to jump on that boxcar's ladders while the train was slowing. The third man was to board the engine and watch for their signal. He would tell the conductor when to stop so that car would be in the Gatling gun's line of sight.

While they waited, the men sat on the ground smoking and passing a jug that one of the men had the foresight to bring along. There was little talk— each man seemed to have deep thoughts on this day. Thoughts that, though private, were uncommonly similar. None of them could get the eight dead comrades from the Virden massacre out of their heads. Nor the dozens more injured, many seriously with wounds that would scar them for the remainder of their lives.

Each of the Pana men had been among the thousands who attended the funerals for the eight martyrs. One of the dead had been a man most of them knew well. Frank Bilyeu was buried at the Oak Hill Cemetery in nearby Taylorville. He had been a widower with a daughter and two sons. During the Virden battle, Bilyeu had continued fighting even after being shot through the head. Several men witnessed his struggle to remain on his feet right up until the moment his heart quit beating.

Now, as the Pana men awaited the train, their thoughts allowed their hearts to grow even more cold toward the strikebreakers. The unpleasant duty would be easier because the scabs were Negro. But even if they had not been black, the union men felt they owed it to Frank Bilyeu, his orphaned children, and all the youth of the future who would never get to know their own fathers. Men whose lives would be cut short trying to make a living in the deep, dark depths of the coal mines.

Tom Downs and his men didn't have long to wait. The train whistle at the Lakewood crossing brought each of them to their feet. Those smoking dropped their cigarettes and stomped on them. Many of them extracted big plugs of tobacco from their trousers and helped themselves to a chaw. Drawing cloth hoods from their coat pockets, they pulled them over their faces. Tom chose to remain unmasked.

The conductor began a series of short blasts of the whistle the moment he saw the wagon full of logs on the tracks. The loud squeal of the braking system came a moment later, and the train began to slow. The men assigned to board the train and secure it came at a sprint out of the woods, grabbed ladders, and swung themselves onto their positions. Then came the loud crash of the bumpers between the cars as the engine slowed more rapidly.

The conductor followed the hijacker's instructions and pulled the engine right up to the wagon full of logs, the engine releasing the excessive steam in a loud hiss as it came to a complete stop. Tom and the men walked straight to the boxcar that had its doors shut. The two men clinging to the ladders along the outside jumped to the ground and formed rank next to their comrades. Every man's weapon was aimed at the door.

"All right, you nigger scabs!" Tom shouted. "We've got a hundred men out here armed with Winchesters. Now, I want you to slowly slide that door open and come out with your hands up. If you do as I say, you might get out of this alive. If you don't do exactly as I say, we are gonna start blasting right through the walls, and then we're gonna burn it with you inside!"

There was a lot of commotion inside the boxcar. Finally, the latch flipped up. The big door squealed slowly open. The Negroes held their hands high above their heads as they took turns sitting and then sliding to the ground. One of the blacks was a young girl about fifteen years old. Her face was full of scar tissue as if she had at one time been badly burnt. The captives remained in a tight huddle. Their eyes were open wide. Most of them were shaking. Except for some whimpering and crying, none of them made a sound. When prodded with the barrels of the Winchesters, they moved as one away from the train.

While his men held the strikebreakers at gunpoint, Tom returned to the front of the train. He recognized that it was the same conductor and fireman as on the last train they had stopped. "Did you gandy dancers know you was haulin' nigger scabs?"

The train conductor looked along the railroad tracks at the Negroes and spat a large wad of tobacco on the iron wheels of the train. "Hell," he said, "I don't see no niggers. I suppose if there were some hid away in one of them boxcars they probably jumped out somewhere betwixt here and Indianapolis."

"You see any niggers?" Tom asked the fireman.

"No, sir, I surely don't."

"Anyone else on the train?" Tom asked.

The railroad men shook their heads.

"You'd best get this train moving then."

A few minutes later, the engine was stoked up again and heading west, leaving the strikebreakers standing along the tracks by the clearing, a dozen armed men aiming rifles at them.

"How many you count?" Tom asked Holiday.

"Twenty-three if you count the girl." Holiday said.

"She counts," Tom said in a whisper, "so when this is over you better have twenty-three bodies. I don't want no niggers making it to the woods. Understood?"

"Understood." Holiday spoke softly to two other miners who immediately went in separate directions and positioned themselves a few feet back from the other men. They stood at the ready to chase down any black who made it through the first assault. The clearing behind the strikebreakers was at least one hundred yards of prairie grass, with woods behind. From within those trees were several white-tailed deer. Their heads raised and ears perked as they looked across the field toward the humans.

Holiday glanced toward the brush where the Gatling gun was camouflaged. "Nice day, ain't it?"

He reached in his breast pocket and retrieved a cigar along with a small box of safety matches. He glanced up in the sky at a noisy flock of geese honking loudly as they flew south in a V-shaped formation.

Holiday lit the match. Just as he put it to the tip of the cigar, the brush pulled back, revealing the big Gatling gun.

Several of the Negroes screamed, but frozen in fear, they didn't move. One of the union men started turning the crank as fast as he could, but the gun seemed to hit empty cylinders.

Though the only unprotected escape route was behind them, the Negroes appeared hesitant. They started backing slowly toward the open field. One of the deer near the timber raised its tail and the herd leapt quickly into the safety of the forest.

"Use your Winchesters!" Tom shouted.

One of the men immediately cocked and fired, hitting one of the blacks square in the forehead. The rest of the union men weren't prepared and either had problems cocking or were too stressed to work the mechanism.

Just as the Negroes made the decision to turn and run across the open field toward the trees, the Gatling gun roared to life, cutting down black men along with much of the prairie grass. The horrified screams from the fleeing strikebreakers became mixed with the screams of pain from the wounded.

At the same time, some of the men with Winchesters solved whatever issues were plaguing them. Three bullets caught the lone Negro woman in the back at the same time, sending her to the ground mid-stride. The assassins stood as calmly as if they were on a shooting range and continued cocking, aiming and firing. Each explosion seemed to either drop a fleeing strikebreaker or kick up blood from one already on the ground. The head-shots brought the worst destruction, bursting the skulls like exploding watermelons.

An angry, bluish cloud of gun smoke rolled above the prairie grass toward the dead and dying. Even while they killed, a gentle kiss of cool morning breeze ran along the backs of the gunman's necks. The current of air swept up the gun smoke, swirling it upwards and away from the bodies. Bodies that lay in grotesque positions, the faces of the blacks frozen in horrified screams, some twitching in death throes.

When the gun smoke rose toward the clear blue sky, Tom signaled with a raised hand for the Gatling to stop. As it did, he used the other hand to order the riflemen to advance. Though all the Negroes were down, he wanted at least one more, clean head shot into each body to make sure they were dead.

A few moments later, the shooting slowed, then, following a few more pops, stopped completely.

Tom wasn't certain if he had lost his hearing because of the loud percussions from the guns, or if there were simply no noise because the animals themselves were in shock. Whichever the reason, it seemed to take several moments of dead silence before he finally heard a rustling in the grass. One of the other union men heard it too and swung his rifle toward a rabbit that hopped over one of the bodies and scampered off toward the timber.

"You know what we gotta do," Tom said. "Bleed 'em out, boys. Then load 'em in the wagon."

Every one of the men had hunting experience, so cutting the jugular vein was only problematic in that the procedure was not being done on animals. When the grisly work was accomplished, Tom ordered half the men to stay and pick up cartridges. They were then to burn the grass where the men and one woman had left most of their blood.

Blood, however, was still a problem. There was considerable discussion on how to stack the bodies on the wagon so as not to leave a scarlet trail.

Being the eldest—as well as the most proficient hunter—Holiday Jones did the stacking.

Tom drove the death wagon, which was now covered with a big tarp. Less than a mile from the scene of the massacre was an abandoned coal mine. After tearing the boards off the entrance, the bloody bodies were loaded into coal cars and pushed down the slope and deep into the earth. Men with lanterns silently led the way, sometimes stopping to light wall lamps that had been left when the shaft was closed. Several of the men had once worked this part of the mine, and they had no trouble finding what had once been an airshaft that went straight down for over seven hundred feet.

The only man who took the job lightly was Cyrus Cheney. He hated blacks with a passion and had been the first to volunteer for the throat-slashing job. When the bodies were ready to be dropped, he laughed a lot and tried to make bets on which would hit bottom loudest.

"That ain't even nothin' to wager on, Cyrus," Holiday said. "It only makes sense the first ones will be loudest, 'cause they'll hit solid rock. The rest will be cushioned by bodies."

Still, Cheney had a good chuckle each time it was his turn to entomb a corpse. Once all the bodies had been disposed, Holiday set the dynamite while the other men left. When he was done, he lit the long fuse and walked calmly back to the surface.

Cheney volunteered to remain outside the mine and board the entrance back up. The remainder of the men were riding the hay wagon a quarter mile away when they heard the explosion, followed by Cheney's cheers. None of them looked back or said a word. Enough rock and dirt had filled the shaft that it would take years for someone to dig down to the bodies—and that could only happen if they knew where to look.

All the men except Holiday and Tom left the wagon when they reached one of the men's home just outside of town. They had more blood on their clothes than a hunter should and wanted to clean up. And, the fruit cellar had a pretty good supply of moonshine. Holiday purchased a brown jug from the miner's wife and joined Tom back on the wagon.

"Maybe we should have buried them proper," Tom said to Holiday as he drove the wagon back on into town. He turned his head to spit a chaw of tobacco.

"Them niggers is dead and buried." Holiday gulped his fourth mouthful of whiskey. "Buried, that is, if you consider seven hundred feet under the surface of the earth as being properly buried." He wiped spittle off his chin. "At least they's closer to their new home. In Hell."

***

The squeeky sound of the wagon grabbed Rachel's attention. She peeked through thie kitchen window.

Tom walked out of the carriage house. He didn't

come inside, but instead filled large buckets of water at the outside pump and made several trips carrying them into the carriage house. She heard splashing against metal as he filled the big hog scalder they used as a bathtub and spent longer than normal cleaning himself. She was still standing by the window when he exited the building, wearing old work clothes and carrying the ones he'd worn when he arrived home. He dropped them in the incinerator, poured kerosene on them, and threw in a match.

Without waiting for the fire to finish, he walked straight through the backdoor and into her arms. It had been a long time since he'd held her so tight, his head resting on her shoulder.

"What is it, Tom?" she asked after several moments. He smelled so strongly of lye soap she thought he must have used the whole bar.

"I killed a whole parcel of nigger scabs today." Tom slowly told her what had transpired that morning, leaving out the most horrifying details. Still, he didn't hide the fact he'd been the man most responsible for the murder of almost two dozen Negroes.

"Why is all this happening?" Rachel knelt on the floor beside his chair and caressed his hand.

"If the Pana union workers lose this fight, all the other coal mines in Illinois will lower their wages." Tom's hands shook as he tried to run them over his wife's hair. "I know you'll think this sounds crazy, but there's a good chance that what happens in this town will affect labor all across the country."

"You sounded just like your father just now," Rachel looked up into his eyes. "It scares me."

"Don't worry about that," Tom said. He attempted a smile but it wouldn't come. His cheeks trembled from trying. "I'm not about to do to you like my pa did to my ma. I intend to win this fight. Not for me or even my pa. We will win this fight for every man, woman and child in America. Someday the workers of this world is gonna be treated with the dignity they deserve."

"But those poor men who died today..." Rachel kissed her husband's hand, tears running down her face.

"Those scabs had to die so that others may live," Tom said, tears now pouring along his chin and into her hair. His mouth quivered so badly he struggled to set his jaw and then almost shouted. "I am willing to bear that cross."

"Oh, Tom," Rachel said. "This is not who we are."

"No," Tom said, "but maybe it's who we must be to survive."

14

"How am I supposed to vote when I can't even read the writin'?" Swain Whitfield asked Myrtle. She and several of the other women had brought the miners into the stockade house to learn how to vote in the local election that was to be held the next day. It was a simple skill that they had never had the need to learn in Alabama.

"I'll teach you the letters for each name," Myrtle said. "All you gotta do is put an X next to it."

"Do I put the X before or after the name?" Quits Simpson asked.

"Well, I don't know. There'll be a little box or a line or something," Myrtle said, getting confused herself. "Oh, just put an X before and after the name. That should take care of it."

"This is just crazy," Bucktooth said, "Why can't you just go vote for me?"

"It ain't allowed," Myrtle explained for the third time that evening. "I'm a woman, and women can't vote."

"That don't make no sense at all," Bucktooth said. "Women is the ones that knows how to read."

A few of the miners got up to leave. Big Henry and Garfield held their seats. They knew Myrtle well enough to know what was coming.

"Now you all just wait one minute!" Myrtle yelled. "I can tell you right now there ain't a one of you knows how to pack your own lunch box. Now either sit back down or learn to wash and darn your own clothes!"

The other Negro women nodded their heads and crossed their arms. The men sat back down. Not being married, Big Henry had no intention of quarreling with the woman who took care of most of his bachelor needs. He wondered often, though, why Garfield tolerated his wife's bossy behavior. Henry didn't think it would be legal for her to withhold her wifely duties to her lawfully wedded husband. He was sure there must be a law somewhere against that. Still, Garfield acted like Myrtle had a way to keep his temperament in check. Maybe one day he would think of a way to ask what it was.

"Now we wrote on the wall the names of those you need to vote for." Myrtle said. "We want you to practice the names by copying them onto the sheet of paper that my sons are passing around. If you men don't know how to use a pencil, some of the children can show you."

Ornery Billy handed Quits a sheet of paper.

"The last time I put an X on something," Quits

said, giving the boy a sourpuss face, "I wound up married and with five brat kids."

Ornery Billy stuck his tongue out at the old man.

***

Jeb and the other deputies spent Election Day patrolling the streets. There were five polling places in town, none of them friendly to the Negro voters. The one closest to where most of them lived was the Opera House.

Soldiers were posted at each of the voting areas, though they made no move to interfere in any way. Almost all of the first Negroes who walked into the building were rejected.

"They says I ain't lived here long enough," Swain Whitfield said.

"They says I ain't old enough," Louis Hooks said.

Bucktooth Daniels held his head low as he tried to sneak past Jeb, but his bowler hat gave him away.

"Why couldn't you vote, Bucktooth?" Jeb asked.

"I ain't rightly sure, Mistuh Deputy, sir," Bucktooth said. "They didn't say, but I think it had something to do with my answers."

"Your answers?" Quits said. "What did they ask you?"

"They asked if these were really my eye teeth or if I was in disguise," Bucktooth said. He took off his bowler and ran a finger around the rattlesnake skin hat band. "I reckon I shouldn't have showed them the skin of the snake that bit me. When I tried to tell them the rattler was the reason my teeth grew so big they laughed at me and told me to get out."

"Did you give them your first name?" Jeb asked, thinking there must have been a different reason. "Or did you tell them Bucktooth was your name?"

"O' course I gave 'em my first name," Bucktooth said. "I ain't stupid."

"Well, what is your first name, Bucktooth?" Quits asked.

"Oh, don't call me that." Bucktooth shook his head and started walking away. "My first name is ridiculous."

"He's right, you know," Quits said to Jeb when his friend was out of sight. "Why in the world would a parent name their child Ridiculous?"

***

The crowd that was gathered in and around the Opera House on the night of the November election was the largest anyone could ever remember seeing in Christian County. Tom Downs easily won the election to become the new county sheriff. He received a rousing applause when he announced his first act when he took office on December fifth would be to fire all the deputies that had been protecting the mine yard and hire union men to take their place.

"We just now got a telegraph saying the Chicago-Virden Coal Company is beat," General Bradley announced later that evening. "The Virden mines will open with union labor at forty cents per ton."

***

When Jeb learned several days later that only fifty-nine Negro votes had counted in the election, he was incensed. He had talked to each miner as they exited the Opera House, and by his count, over one hundred had been allowed to cast ballots. Several times that number, though, had been turned away for one reason or another. Jeb found no one to hear his complaint in Pana, since the union supporters had won every election from sheriff to mayor. The county building in Taylorville was no better. All the coal towns in Christian County were already strongly in favor of the United Mine Workers.

Fearing that Big Henry would rally his people to riot when he got the news, Jeb went straight to the Alabama Hotel. When he entered the community room he saw Garfield comforting his wife Myrtle. She was crying with great, deep sobs as many others in the room stood nearby, watching with tearful eyes. Jeb knew there was something terribly wrong when he saw the four Wallace boys standing resolutely beside their parents, even Ornery Billy being quiet and respectful.

Big Henry walked toward Jeb. The huge man's eyes were teary, but his giant-sized fists were clenched.

"You'd best let these folks have their time," Big Henry said. "This ain't no place for a white man right now."

"What happened to Myrtle, Big Henry?" Jeb asked.

"Her sister's husband was killed in Wilmington."

"You mean when the Negroes rioted the other day?"

"You call it a riot?" Big Henry demanded. "Near on one hundred coloreds murdered, but not one white person. We call it a massacre. Now leave, white man."

Jeb was confused, but he did as he was told. He went straight back to the boarding house. In his room, he read for a second time the newspaper article about the riots that had occurred in Wilmington, North Carolina, on November tenth.

According to the paper, it had all started because of an editorial by a black man named Alex Manly who ran the *Daily Record*, the only Negro newspaper in the state. In the editorial, Manly denied charges that Negro men were sexually attacking white women in the city, claiming they were consensual relationships. He argued that "poor white men are careless in the matter of protecting their women...our experiences among poor white people in the country teaches us that women of that race are not any more particular in the matter of clandestine meetings with colored men than the white men with the colored women."

Clandestine meetings...white men with colored women. Fanny's words had haunted him since that day at the pond. "Even proper white men down south don' mind a dalliance with a colored gal now and again."

The article went on to state that because Manly had defamed white women, the white community in Wilmington had destroyed and burnt his newspaper building. It went on to claim that the benevolent white supremacists had restored order to the city following the Negroes' attempt to riot. *Benevolent white supremacists?*

A loud knock sounded on Jeb's door. With newspaper in hand, he rushed to see who could've had such a heavy hand. He opened it to see Big Henry's massive frame filling the doorway.

"I think that old lady downstairs might have fainted," Big Henry apologized. "The other boarders are givin' her some smellin' salts."

"Come in, Big Henry," Jeb said. He held the newspaper. "I was just trying to figure out what happened in Wilmington. I'm real sorry for Myrtle."

Big Henry turned his head to the side to avoid the top of the door frame and walked inside. Jeb shut the door and offered him the only chair in the room. It gave a painful creak as the big man sat down. Jeb took a seat on the edge of the bed.

"I came to apologize for talkin' to you the way I did," Big Henry said. "You didn't do nothin' to deserve that."

"What happened in Wilmington, Big Henry? The newspaper says seven Negroes were killed."

"All I know is what Myrtle's sister wrote in the letter," Big Henry said. "She said there was about one hundred killed, and the Cape Fear River was running red with blood. The colored folks had to run from the city and hide in the swamps."

"Didn't anyone try to help them?"

"The governor sent the Wilmington Light Infantry, but even they started killing colored folks."

"Was this all because of the newspaper article?"

"That was their excuse," Big Henry said. "The real reason is because the majority of folks in Wilmington is colored, so a lot of Negroes and other Republicans got elected November eighth. The white folk is mostly Democrats. They had a bunch called the Red Shirts try to stop coloreds from votin'. They used to be called the Ku Klux

Klan. When the Republicans won and a bunch of Negroes got elected, the Democrats ran the coloreds out of town and took over the government."

"A coup d'etat," Jeb whispered.

"What?" Big Henry asked.

"It's what they call a violent takeover of government," Jeb said. "I never heard of such a thing in the United States."

"Well, you heard of it now," Big Henry said, rising from the chair. "Anyway, I'm sorry I wasn't respectful earlier."

"I think I understand," Jeb rose, and the two men shook hands.

"Oh," Big Henry said as he opened the door. "Be a little careful around the colored folk. They may not be real hospitable for a while."

***

After stopping by the Sunrise Tavern for a drink, Big Henry walked to the Alabama Hotel to check on Myrtle. He looked into the Wallace room, where the boys were asleep in their bed. Garfield was cuddled in the small bed with his wife, and though she was sound asleep, he was softly singing to her.

I love you as I never lov'd before,
Since first I met you on the village green

Come to me, or my dream of love is o'er.
I love you as I lov'd you
When you were sweet, when you were sweet
sixteen

***

A few days later Jeb, and Big Henry were sum-
moned to the coal company office building. Though
they wore expensive-looking suits and broad-
brimmed hats, the men Eubanks introduced as
the "trusty six" were the hardest looking men Jeb
had ever seen. Their expressions of anger and hate
as they stood in the front of the big company conference room brought an awed silence to those in
attendance. Only Big Henry's eyes seemed able
to study the sun-dried faces that held many scars
from countless battles. Though each man wore a
side arm on their hip, they also had small bulges
on either side of their vest coats that Jeb suspected
held shoulder weapons.

"I don't like that nigger staring at me," the small-
est of the six said. He was called Nelson Macnee
and had been introduced as the leader of the hired
gunman.

"Big Henry don't mean no harm," Howard
Smithson said. "He's just simple-minded and
don't know no better."

Recognizing that Big Henry resented the two

insults, Jeb made eye contact with his friend and motioned with a slight nod of his head. The black man's eyes narrowed, but he finally turned his face away from the six.

"Our numbers have dwindled since Tom Downs announced he will be firing our deputies when he takes office," Eubanks explained. "Since the county will no longer be financing them, our mine operators will be taking up that burden. Hence, the reason for us hiring you six. Your first job will be to evaluate and select among the deputies who will be the most useful. They will be hired and paid for by the coal company. Your next assignment will be to train the coloreds as best you can."

"You want us to train the niggers to fight?" Macnee said. "Hell, if they could fight, you think they'd ever been slaves?"

When Jeb saw Big Henry's head jerk back toward Macnee, he jumped in front of the black giant. "That's what I've been telling everybody!" Jeb shouted, accidentally spitting in Big Henry's face. "You coons can't hold a candle to white folk!"

Jeb shut his eyes when he saw Big Henry's fist draw back, but instead of a blow to the jaw, he felt himself being lifted high off the ground and flung across the room into a wall. When he opened his eyes, half a dozen men were attempting to restrain the big Negro.

He looked at Nelson Macnee, who had half a

smirk on his face.

"Well," Macnee said, "I guess we can use that one."

***

"It was the 'dirty six' burnt down my barn and kilt my milk cow!" Ora Langford yelled at the guardsmen gathered in front of the jailhouse. The old farmer was so loud, church goers next door came out right in the middle of the preacher's sermon. "They shot right into my house and kilt my milk cow."

"What was your cow doing inside your house?" Captain Gibbs asked.

"Well, with all the shooting going on lately, she quit giving milk. Everyone knows how I love a cool glass of buttermilk. So, I let her live inside the house with me. I guess she took a likin' to livin' there, 'cause when I tried to get her back outside, she threw a fit and tore the place up. That's when the bullets came through the window."

"Did you see 'em shoot?" Captain Gibbs asked.

"No, 'course not!" Langford shouted. "I fell flat on my back and knocked myself out."

Holiday Jones had been the one to see the smoke and hurried to Langford's farmhouse. He found the farmer lying unconscious in a pool of the dead cow's blood. Langford had a large bump on the back of his head.

"They musta been usin' ol' Betsy for target practice," Holiday said. "The cow had over fifty bullet holes in her. Now, what you soldiers gonna do about it?"

"We ain't doin' nothin'," Gibbs said. "We're here to protect people, not livestock."

"But they burnt his barn!" Holiday shouted. The church was emptying rapidly and a sizable audience formed. "You're supposed to protect property, too."

"Well," Gibbs said, then grabbed Holiday by the coat collar, "how do I know that you didn't set the fire yourself just so I'd arrest the company guards?"

"Sure," Holiday shouted, "and if my sister had balls, she'd've been my brother."

He was older and a thin man, but had big hands that when fisted were quite formidable. The right he delivered to the captain's cheekbone might've dropped an average-sized man, but Gibbs was no average-sized man. The guardsman raised their weapons.

"I can handle this old geezer." Gibbs motioned his patrol to stand down.

Neither the soldiers nor the town deputies seemed inclined to take part in the fight, although several of the church women wrestled to remove young children from the scene.

The thrashing that Gibbs received from the lanky man was nothing compared to the laughter the captain heard from the townspeople as his soldiers helped him back to the barracks. As soon as he was able to sit at his desk, he wrote an ordinance, "I am here to do my duty, to protect life and property, and I intend to do it. Henceforward, no insulting or slurring remarks will be borne with on the part of any of the officers and the soldiery, and any persons, white or black, using ill-meaning or insulting remarks must stand the consequences. When an order to halt is given by any soldier to any person, the order must be obeyed, or the person must stand the consequences."

When Swain Whitfield heard this, he thought it would be good to stir up the militia a little. He invited a couple of the better Negro marksmen to stand guard with him at the top of the mine tipple. The house of an old widow named Beatrice Jamison was within easy rifle range of the tipple. She had a yard full of fat Cornish hens that she refused to sell to the blacks. Periodic violence being common throughout the day, Swain and the marksmen didn't have long to wait before they heard gunfire coming from somewhere in town. They opened up on the widow Jamison's poultry. When the smoke cleared, the only thing moving around her house was a yard full of feathers.

This fowl massacre caused such a stir in Pana,

Tom Downs and his union boys were out in force every evening for the next week. Swain got the notion that if he and his sharpshooters could eradicate the chicken population that easily, they should be able to do the same before the new sheriff and his deputies took office. His plan was to have one of the Negroes sneak into town at night and fire a couple of gunshots in the air, and then run back to the mine yard. The hope was they could lure Tom into rifle range of the mine tipple.

The result was a hide and seek every day from dawn until dusk. The shots would bring the militiamen running down one street, and Tom and his men down another. The two groups would often meet and have a heated exchange before heading off in different directions. While the cat and mouse game proved to be entertaining for the colored marksmen watching from the mine tipple, it did little in the way of bringing about a successful assassination.

Fistfights erupted almost every day. Sometimes it was between union and non-union men. Often as not, however, it was between colored strikebreakers who were getting bored from being in the stockade and more than a little rattled by the stress of the mine war.

When Governor Tanner got word that his militia were not being respected in Pana, he posted a notice that the soldiers were to use their bayonets if anyone assaulted them or even threw missiles at them.

The town of Pana was on the brink of a major storm.

15

"My shit don't stink," Garfield announced one evening during dinner. The unpleasant conversation had started when, out of pure boredom and refried beans, he and his sons began a farting contest. When the competition spread to children and fathers at other tables, Myrtle decided to end it by loudly accusing her husband of the disturbance. The Wallace couple's arguments were the only entertainment many of the Negroes in the Alabama Hotel had each evening.

"No?" Myrtle said. "Well, the shoats back in Alabama sure liked to follow you to the outhouse, didn't they?"

"That's because I'd throw them one of your turds now and again," Garfield said. "They probably liked all the corn you was always eatin'."

Myrtle couldn't disagree with that. She liked her corn-on-the-cob, and that was a fact. Everyone in the room fought to hide a chuckle except Dr. Mills, who was trying to get a button out of Ornery Billy Wallace's nose. The doctor had the little six-year-old standing in front of a window with the boy's head tilted as far back as it would go. This was the second object Billy had stuck up his nose that month. Had there been more evening sunlight and had the conversation at the dinner table not been so lively, the doctor most likely would've completed his retrieval of the button. But he paused with his long pincers midair for a moment to hear Myrtle's retort.

"Don't be tryin' to cover your tracks with my shoes, Garfield Wallace." Myrtle shouted at her husband.

A bullet shattered a nearby window. Everyone in the dining room screamed and dove for cover under the tables. A dozen more shots ricocheted about the room. On hands and knees, mothers herded their children toward the safety of the windowless hallway.

The men followed Big Henry, who pulled a revolver from his belt. They hurried to get in position alongside the windows. Without taking aim, Henry fired several shots out the window toward the nearby Opera House, from where he was certain the first shot had come. By the time he'd emptied his gun and leaned against the wall to reload, the rest of the men were in position. They began holding their own guns up to other windows and blindly firing at the same building.

Jeb Turner stumbled over the women and children in the hallway and slid head first across the cafeteria floor. When he put his hands down to crawl, they came up bloody from the glass heavily strewn across the room.

Another round of shots came from the Opera House. Dr. Mills screamed, and with hands over his face, fell backwards onto the floor. Jeb looked up just in time to see the doctor pull an inch long piece of glass out of his own eye socket.

"You men quit wastin' ammunition!" Jeb yelled.

The Negroes immediately stopped firing and sat with their backs against the wall. Some began reloading.

"Don't shoot unless you have a target," Jeb said when shots from the adjacent building also stopped.

"I ain't raisin' my head to look out that window, I sure ain't," Swain Whitfield said.

"Then don't," Jeb said.

Gunshots from blocks away sounded, but no more bullets seemed to hit the hotel.

"Just sit tight and let's see what happens."

Staying low to the ground, Myrtle scampered out of the hallway, took the injured doctor's arm, and led him back to the other women.

After a few minutes of listening to the distance shots, Garfield held his hand up. "Mistuh Turner, sir," he said. "It sounds like maybe they's havin' a gunfight over at the Sunrise Tavern."

Jeb looked at Big Henry, who nodded.

"That saloon's in a bad spot," Big Henry said. "Them folks in there'll like to never get out."

Jeb felt guilty that his first thought was of Fanny, whom he assumed would be there. "Big Henry, you come with me," Jeb said. "Garfield, you're in charge here. Keep the doors blocked until morning, and keep everyone away from the windows."

Holding their Colt revolvers at the ready, Jeb and Big Henry ducked low and ran out the door of the building and into the street. They both leapt back when a pair of horses pulling a farm wagon roared toward them. When he didn't see anyone in the driver's seat, Jeb assumed the horses must've been runaways. Then he saw a man driving the team from beneath the bed of the wagon.

The wagon didn't slow as it took the next corner on two wheels.

In the distance, women herded children toward the country road that led out of town. Two soldiers stood guard in the street to ensure the frantic evacuation, their bayoneted guns silhouetted against the red rays of the evening sun.

Captain Gibbs and two lieutenants emerged from the building across the road. Jeb approached them as the captain stood calmly donning his gloves, gunshots echoing from every direction.

"Where's everyone going?" Jeb asked the captain.

"They're leaving," Gibbs said. "I'd 'spect to other

towns or to stay with friends in the country."

"Why isn't your militia doing anything?" Jeb asked.

"I've had less than seventy men here ever since the riot at Virden," Gibbs said, a hint of irritation in his voice. "We are guarding the roads into town, the jailhouse, and the railroad station. We can't be everywhere."

With a theatrical flip of his head, Gibbs turned and proceeded with his soldiers toward the Eubanks mine gate. Big Henry headed off in the direction of the Sunrise Tavern, so Jeb followed after him. Jeb wasn't accustomed to following anyone except Sheriff Cogburn. The muscular Negro, though, was so confident in his actions, following him seemed the natural thing to do.

Gunshots rang all around, but not near them until they were a block from the tavern. The sky was turning black, so rifle flashes gave away the position of union men as well as the Negroes defending themselves inside the tavern. Jeb and Big Henry took a knee at the edge of the alleyway and peered cautiously around the corner, trying to decide their next move.

A sound behind them caused them both to spin around, their Colts pointing into the dark alley. Nelson Macnee and the other five hired gunmen stepped slowly into the light.

"You and the darkie come with me," Macnee

said without prelude.

Jeb wondered if Big Henry would take orders from the gunman, but when the black man rose to follow Macnee, Jeb did the same.

***

Fanny wasn't struggling, but two men held her arms anyway. During a lull in the gunfire, they had rushed into her room from the outside staircase, grabbed her off the floor, and threw her on her back onto the little dining table. She knew the plate and silverware beneath her would be more uncomfortable than anything the men were about to do. She smelled whiskey on their breath as they laughed and made rude comments about the color of her skin. The man at the end of the table, Holiday Jones, was one of her paying customers. He had been sporting a sawed-off shotgun when he burst into the room, and she heard it drop beside the table when they took up positions around her. She couldn't remember having been acquainted with the other two men. It didn't surprise her that Holiday would prefer the excitement of rape to something he could have for just a day's wages. He liked to spank her during tricks.

The man on the right leaned over and put his mouth over hers while Holiday stood near her feet, working to unbutton his fly with trembling hands. When Holiday finally managed the clumsy task, he let his baggy long johns drop to his ankles, grabbed Fanny's knees, and spread them with more violence than was necessary. The third man let go of her left arm, and using both hands, pushed her pink sateen corset down off her ample bosom. He was howling like a coyote and giving the nipples a hard squeeze when Fanny used her freed hand to grab a whiskey bottle pressed against her ear. Holiday's face was closest, since he had lowered it to look beneath her petticoat at the flower-like tunnel between her legs. The bottle, being unopened, offered a suitable bludgeon for the Alabama girl who had plenty of experience cold-cocking uninvited liaisons.

Holiday was knocked unconscious by a blow from the heavy end that, to Fanny's dismay, didn't break the bottle. She had counted on using the sharp edges to cut the face of the man kissing her. Instead she rolled toward him and let her own body weight break the hold he had on her right arm. His inebriation slowed his ability to recover and straighten up. Fanny took advantage by switching the bottle to her right hand and backhanding it against the top of the man's head. This time the bottle did break, leaving the menacing, sharp-edged half to jab toward the tit man, who was still staring with glassy eyes at her naked breasts. The motion of the edges of glass coming inches from his nose caused him to turn his attention to the crazy girl's face, which was more demonic than any bad dream he'd ever had. He turned and dashed for the door.

Fanny's dander was still up. She reached to the floor and grabbed the long end of the sawed off shotgun, then swung it toward the retreating would-be-rapist.

"Hold on there, little lady!" the man shouted when he glanced over his shoulder. He had one hand on the doorknob while the other waved frantically toward Fanny. "An instrument like that ain't meant to be used during no simple train pull."

If she hadn't had to look down to cock the hammer, he wouldn't have gotten the door open. Instead, she pulled the trigger from a blind hip shot. The kickback ripped the gun from her hands. When she looked up, she saw a short, well-dressed man in the doorway, a dumbfounded look on his face. He had a mine security badge on his chest. Then she noticed the blood. Half his right hand was missing below the wrist.

***

"I ain't gonna get myself kilt for these mine owners, no matter how much they pay me," Frank Cogburn said the day after the shootout. He dropped his Winchester and his badge onto his father's desk. "I'd say it's time to turn tail to the wind and hunker down. After all, a livin' dog is better than a dead lion. If a tough son-of-a-bitch like Nelson Macnee can lose an arm, then I'm out."

Jeb didn't know what to tell Frank. The two had been friends for as far back as he could remember. Frank's resignation wasn't a surprise. A dozen other deputies had already done the same, claiming that when Tom Downs took office as sheriff on December fifth, and with most of the rest of the town supporting the UMW, they would all be easy targets. Jeb figured men weren't as much afraid of dying as long as it didn't involve pain, appendage loss, or a slow death.

The sound on the street that had become familiar in Pana caused Jeb and Frank to turn their heads. A column of National Guardsmen stomped in marching order outside the window, their bayoneted rifles slung smartly over their shoulders. That morning an irate governor had returned several companies to the town, which was now under martial law. Tanner had again ordained that all citizens turn in their weapons and ordered the Guard to search everyone who ventured out into the streets. Even the sheriff's deputies were treated with suspicion, although they were allowed to carry their side arms.

The morale of the coal company guards was further damaged by the fact that Dr. Mills had butchered his first attempt to remove Nelson Macnee's arm stub by cutting too close to the wrist. For the second effort, he took the arm just above the elbow. No one really blamed the doctor, since he was performing the operation with one eye, the other having just been covered with a bandage. Jeb and Big Henry were the only ones who knew it had been Fanny who had reduced the "trusty six" by one, and Macnee wasn't likely to admit a woman had destroyed his gun fighting career.

"They say that it all got started when some of the union boys took a few shots at Howard Smithson," Jeb said. He wanted to talk. "They missed, but he took cover in Eubanks' store, and there were some coloreds in there who started shooting back."

Jeb wanted to see if Frank might have any type of respect for the Negroes. He had seen his best friend drinking and shooting dice with them. He also knew the sheriff's son had developed a thirst for Fanny Cahill that took him up the back steps of the Sunrise Tavern at least once a week. Frank, though, hadn't seemed to have acquired the degree of regard for the Negros that Jeb had.

"Them coloreds do put up a good fight," Frank admitted, "but I ain't riskin' my neck for 'em. One of the union leaders suggested they recruit the niggers into the union, but the strikers voted it down. I doubt the scabs would have accepted it anyway. There's just way too much animosity between whites and blacks right now. I just wish those jigaboos would go back to Africa."

"You mean *Alabama*." Jeb corrected.

"No." Frank turned and started for the door. "I mean *Africa*."

***

To everyone's surprise, it was Buffalo Butts Bertha, the prostitute from the Sunrise Tavern, who assisted in both amputations. Bertha was especially good at keeping Macnee sedated with chloroform, a skill she claimed to have learned when her mother was the housekeeper for a doctor.

After the second amputation, Dr. Mills wrapped the fingerless hand and the piece of forearm in a towel and handed it to Bertha. The big woman stood for a moment and looked from the towel to the doctor to the unconscious man. Finally, she carried the leftovers out of the room and into the courtyard, where she promptly buried the remains in a shallow grave beneath a Chinese elm.

Bertha reveled in the quiet notoriety from her skill as a healer and briefly considered giving up the sporting life. Over the next days, a few of the other colored women even came to her for medical advice, mostly for themselves or their younger children. The big woman meticulously cleaned cuts and made more poultices than she could count. The wives of the coal miners, however, refrained in trusting their husbands or older boys to receive such treatments.

The fact that her nursing only paid in gratitude or an occasional mincemeat pie drove the toothless prostitute to slowly return to the more lucrative trade in which she was more famously known as Buffalo Butts. Still, for the first time in her life, Bertha was able to enjoy a reserved respect from some of the women who had known her for years.

Thanksgiving a week later was a warm and sunny day, so over one hundred of the Negroes living in the Alabama Hotel set up tables in the courtyard and roasted the biggest of the three razorback hogs they had bartered from a local farmer. After the meal, the men sat at the tables talking while some of the children took turns riding around the yard on the two surviving hogs. The women set up a big wash tub near the tables to clean the dishes. When they started dumping the used water at the far end of the yard, Bertha got real nervous. Matters were made worse when one of the hogs took a bite at Ornery Billy Wallace, who had been beating the animal with a stick. After that, the children started up a game of kick-the-can, and the hogs hurried over to the new mud hole beneath the elm. Bertha kept her eyes on the animals as she stood with the other women. They were all chatting away as they dried the pots and pans and handed them to little girls to carry back inside.

It only took a few minutes before one of the hogs found Nelson Macnee's appendage. No one but Bertha paid the animals any attention as they began a tug-of-war with the gunfighter's remains. When the last of Macnee disappeared into the stomach of the hogs, Bertha breathed a sigh of relief and turned her attention back to what the women were saying.

"Ain't nothin' taste better to our men than a fat hog," Myrtle was telling the women.

"Or da other way around," Bertha muttered under her breath.

Fanny May Cahill couldn't get warm enough anywhere except in her own room above the Sunrise Tavern. She kept the potbellied stove topped off with so much coal her customers usually worked up a fast lather of sweat before they even finished with her. Fanny liked that white men in particular didn't appreciate the excessive heat of the room. It meant they'd be out the door quicker after they'd finished their business. She was told this December was unseasonably cold for central Illinois, a factor that seemed to have contributed to the sudden decline in violence in the community of Pana.

Since Fanny was usually up most of the night entertaining, she was accustomed to sleeping until noon each day. She liked to lounge in her big chair in front of the window. Sometimes she sat in the chair to relax before getting into bed, often until around four in the morning. She knew it was that time because Swain Whitfield always drove a pair of mules hauling a big heavy wagon of mining materials each morning. He was regular as clockwork. She would imagine shooting him from the window with a shotgun. The pleasant thought would help her lie down and sleep like a baby.

When she rose from bed, it would be the lunch hour, and she'd return to her chair to drink coffee and to watch people hurrying from the warmth of one building to another. Many of these comings and goings were so routine, she began watching for each person's turn on the street.

The most interesting was the departure every day of Frosty O'Brien from his store and the prompt arrival of Major Samuels a few moments later. Having heard about Mrs. O'Brien's youth and beauty, it didn't take long for Fanny to put one and two together. Fanny hated the major. Several of the militiamen had been good-paying customers until the incident with Samuels and his two soldiers. Rarely now did his men sneak up the back steps of the tavern to visit the three Negro women. Business had slowed. The cold weather added to the recession.

One especially frigid afternoon, Fanny awoke feeling mischievous. Throwing on some clothes and her coat, she walked across the street just as she knew Mr. O'Brien would be leaving. When she entered the store, she expected Mrs. O'Brien to scold her away. Instead, the grocer lady gave her a smile and a look that Fanny had occasionally seen on women who admired other women.

"May I help you, Mrs....?" Mrs. O'Brien asked. She wore a brown cotton blouse and skirt with a dark fur stole around her shoulders. She had fingerless gloves that matched her fur.

"Names Miss Cahill, not Missus. I ain't never met a man up to changin' it."

Fanny turned when the door opened behind her, offering up a whiff of witch hazel and shaving cream. She looked in time to see Major Samuels pull it shut and then continue on his way down the street. Probably because of her heavy coat and broad-brimmed hat, he showed no signs of recognizing her.

"I'm not interrupting anything, am I, ma'am?" Fanny asked with as much innocence on her face as she could muster.

"Nothing that can't wait," Mrs. O'Brien replied, a twinkle in her eyes. "I've seen you coming and going across the street. You're very popular with the men, I hear."

"And the women, I'd 'spect, ma'am," Fanny said, lowering her eyes and tilting her head just enough to portray shyness. She knew how to play the game, if only through hearsay from other women in her profession.

Mrs. O'Brien's face went flush just like the faces of men did when Fanny insisted they were the best she'd ever had.

***

Fanny arrived at her plan to frustrate Major Samuels' love life the moment the young grocer lady had given her "the look." After a fine romp in the backroom and the expected invitation for a return visit, Fanny announced that the only time she could get away each day would be right after the noon hour.

"That would be perfect," Bette O'Brien said without hesitation.

Fanny knew exactly what Major Samuels' reaction would be to the loss of his regular liaison, as well as the need he'd soon have for a sporting girl. When, a few days later, a grizzled sergeant chanced a day in the brig to visit her, Fanny made a deal the red-blooded soldier couldn't refuse.

Within the week, the sergeant brought her a very drunk Major Samuels, whom she immediately bedded. He was so inebriated she was able to satisfy his urges with nothing more than the palm of her hand. Fanny was familiar with what followed such pleasure, especially when mixed with excessive alcohol. She let Samuels sleep and ignored the knocks on her door, most of which could be heard across the hall where Buffalo Butts shared a receiving room with young Sissy.

Fanny waited until three-thirty that morning before killing Samuels with a hard blow to the head with a sledge hammer. She then flipped her feather mattress over and pulled out one of the long two-by-twelve pieces of lumber that made up the bed frame. She rolled Samuel's body onto it, and then, using both hands and all her might, she lifted one end of the board and rested it on the window sill. Then she snuffed out her oil lamps and opened the window that looked out onto the empty street. A strong wind brought a biting snow into the room and blew the curtains inward. She hurried to the opposite end of the board, took a deep breath, squatted down, and took a firm grip on either side of the thick lumber. With all the wrath she could muster, Fanny raised the board and pushed it toward the opening. Major Samuels' body flew over the sidewalk and clear into the snow-covered street. She almost lost the heavy piece of wood along with the major, but managed to get the weight of her body on the end and see-sawed it back inside. She shut the window quickly and closed the curtains.

After getting her room back in order, Fanny pulled her chair closer to the window and watched for twenty minutes as the blowing snow partially covered the body. Another brilliant idea came to her. She hooted aloud. She had not expected the major's body to land in the street, but since it was there, and if luck was on her side . . . .

The supply wagon was late by several anxiety-filled minutes. Finally, the mules, straining against the harness, rounded the corner at the end of the street. Swain Whitfield was tucked low in the seat, a dark scarf wrapped around his head. He held a gloved hand before him to thwart the sting of the icy blizzard on his eyes. Fanny thought God—or, more likely, Satan—must be pulling some strings for her.

In the seconds before the wagon rolled over the dead body in the street, Fanny May Cahill recalled the moment her innocence had been forever lost. It had been a pleasant spring morning in her eighth year on earth. She remembered the sound of her bedroom door creaking open as she lay in her bed enjoying a gentle breeze from the open window that billowed her bed sheet. Then a hard body crashed down on her back, a dirty hand grasped tightly over her mouth, her favorite nightgown was ripped from her body, and then—the cruel pain. He mounted her like a dog and put his boot heels to her feet every time she tried to throw him off.

The moment the wagon wheels touched the major's body, Fanny pushed the window open and screamed as loudly as she had wanted to that morning so many years before. The haunting scream that echoed even above the sound of the howling wind caused Swain to pull hard on the reins and raise up in his seat. He turned his head in every direction as the shrieks changed to a call for help. The old colored man spotted Fanny's face in a window just as men and women began emerging from the buildings around him.

Shouts of "murder" echoed down the icy street as Swain was ripped from the wagon seat. He screamed and pointed toward Fanny's window, but his cries were ignored by the angry vigilantes.

Fanny was the last of Swain's people to see him, his eyes staring up at her, begging for the mercy he'd never offered her on that warm spring day in Birmingham eight years before.

***

When Swain didn't make it to the mine yard with his delivery, Jeb was sent looking for him. He arrived in front of the Sunrise Tavern as they were digging Major Samuels' body out of the snow. He watched as the top half of the man's body came loose from the bottom half where the heavy wagon wheels ran over him. The guardsman quickly loaded both halves of their officer on the back of a sled and, using one of Swain's mules, hurriedly pulled it back to the warmth of their camp. Since no one present seemed to know what could've happened to Swain, Jeb knocked on doors to ask questions.

As he was leaving one of the buildings, he

glanced up to Fanny Cahill's window. It was more of a habit than anything, but he did spot her peeking between the curtains onto the street. Half reluctantly, he walked up the back steps to her room. The door opened before he could knock.

"Well, get in here, deputy," Fanny said.

"I didn't come here to—" Jeb's face turned red.

She stood before him wearing a pair of thick blue long johns partly covered by a white robe. Not being able to look her in the face, Jeb stared down at her feet. That didn't help, though, since she was wearing slippers that exposed the most beautiful toes he'd ever seen.

"Don't you think I know you ain't here for pleasure?" Fanny said. "The great Deputy Jebediah Turner would never want nothing to do with a whore, would he?"

"Yes, ma'am." Jeb took a step backwards and shook his head. "I mean, no, ma'am. I ain't no deputy no more. I'm here on behalf of the coal company to find out if you saw anything when the major got run over by the wagon. We need to know what happened to Swain Whitfield."

"You ain't a deputy?" Fanny asked, shaking her head. She closed the gap between them with a step forward.

"No." Jeb took one more step backwards and felt his back against the door. "Not no more."

He smelled her now, and it filled his senses. He

wanted to take her not just for the pleasure, but to hold her and—to save her from the cruel fate that had fallen her.

"Well then, you can stay for coffee." Fanny's face was suddenly inches from his. "If'n you've a mind."

He looked in her eyes and was shocked to see they were watering. Then came a tear along her smooth, dark cheek and down into her mouth.

"This ain't right." Jeb reached with his hand behind him to turn the doorknob, and as he spun out into the cold wind, for just a moment, he felt the warm skin of Fanny's hand in his. Then he was gone.

17

A few days later came a break from the bad weather. Armed patrols once again prowled the streets. Groups of union men and black strike-breakers taunted one another with words that always led to fistfights, and from the fistfights would inevitably emerge a revolver, followed by a gunshot and a mad scamper by all to find cover. National Guardsmen would come running, but almost always too late to do anything except rush the wounded to Dr. Mills.

Even Christmas Day brought no peace to Pana, Illinois, with three separate shootings. The year 1898 ended with no resolution in sight.

"Why don't you follow the city councilman's advice and disarm the citizens?" Rachel Downs asked her husband on the first day of the New Year. She had decided early in their marriage she would never tell her man what to do, but she would encourage him to think things through by asking him questions.

"Hell, Rachel," Tom said, "that would give the advantage to the coal company."

"Well, why do you want to get the National Guard to leave town?" Rachel asked. "Don't they keep the peace?"

"The militia are a hindrance to the United Mine Workers' cause." He was less confident on that point. Any mention of the soldiers reminded him of the Gatling gun.

"How?" Rachel asked. "Aren't they often harder on the Negroes than the union men?"

"Yes, but the soldiers break up several skirmishes that could've reduced the number of scabs. Since there are approximately six hundred nigger miners fighting against several thousand picketers in Pana, a war of attrition can be easily won by the United Mine Workers."

"You would let six hundred of your friends and neighbors die to win this mine war?" Rachel asked.

Tom looked down at the picture of his father that sat on a small table. The muscles in his face began to twitch as they had been doing so regularly these past few months.

"Yes. I would," he almost whispered. "If we don't win this war, if the United Mine Workers are not successful, then during our lifetime thousands of men will be killed in the coal mines and other workplaces, and tens of thousands of impoverished women and children will die from starvation or disease or hopelessness. All because of the greed of capitalists. We must win this war, at any cost."

Tom lowered his head and slapped his hands to his face. As was happening more and more often lately, he was suddenly struck with images of blood and brain matter exploding from the heads of black men. In his mind's eye, he saw bullets riddling the back of a Negro woman whose face was horribly disfigured. Then came bodies being tossed casually down a mine shaft into a common, eternal grave. The sick laughter of Cyrus Cheney echoed between his ears.

Suddenly gasping for breath, Tom dropped to his knees, tears showering his face and hands. Rachel was, as always, instantly on the floor next to him, cradling his head against her bosom. It took several minutes for her husband to stop sobbing. Finally, he raised his head and pulled his shoulders back. "We must win this war," he repeated firmly. "At any cost!"

***

"Your guardsmen are hurtin' business in Pana, Governor," Sheriff Tom Downs said. "They stop folks and search 'em for no good reason other than they're walking down the street. Even nearby farmers are travelin' to other towns to do their business. If this keeps up, we're gonna be a ghost town."

Tanner stood up and started pacing, so Tom

continued talking. "Why we haven't had nobody but striking union men come to our town since this all began, and they ain't got no money to spend. Other towns won't even let their school kids come to Pana. We had to cancel this year's literary contest. Even the Opera House has been closed because no theatrical groups will come do shows there."

"That's probably because the theater is so full of holes from the gunfights," Tanner pointed out.

"Well, there's that," Tom agreed, "but the theater folks are afraid the niggers will come to watch the show and a fight will break out."

"Damn those coal companies for hiring Negroes," Tanner said. "If they'd have hired white strikebreakers, they might've blended in better."

"I doubt it, Governor," Tom said. "Low-life scabies are pretty easy to recognize no matter what their skin color or how much they bathe or dress up."

"Tell your mayor I want him to do more to eliminate weaponry." Tanner said. "If we can disarm your citizens perhaps we may better keep the peace."

***

When Big Henry got wind that some of the city council members were going to do more to disarm both sides, he instructed the black miners to start hiding guns and ammo down in the mine. Jeb recognized that the weapons in the arms room were disappearing and confronted him one morning when he caught the colored man carrying two silver dinner buckets out of the ammo room.

"You takin' your meals during target practice now?" Jeb set the big sack he was carrying on the ground.

Big Henry turned toward him but kept his silence.

"You fixin' to pay for those weapons you're hiding in your dinner buckets?" Jeb continued. He wanted to make light of the situation but still make his point.

"Hell, Mistuh Boss Man," Henry said, "after paying for black powder at the company store, I ain't got enough script left to buy supper for a mine canary. I figure the coal company at least owes colored folks a means to stay alive."

"There's a whole passel of grits over yonder," Jeb said with a nod toward the potato sack he had been carrying. "And it's my job to keep you boys alive."

"It'll take a heap more than the likes of you to get that done," Henry said. "Two or three of us are disappearing every week, and I don't see any of them getting' on no trains, do you?"

Jeb didn't know how to answer. Not only had

the number of Negroes been dwindling, but since Tom Downs became sheriff, several more coal company guards had resigned.

"All I got to my name is my knowin' how," Henry said after an awkward silence. "And so far, I knows how to keep white folks from killing me."

"There's a colored fellow from back east wants to talk to you boys about forming an organization called the Afro-Anglo Mutual Association," Jeb said. "He wants you boys to lobby the state government to ensure that black and nonunion miners receive the same protection as union men."

"Talk to us *boys*?" Big Henry raised his head and stuck out his chin. "Garfield's children are *boys*. When whites talked to Indians, they called them *warriors*. Talk won't do no good until whites start thinking of us as *men* and not *boys*."

Jeb looked off toward the town for several moments and pondered the meaning of the colored man's words. "That sky's a fixin' to bust loose directly," he finally said as he ascended the mine tipple steps.

***

A week later, the Afro-Anglo Mutual Association met in Douglas Eubanks' office to prepare for a visit to Springfield to meet with Governor Tanner. The small, bespectacled Rev. Horace James paced rapidly in front of the table where Eubanks and Howard Smithson sat puffing on thick cigars while he talked constantly. Since Big Henry hadn't been offered a chair, he stood in front of the table trying to keep up with the conversation and stay out of the little man's way as he paced.

The reverend had an energy that made Big Henry nervous. He remembered their first encounter the day of the tornado, and how the pastor had encouraged a truce with the union. That had been just days before the first battle with the United Mine Workers. Any trust he had of the preacher's ability to negotiate had faded with those first gunshots.

Jeb arrived to the meeting late. When Eubanks offered him a chair, he declined and stood next to Big Henry.

"We will, of course," James was saying, "make an appeal to the governor to keep the state militia in Pana for the duration of the conflict."

"Let him know," Eubanks said with a wink to Smithson, "that if he doesn't, there will inevitably be consequences."

"And it would be good," James continued, "for us to explain that Negroes, being United States citizens, cannot be legally restrained from migrating to another state to obtain gainful employment." The reverend suddenly stopped pacing and pointed a slender finger at Big Henry. "Do you have anything to say, Big Henry?"

"I don't like folks who are always shootin' off their mouths," Big Henry growled, "always wrasslin' 'n a-wranglin'. If youse got something important to say, then say it straight. I see your lips moving but don't understand a damned thing that's coming from betwixed them."

Smithson's chair skidded backwards on the wooden floor as he leapt to his feet and glared at the big miner. James, with a wave of his hand, ushered him back to his seat. "No, Mr. Smithson," James said with a smile, "Big Henry and I have a stormy history, but I think he will be just fine as my aide-de-camp. However, do you think we might find him a suitable set of clothing?"

"Wait a minute there, Reverend," Big Henry interjected. "I never agreed to go to this meetin' with youse."

"You'll do what you're told, boy!" Eubanks shouted.

Boy? Jeb immediately realized why Big Henry had objected to the use of the word. He stepped forward. "Gentlemen, may I speak to Big Henry in the hallway for just a moment?"

Eubanks waved the hand that held his cigar, crossed one leg over the other and turned his face toward the window.

"Henry," Jeb said when they were alone, "you must go to that meeting."

"You bein' downright unreasonable. I ain't no

speaker, Mr. Jeb. My fists do my talkin'."

"Well, you can sure talk bullshit about catfish, Big Henry. And you're smart enough to steal guns and hide'em in the coal mine, ain't ya?"

"Things bad enough around here, Mr. Jeb. Now you gotta team up with that preacher fella and ride double saddle. Well, I'll go if you want me to, Mr. Jeb, but I ain't sayin' nothin' lessen they insults me. And if they do that, I might just put an extra hole in their noses." Big Henry walked to the office door and put his hand on the doorknob. "Boy, that Devil sho' is busy today."

***

Myrtle and several of the other women labored for an entire day attempting to put together a set of proper clothes that would fit the gigantic frame of Big Henry. When he tried the suit on, his broad shoulders immediately split the seams. They were about to give up when the door to the Alabama Hotel burst open.

"Why, I declare, it's that Cahill gal," one of the older ladies said.

Fanny May set the large package she carried on a table and began unwrapping it.

"Haven't you hooked a man yet?"

"I ain't engaged," Fanny answered, then decided if she offered up a lie it might keep the peace. "but

I's keepin' steady company."

"Hummf, fancy that." The woman put her nose in the air. "Well, you'd best be catchin' one while the bait's fresh."

"Just slither back under that rock where you came from, you ol' biddy." Fanny pulled an extremely large suit jacket from the wrappings and proudly held it up.

"How in the world did you get this?" Myrtle put her hands on either side of her open mouth.

"Compliments of O'Hara's Store," Fanny said. "I won't be havin' my Big Fist Henry Stevens standing in front of ol' Gov Tanner looking like no low-life jigga-boo."

"Hush now, Fanny May," Myrtle scolded, "we don't talk that way 'bout our own."

***

When Governor Tanner learned the spokesman for the Afro-Anglo Mutual Association would be a minister, he requested a local pastor attend who he was told had an interest in labor strife. Though Tanner's own sympathies often leaned toward the workers, he thought that since his Bible knowledge was a little rusty, he might need some theological backup.

After introductions were made, the Governor and Rev. Jacob Walsh took seats on one side of the big conference table. Since no chairs had been placed across from them, Rev. James and Big Henry stood facing the two white men.

"Governor," Rev. James said when the meeting began, "your refusal to permit laborers to be brought into the state under guard is a virtual declaration of war against the United States and is a violation of the National Constitution. Negroes, being citizens of the United States, cannot be legally restrained from migrating to another state. The continued lawlessness in Pana is attributed to your refusal to permit additional Negroes to be imported to Pana."

"I'll admit," Tanner replied as he leaned back in his chair, "that the Illinois Constitution does not contain any direct authority for me to use state troops to prevent the importation of labor, but the desperate conditions at Virden and Pana required drastic measures. I am willing to accept that responsibility."

"The fact that these Negro laborers were once slaves," Rev. Walsh interjected with his elbows on the table and his fingers interlocked, "does not detract from the calling of the free worker today to submit, but emphasizes this calling even more strongly. If slaves had to submit for God's sake, how much more, workingmen today, whose circumstances are in any case far better than those of slaves? First Timothy Six says, "Let as many servants as are under the yoke count their own masters worthy of all honor."

"And the scripture also says," Big Henry's deep baritone voice suddenly filled the room, "'muzzle not the ox that treadeth out the corn.'"

The mouths of the three men fell open. They tilted their heads back to look up at the giant.

Preacher Walsh turned red. Though a man of immense girth he leapt to his feet and shouted, "Colossians three, twenty-two says, 'Servants, obey in all things your masters according to the flesh!'"

"Deuteronomy twenty-four, fourteen says," Henry said calmly, "'you shall not oppress a hired servant who is poor and needy, whether he is one of your countrymen or one of your aliens who is in your land, in your towns.'"

"James five, one," the preacher screamed, "says something about the description of the godly conduct of the worker is, 'he doth not resist you!'"

"Leviticus nineteen, thirteen," Henry countered, "says exactly, 'you shall not oppress your neighbor, nor rob him. The wages of a hired man are not to remain with you all night until morning.'"

"Titus two, nine." Walsh gasped and wiped his chubby cheeks with a handkerchief. "'Exhort servants to be obedient unto their own masters.'"

"Deuteronomy twenty-four, fifteen," Henry said, "'you shall give him his wages on his day before the sun sets, for he is poor and sets his heart on it; so that he will not cry against you to the Lord and it become sin in you.'"

"S-so you can read," the preacher said, returning his wipe to his breast coat pocket. "All you have proven is that you are a credit to your race."

"No, I can't read at all," Big Henry said. "Maybe that's why the passages are more to me than just letters and words. Now, why don't you sit down and shut up?"

Rev. Walsh fell back into his chair, and all three men stared up at Big Henry.

"Would you two pastors please allow me to speak to Mr. Stevens privately for a moment?" Tanner asked, suddenly realizing he had been wrong to invite Rev. Walsh to be part of the discussion. Cora would have been outraged if she had been present to hear the disgusting man's views.

Walsh and James looked at one another, then rose and left the room.

"Please sit down, Henry," Tanner said. When the big Negro didn't budge or change his defiant expression the governor brought two chairs around the table. This time when he motioned with his hand the two took the seats facing one another.

"Governor, I agree there's time when a scab ought to have his head knocked off his shoulders," Big Henry began without being asked to, "but first the union should try to talk to him like a brother. If a black man were allowed to be a member of the UMWA, he would pay a dollar a month to the coal miners' union, and the UMW would use part of that money to help the streetcar strikers. But if they catches that same black union man ridin' in a street-car, he gets fined twenty-five dollars. Is that all right?"

Tanner nodded. He couldn't take his eyes off Big Henry.

"If I kill you," Big Henry went on, "everybody says: "Henry Stevens, a Negro, kilt a white man. Now, I got a little Indian blood in me, but that wouldn't count. We are standing here right now in Springfield, Illinois, Abraham Lincoln's town. But there's only eight mines out of twenty in Sangamon County where the white miners let a Negro work. If I buy a house right next to the mine gates, that won't do no good. Only white men digs coal there. I got to walk a mile, two miles farther to where the black man can dig coal.

"The United Mine Workers is one of the best or-gan-IZ-a-tions there is," Big Henry stood before continuing. "United means union, and union means united. But they's a lot of mines been runnin' for years, and the white man never lets the Negro in. If they's a cause to strike for, I'll strike. I'd live in the fields on hard corn for a just cause. Yes, sir, for a just cause, I'd live in the fields on hard corn."

After a long silence, Tanner also rose. He reached up and placed a hand on Big Henry's massive shoulder.

"Henry." Tanner rose up on his toes so his eyes were almost level with Big Henry's. "I want you to know that I was the only governor in the United States to allow colored troops and colored officers to fight in Cuba. Those Negroes fought gallantly for their flag and country. I shall never rest until I see your people achieve equal rights in this great country."

Big Henry pondered the governor's words. He was aware of the black troops that fought in Cuba and had heard that even some white southerners had said those Buffalo Soldiers were a credit to their race. He thought about how he would have reacted if he'd been called to duty for the country.

"I'd 'spect," Henry said slowly, "them colored soldiers had to do a lot of forgetting befores they picked up a gun for this here United States."

"How so, Big Henry?"

"I'd spect that before I faced death to defend that flag, I'd have to forget a lot of things. I'd have to forget that when I got home from the war, I'd have to ride the train in a Jim Crow car and eat my meals standing up in the kitchen instead of in the fancy dining car with the white folk. I'd have to forget that if we followed the white man's rules and won a place in government like them coloreds did in Wilmington last November, we'd be chased, shot and lynched, and the democratic rights we fought for and won would be stolen from us. Yes, Governor, them colored boys you sent to fight surely do have bigger hearts than I's got. They fought for that flag with the hope that white men would pay attention and maybe tell others back home how the black man deserve to be treated as more than just a servant." Big Henry paused for a new breath. "Well, Governor, I ain't no man's servant, and I ain't dying for no flag that don't stand up for my rights."

Tanner's shoulders drooped. He placed his finger tips on the back of the chair and pushed it under the conference table.

"I have met with Sheriff Downs," Governor Tanner said quietly, his eyes toward a nearby window. "He assures me that he will do an honest and fair job of protecting all the citizens of Pana, including the black population."

Big Henry stared at the governor. "Then God help us all."

***

The conversation taking place in the hallway between the two ministers was not quite as civil.

"Damn." Rev. James growled. "I know the Bible from the conception to the resurrection, and don't need no nigger-loving governor giving me the bum's rush."

"There are Negroes in our southern Illinois mines who have joined the United Mine Workers," Rev. James stated in an attempt to calmly rationalize with the pastor. "They actually get along quite civilly with the white populace."

"Well, maybe your niggers are a little higher on the monkey scale down that way, Preacher," Rev. Walsh hissed quietly so as not to be heard by the people passing through the hallway. "We've had a few jigaboos that can be trained to act civilized, but then soon as our backs turned, they's right back to actin' like savages. No, sir, I figure our society has higher standards than to allow Africans to be members."

Horace James was a civil man who had practiced passive resistance his entire life. His vocabulary had won him many battles during his long career.

"Did you know, Rev. Walsh, that during the slavery days, Pana was a sanctuary for runaway slaves?" James asked. "Isn't it ironic that in that very city in this modern age, the descendants of those slaves are now being held in servitude by capitalist coal companies?"

"Why, my good Rev. James." Walsh put his face closer to the black man and continued, "did you know that Pana stands for People Against Nigger Associations? Now, why don't you take that big ape in there and go back down to the Alabama Coon House and tell those scabs to get the hell out of the white man's town?"

"I tell my congregation that inside every man there are two sets of twins fighting a constant battle," Rev. James answered. "One set is called love and hope. The other is hate and evil." He took off his glasses and looked deep into Walsh's eyes. "Do you know which set of twins will win, Reverend? The ones you feed."

18

Toby Eubanks had been checking his willie at least once a week since he was five. That was the year he'd watched his father wrestling the upstairs maid. Since both adults had all their clothes off, Toby had chosen to remain hidden in the bedroom closet until one of them won the tussle. The maid was a heavy set Mexican woman, but Toby's father finally managed to throw her and pin her against the bed. He knew the woman's English wasn't very good, because she kept calling his father God and yelling "Rapido! Duro!"

The thing that disturbed Toby was not that the two were wrestling naked, but rather that his father's wee-wee was so big. It looked to the five-year old as if it had grown to such a size that it was about to burst like a balloon.

That experience had started Toby on a lifelong pursuit of the weekly inspections. Even after he'd become a teen and learned from other boys the copulation purpose of his willie, Toby checked often for growth and even used girls' pictures in the Sears magazine to practice some of the techniques the other boys so often discussed. Now, at close to twenty years of age, he still took a peek between his legs now and again when he went to the outhouse.

Despite his frequent inspections, Toby wasn't overly concerned that he was different from other boys in this respect. After all, no one but he knew of this deficiency. The thing that bothered him most was that his father didn't seem to think of him as an adult. Time after time, Toby was given menial tasks that a child could perform.

Therefore, it came as a complete surprise to Toby when one evening after dinner his father ordered him to take some papers over to the Springside Mine. Such assignments were normally carried out by the company guards or, if the papers were important enough, by one of the hired gunman. Toby felt that his time had arrived. As he departed the house and approached two of the guards who stood at the front gate, he paused for a moment to light a cigar. He rubbed a match hard against a column to the wooden fence but it broke. a second try brought the same result. One of the guards pulled a match out of his shirt pocket, and with a quick movement against his trousers, lit it and held it up for the young Eubanks.

Toby leaned forward into the flame and puffed his cigar lit.

"Much obliged, Bert," he said, and then struggled to stifle a cough. "I'm just gonna run these important papers over to Springside. I'll see you boys in a little while."

Toby Eubanks walked into the darkness of the moonless night, whistling a merry tune. That was the last thing he remembered until he woke up the next day on Dr. Mills' examination table.

***

STRIKERS ATTACK MINE OPERATOR

Myrtle glanced at the headline again and tossed the newspaper onto the counter behind the dirty dishes. Just an hour earlier, she'd read the article to her husband and Big Henry before she left for work at Harrison's Restaurant. She saw Carole Felix, the cook, pick up the paper and start reading it. Myrtle wondered what a white lady like Mrs. Felix would think about the incident, but knew better than to ask.

"Hard to believe even union boys would beat up a nice fella like Toby Eubanks," Garfield said when his wife finished reading the story aloud.

"Doubt that they did," Big Henry said. "Jeb Turner thinks Boss Eubanks had his own son bushwhacked so the governor would keep the troops in Pana."

"He had his own son whooped?" Garfield said. "Boss Eubanks is sure one determined man."

When Mrs. Felix finished the article, she folded the newspaper neatly, set it on one of the dining tables, and began sweeping the kitchen floor. Myrtle liked the older lady, even though she'd only known her a few days. The two had hit it off well enough when it came to idle chatter, but Myrtle was still not bold enough to talk politics. She spotted a swarm of big reddish-brown bugs fleeing down the sink.

"Your restaurant is full of cockroaches," Myrtle said.

"So is every other place in this God-forsaken town," Mrs. Felix said.

"Yes," Myrtle said, "but your cockroaches are bigger than in the other places."

"That's because my food's better," Mrs. Felix said. "Now get started on those dishes. We'll be getting customers soon as the noon hour whistle blows."

"Where's the soap?" Myrtle asked.

"Soap?" Mrs. Felix said with a laugh. "Just pour a little of that moonshine in the dishwater. But don't let much of it get on your hands or they'll turn as white as mine."

That evening Myrtle was putting on her hat and coat to leave work when she heard soldiers marching on the street. When she opened the door, Mrs. Felix and her husband rushed up behind her in time to watch a large contingent of guardsman filing down the street toward the rail yard. There came a mixture of cheers and heckles as union men came out of saloons and houses to taunt the soldiers.

"The militia is leaving!" someone yelled.

"Now, by God," one of the union men shouted from the street, "We'll be able to give them scabies what fer!"

***

A few nights later, two black men stood toe-to-toe in the Sunrise Tavern, swaying in a drunken stupor while a dozen of their fellow miners looked on with indifference. Fights were a normal part of every evening. This one had been brewing since the Negroes' first week in Pana when Ike Alexander had accused Lindsey Duncan of being one of the coal company cronies.

"I whacked ya cause you lied to us back in 'Bama," Ike said. "You knew they was bringin' us up this a way to be scabs."

"Up 'til now, we been passing the time kinda pleasant," Lindsey Duncan said, "but I'd 'spect those knuckles on my jaw spoilt that associatin'."

"I'm kinda ever so good with a gun, don't you see?" Ike said. His bragging was what had provoked Lindsey's wit, a wit that historically caused many a confrontation, especially when combined with good corn whiskey.

"Well, sir." Lindsey put one hand on the pistol beneath his belt. The other hand held a bottle. "I ain't carryin' this gun for balance."

"I got the strength of a blacksmith," Ike said, puffing his chest. "You ever shod a horse?"

"No," Lindsey said. "I never even pointed a gun at one."

"Well," Ike said, stumbling back a step, "maybe I shod you before. You got ears like a jackass."

"Well, that's better than being one," Lindsey said. He slowly drew his pistol from beneath his belt. "I'll not be kilt today, I'm thinkin'."

Ike's gun was out of his belt. The blast tore a big scarlet hole right into Lindsey's chest and slammed him flat up against the wall. His eyes and the veins in his forehead looked like they were going to bulge right out of his head. His body gave a violent jerk as he dropped to his knees. The pistol in his hand was pointed toward the ground. It gave a blast that kicked up chips of wood. Somehow, he stayed upright and walked three steps forward on his knees, cocking and firing another shot into the floor with each spasmodic movement. He finally fell, his face making a loud thud when it hit the floor. Ike aimed his pistol and placed one more bullet in the back of the dead man's head.

"Well, I guess you was thinkin' wrong, Duncan." He spat on the floor, adding, "Anyhow, I promise not to kill ya no more today."

There was a mad scamper as a dozen patrons of the tavern rushed out the door. Those that remained were too drunk to care.

"Why, he died real nice, I'd say," Ike said, then drained his shot glass. "How 'bout another whiskey, barkeep?"

Quits Simpson stumbled forward and squatted over the body. "W-why, t-this fella got shot right through the whiskey bottle," he stuttered. "T-to make it worse, the bullet went through his heart, too."

**

"After a killing," Sheriff Downs was quoted in the newspaper the next day, "all the Negroes knows the dead but none of 'em knows the killer. There are no witnesses to the murder of Lindsey Duncan."

The article went on to state that the colored strikebreakers displayed no signs of morality. To prove his point, the reporter provided a long list of fights the blacks had provoked since they'd arrived in town the summer before. He went on to point out that in several instances, Negro men openly made unwanted advances toward white women.

Many will remember that Negro

strikebreaker Garfield Wallace assaulted a female store owner last September. Complaints have also been made against a black brothel being run in the upstairs of the Sunrise Tavern. The tavern is owned by Horace Cowan, a man who himself came to Pana as a strikebreaker during the 1896 strike.

Some of the Pana residents sided with the Negroes. One of them was Rev. Collins, who presided over the funeral proceedings the next morning.

"Since the governor withdrew the National Guard," Rev. Collins said at the graveside of Lindsey Duncan after he'd finished the prayer, "young union men with no legal authority are roaming the streets and alleys of Pana searching for Negroes and shooting them randomly. Our sheriff and his deputies do nothing. They have put our city into the hands of cowardly, irresponsible and bloodthirsty mobs. Further, every day more union men are being brought into Pana from other communities with the intention of running the Negro out of town. This week I will join a committee of Pana citizens that will travel to Springfield to make one more appeal to the governor to return the troops. God help our community if he refuses.

Now, I would like to invite the friends of Lindsey Duncan to say a few words if they so wish."

When no one stepped forward, Myrtle gave her husband a little shove with her elbow and whispered. "Your friend'd be wantin' at least one prayful thought from his friends, I'd 'spect."

"I'd say amen to that." Garfield whispered back, fidgeting from one foot to the other. His voice came louder and shriller than he intended. "Well, Lord, here he is. As far as I know Lindsey ain't never leant his teeth to no meat he ain't never shot his self or paid for."

Myrtle shook her head and rolled her eyes. Then she heard Big Henry's deep voice speak up from behind her.

"Lord," Big Henry said, "I hope you'll give ol' Lindsey a little extra consideration before you make a final up or down decision. I know I ain't earned many pluses on your tally book, but I'd be obliged if you'd give ol' Lindsey any points I do have. I reckon I'll deserve whatever punishment you want to give me, but I think ol' Lindsey oughta get a second look."

When no one else spoke, Myrtle took Garfield's arm, piercing his skin with her nails. He gave a quiet squeal as she led him back down the hill.

"Was that the best thing you could think to say about Lindsey Duncan?" Myrtle demanded when they were out of earshot of their friends. "You've known him for nigh on twenty years."

"Well, what I said was the gospel truth, I tell you." Garfield said. "Lindsey told me that his own self."

19

Henry Stevens had finally had enough. Over two dozen Negroes were in the city lockup for everything from burglary to making advances toward white women. Many had accepted the United Mine Workers offer to return to Alabama, and had not been heard from since. April tenth was a wet, dreary day. Big Henry was in a melancholy mood. He decided to go talk to his jailed friends and find out if they were all right. Knowing the deputies would refuse him visitation, he circled around to the back alley and looked in through the cell window.

"Why it's Big Henry hisself, come to visit us." Bucktooth Daniels stuck his hand between the bars. "By grannies, put 'er there."

"What in Sam hill you been doing, Bucktooth?" Big Henry said, shaking the man's hand. The rain started coming down faster, so he stood closer to the building to be under the eave.

"Why ol' Quits was just showing me how to make a silk purse out of a sow's ear," Bucktooth said. "He' fixin' to leave tomorrow on the train."

"I never meant no such a thing. I'll join up with you directly. I done told you that," Quits said, growing louder with every word. "I can practical guarantee it! I'm just hungry, that's all. There's nothin' I'd like better than a greasy mallard duck right about now."

"Okay, okay, I heared already," Big Henry said. "Now don't talk so loud. How they treatin' you men?"

"Oh, they's just the orneriest people you'll ever meet," Bucktooth said. "That Deputy Cheney's got some fearsome temper, all right."

"You fellas need anything?" Big Henry asked. A loud clap of thunder sounded behind him.

"I want you to go fetch me some vittles," Quits said. "Something that will fit in betwixt these here bars. If I get some good vittles, I might stay."

"Quits is a might backwards, some say," Bucktooth whispered then turned to his friend. "That there ain't your fault though, Quits."

"Smarts don't make no never mind," Quits said. "The most importanence thing is—"

"Would you quit palavering in my ear and let me do some figurin'?" Bucktooth spun toward Quits to interrupt, then looked back through the bars at Big Henry. "You fixin' to get violent, Big Henry?"

"Seems to be the times require it," Big Henry echoed the words he had heard from Jeb Turner. "But I'm sorrier for that than you'll ever know."

"Then get us outta this here lockup, and let's get it did."

"Get away from that window!" a voice yelled from the entrance to the alley. "Them are jail birds, and they got nothing to say to the likes of you."

Bucktooth and Quits jumped away from the window just as a streak of lightening flashed across the heavens. The wind began to pick up and the sky transformed into dark, swirling, thunderhead clouds.

"These miners don't want to go back to 'Bama." Big Henry turned toward the deputy. "If they go missin', I'll be comin' for you, Cyrus Cheney."

"By God, you ain't threatenin' me, nigger!" Cheney shouted.

A flash of lightning reflected off the silver revolver. Big Henry dove behind an empty beer barrel. The first bullet the deputy fired split through the wood. Something stung like a bumblebee against Henry's neck.

Two more deputies ran up and started firing at him. He pulled his own revolver tucked under his belt. Raising it, he fired two quick shots over the barrel toward the men, and then ducked low as he ran to the end of the alley and turned quickly behind the protection of the building.

A dozen men and women stomped through the muddy street toward the nearest doorways. He was about three blocks from the safety of the Eubanks

Company Store, but he needed to cross the street. Blood ran down beneath Big Henry's shirt, so he decided he'd better get to the other side while he still had the chance. At a full sprint, he crossed the road and dove behind a horse trough just as he heard more gunshots and the buzz of bullets passing near him.

A union man he recognized as Xavier Lecocq stepped out from the door next to him with a pistol aimed at his head. "Drop it, Big Henry," Lecocq said with a French accent.

Big Henry was setting his gun down on the ground when Lecocq's left eye socket exploded in a gush of blood and gray matter. Before the man's body hit the ground, Big Henry sprinted along the boardwalk toward the Eubanks'. He didn't slow as bullets tore into walls. Windows shattered all around him. Just as he crashed into the company store door, knocking it off its hinges, a bullet ricocheted off a pewter plate and hit the heel of his boot, the force of which spun Big Henry to the floor. Seeing no one in the establishment to help him, he stumbled to his feet and raced up the stairs and into the storage room.

A few moments later, angry shouts sounded from outside and below. The rain grew heavy, pounding the tin roof with such power it silenced even the thunder and loud cracks of lightning.

Big Henry's neck wound sprayed blood like

a fire hose. Trying to pinch it shut with his fingers, he began to feel faint. Finally, with both hands around his bloody neck, Big Henry stood and walked toward the stairwell. When he tried to shout that he was coming out, he found he had no voice at all. Tossing his gun down the stairs, he struggled to move on weakened legs. The last thing he remembered was the world spinning, and then he was rolling end over end.

***

With Big Henry arrested, none of the Negroes knew who to follow. Garfield was one of the miners who tried to offer a calm and thoughtful decision, but he was vastly outnumbered by those who were in favor of confronting the union men.

"Let's end it now!" Ike Alexander shouted. He had been itching for a fight for weeks and had been working hard to convince his friends that they could win a direct assault on the union men.

The streets outside the stockade were filled with men stomping through mud as they hastily gathered horses and hooked them to buggies. Women and children rushed out of houses and buildings carrying small valises. After fleeting hugs and kisses, the union men slapped the horses on their rumps and watched until their families were safely on their way out of town.

Jeb surprised even himself by the anger he felt toward the white community he'd known his entire life. Since the day several weeks before when the National Guard was removed, the blacks had been harassed, beaten, and arrested. It seemed that every day, two or more disappeared from Pana. He didn't know if it was because they were running away or because they were dead and buried. Rumors of the latter fate abounded, including stories of a mass murder and disposal of two dozen black bodies around the time of last October's gunfight in Virden, Illinois.

None of the white security guards tried to stop them when hundreds of blacks began helping themselves to weapons in the coal company arsenal. That was when Jeb got word that the entire Eubanks and Smithson families had left town on a train for Chicago. He called his men together under the tipple to tell them the news.

"If any of you men want to skedaddle, no one is going to blame you," Jeb told the white guards. The rain had slowed to a drizzle, but water still trickled from their hat brims.

"What're you gonna do, Jeb?" Mert Whitmer asked.

Jeb hesitated. He didn't want to live the rest of his life with a guilty conscience for having influenced another man to get himself killed defending scabs, much less colored ones. Still, he had grown to respect the dark-skinned men and women from Alabama. Many of them had not been told they would be strikebreakers until they arrived. They had journeyed to Illinois to provide better lives for their families. Even women of ill repute like Fanny Cahill had come with hopes of escaping the horrible life of the Jim Crow south.

"I reckon I'll finish the job I was hired to do," Jeb finally said.

Several of the guards shook their heads, laid down their guns, and headed for the gates. Others stood their ground, their eyes going from the mine gate to the black miners they had protected for so many months.

"I suppose it won't hurt to provide cover fire for the coloreds from the mine tipple," Whitmer said. He checked his Winchester and began climbing the steps. Several white guards followed him.

Jeb wondered why so many of the men were willing to risk their lives for the Negroes. Was it the money, or were their reasons similar to his own? He saw Garfield standing alone, looking down at his revolver.

"I fear men are going to die today," Garfield said quietly.

***

As Sheriff Downs heard gunfire coming from the

Eubanks mine tipple, the mine gate opened wide and five hundred heavily armed Negroes rushed into the streets firing their weapons.

Tom joined the mad rush of picketers hurrying through muddy roads to seek cover. Men dropped all around him, only to be lifted up and carried by fellow union men. The gunfire was at first behind him as he ran, but then a hail of gun smoke and shots from the United Mine Workers in front of him ended the assault by the charging Negroes. They, too, began seeking shelter as they picked up their wounded and hurried behind buildings and outhouses.

After that, most of the constant barrage of gun-shots seemed to come from second floor windows and the mine towers, as both sides tried to snipe the other from the high ground. Tom found him-self squatting in an alley between two buildings along with several of his deputies. He heard the rumbling of thunder in the distance as the storm began moving further away. The responsibilities associated with his new job was weighing heavy on his mind. He was just now realizing that the decisions he would soon make might affect the entire town for generations to come.

"Sheriff!" Holiday yelled as he limped towards them, "I been lookin' all over for you. The union boys is fixin' to hang that big nigger for killing Xavier Lecocq. One of 'em nearly broke my leg when I tried to stop 'em."

"This is getting out of hand," Tom said. "Can't those boys think of another use for a rope? The governor will be sending the militia back. We need to stop that lynchin'."

"Hell, I ain't riskin' my neck for no scab nigger," one of the deputies said. "I'd just as soon help hang him myself."

Several other men nodded their agreement. Knowing he would have to act alone, Tom ran out of the alley, followed by a slowly hobbling Holiday. Staying close to the walls of buildings, the sheriff worked his way toward the jailhouse by going from one doorway to the next. He arrived just in time to see a badly beaten Big Henry being dragged out of the jailhouse. The black man was barely conscious and blood ran down both sides of his face. Though the shouts of anger from the union men was loud, it was almost drowned out by the screams and shouts of protest coming from the two dozen black men behind bars within the building.

"This is my prisoner!" Tom shouted. "You men are needed back at the mine gate."

"We're fixin' to hang this nigger first!" Cyrus Cheney shouted.

"Looks to me like you're just tryin' to avoid the gunfight!" Tom shouted. The union men grew quiet. "What's wrong? You boys would rather lynch a defenseless nigger than help your fellow United Mine Workers fight your battle for you?"

"I'll show you fightin', by God," Cheney said. He and the other men dropped Big Henry and hurried in the direction of the gunfire.

**

When Jeb ran through the mine gate alongside the Negroes, he had no idea the battle would be so intense. He couldn't bring himself to fire his gun at his friends and neighbors, but he still felt the need to stay near Garfield. At first, when he saw union men running away from them, he thought they were going to abandon the fight. Then came the bombardment of return fire from a second wave of picketers who had been in the buildings.

Garfield stumbled and went down. Jeb grabbed his arm and led him to shelter behind an outhouse.

"I'm all right," Garfield said. "Just tripped over my own big feet."

Jeb took off his hat and peered around the corner of the building. Small groups of men from both sides were running from building to building, trying to outflank and outnumber their enemy. Six Negroes crawling under a barbed wire fence were suddenly pounced upon by about thirty union men. Only a few shots were fired before each of the black men were wrapped up in the barbed wire and escorted off toward the jail.

Afterwards, two of the men who had been in on the capture walked off toward Frank Cogburn's house. Since Frank had resigned, he was neutral, but many of the union men still blamed him for his father's actions when he had been the county sheriff.

"I'm gonna go to that house, Garfield," Jeb said.

"Why for, Mistuh Jeb? You's oughtened not be out in the open like that."

"I have to go. My friend lives there."

"Then, I'll be goin' with you. You's my friend, too."

After the two union men rounded the side of the Cogburn barn, Jeb and Garfield raced across the yard to the front of the house.

"Frank!" Jeb yelled. "It's Jeb Turner. Can I come in?"

"Come on in, Jeb, but leave the darkie on the porch."

Jeb looked at Garfield, who nodded and ducked down behind the porch swing. When Jeb entered the home, Frank stood at the open back door looking out toward the mine gates.

"The niggers are trying to get the wounded back into the stockade," Frank said.

"Frank, you need to get away from that door," Jeb said. "I saw two union men sneaking around the house."

"Oh, hell, those boys ain't mad at me," Frank said. He stuck his head out the doorway again. "Look at them colored boys run."

A bullet hit with a dull thud against the door behind Frank's head. At first Jeb thought it had missed his friend because he remained standing for several seconds. When he dropped to a knee and then rolled backward onto the floor, Jeb could see by the gaping hole in his forehead that he had died instantly.

Jeb rushed to the doorway and fired a shot at two men fleeing the scene. Just then a series of bullets pelted the walls of the house, causing Jeb to drop and cover his head with his arms. These shots were coming from the mine tipple. When he looked up, Garfield stood at the front door, his revolver at the ready but his eyes wide with fear.

***

Myrtle stood in front of the kitchen window doing the dishes at Harrison's Restaurant when she heard the first gunshots coming from the direction of the city jail. Carole Felix heard them too, but that didn't stop her from preparing food for the noon meal.

"Land sakes," Mrs. Felix said as she continued slicing pies, "there they go again."

Myrtle had a bigger pile of dirty dishes than

usual. She scrubbed faster as she listened. Gunshots from the direction of the Eubanks mine was what would put her in a panic. At this time of day, her four boys would be playing in the mine yard with the other children, but her husband would be standing guard at the gate.

A few minutes later, the shooting stopped and Mrs. Felix interrupted Myrtle's dishwashing to have her clean tables and sweep. She continued to listen, but only heard the wind and rain and thunder and lightning. Just as she was about ready to return to the dirty dishes, the storm stopped, but all hell broke loose in the direction of the Eubanks coal mine. Myrtle didn't even take time to remove her apron. Ignoring Mrs. Felix's screams for her to come back, she dashed out the back door.

"Land sakes, Myrtle," the cook yelled, "you didn't even finish the dishes!" Mrs. Felix watched the colored lady sprint across the road and toward the gunshots.

"My goodness," Mrs. Felix said as she watched her, "those people can really run."

She picked up a jug of moonshine and was pouring it in the dishwater when a bullet broke the glass window and struck her in the shoulder. Her husband rushed in and knelt at her side. He placed a towel over the flesh wound.

"That Myrtle didn't even finish the dishes," Mrs. Felix said.

***

The hair on the back of Tom Downs' forearms were becoming patchy and the bared skin red. Big Henry was growing annoyed by the sheriff's habit of sucking on his own arms. He wished he would just roll his sleeves back down and look out the window of the train. Downs was clearly distressed. The doctor that had treated Henry's neck had scolded the sheriff as if he were a school boy.

"You'd better get this man out of town before they lynch him," Doc Mills warned as he bandaged the wound.

"I don't care what they do with this scab," Downs said, though he held a shotgun toward the jail door.

"Well," Doc Mills said, rubbing his hand through his moustache, "the governor will hold you responsible, you know."

Twenty minutes later, Henry had found himself in the passenger car of the train watching a wide-eyed Downs sucking the hair off his arms.

"Where you takin' me?" Big Henry asked.

"To the jail in Taylorville," Downs said. "It's the county seat and the only place you might be safe."

"Why you care what happens to me?"

"I don't," Downs said. "But if I get you out of town, maybe the fighting will stop."

"Fighting?" Big Henry's head was still spinning and his thoughts fuzzy from the beating.

"When your Africans heard you were arrested, they charged the town."

"Charged the town?" Henry shook his head. "How many?"

"All of 'em."

***

Despite gunshots all around and bullets buzzing past her head, Myrtle held her skirt high so as to not impede her legs as she raced across the open ground toward the mine gate. She sensed that the puffs of smoke coming from the mine tipple was meant to provide her with cover fire. When she got near the gate, it opened and then immediately closed behind her.

"Where my boys?" she asked the first man she saw. Before he could answer, a guard nearby was spun toward the ground from a bullet to the side of his head.

Myrtle took a loud, deep breath. Next to the steps to the mine tipple were five bodies laid out on the ground covered by gunny sacks. Rushing to them, she quickly threw the covers off each face. Relief was followed immediately by sorrow. Three of them were lifelong friends from Birmingham. First, she recognized Hank Turner, Louis Hooks and Jimmy Jones. Another was Charles Watkins from Georgia. The last was Julia Dash, wife of a black miner and a woman Myrtle had heard sometimes worked the Sunrise Tavern as a prostutute. Myrtle said a quick, silent prayer and tried to not think ill of any of the deceased.

"Your husband is still in town," one of the white security guards told her. "He's with Jeb, so I reckon he's okay."

"My sons?"

"In the stockade room with the other children."

Myrtle hurried inside the building. The sight before her made her feel she were in a dream. While gunshots rang in the distance and bullets ricochet off the outside of the stockade, two dozen children inside the building were in a circle, holding hands and singing "Ring Around the Rosie." The cots had been folded up along the walls except for those holding seven wounded Negro miners and Mert Whitmer, the young white security guard.

When her boys spotted their mother, they broke the circle and ran to her side.

"Mommy," her youngest son asked, "why are people throwing rocks at the building?"

***

After laying Frank Cogburn out on his davenport, Jeb and Garfield went out the back door. They carefully made their way through the town, looking to see what had become of the Negroes who had scattered during the assault. Keeping their backs close to the buildings, they darted from one safe area to another, their guns at the ready. Near the ballpark where the National Guard had bivouacked, they found about fifty strikebreakers huddled together in a series of sheds that lay between a barn and a hen house.

"Get down, Mistuh Jeb!" Ike Alexander hissed in close to a whisper. "Those union fellas knows we's here and sent for reinforcements. We getting ready to make a break for the mine yard."

"Don't do that, Ike," Garfield said. "We just came from that way. They got a hundred sharpshooters just waiting for you to make a try for the gates."

"What we gonna do then?" Ike asked. He looked to Jeb.

"You can fight it out here but I'd 'spect they'll flank you," Jeb said. "I think you'd have a better chance with the sheriff and his deputies. Best we split. Head for the jailhouse as best you can."

"Turn ourselves in?"

"I know Sheriff Downs," Jeb said. "He don't much like scabs—and coloreds even less—but I think he won't want a massacre. He'll probably arrest you and find a place to hold you 'til you can have a fair trial."

The talk among the Negroes commenced immediately. Some were for fighting, but many others for turning themselves in. Jeb was about to suggest a vote when the matter was decided by gunshots and a full scale attack from hundreds of union men. Jeb stood and raised his arms. Garfield and the other blacks fled the barnyard, many of them dropping their weapons so they could quickly skirt the wooden fence.

The union men ignored Jeb as they raced past him, firing as they advanced. Those Negroes who didn't make it to the fence in time were given a blow from the gunstock of each man who passed them. By the time Jeb was able to follow the pursuit, he had to step over several of the dead or wounded.

He reached the jailhouse in time to see Deputy Holiday Jones standing on one leg while holding an injured one off the ground. He was clutching a shotgun that was level with Cyrus Cheney's stomach.

"There won't be no lynchin' today, boys," Holiday said. "Least not 'til Sheriff Downs gets back."

The lynch mob laughed and started moving toward the jailhouse. Holiday fired off a shot into the air, and the union men froze in their tracks.

"I still got a barrel left for you, Cyrus Cheney!" Holiday yelled and gave a maniacal cry.

"Well, that ain't exactly true, Holiday," Cheney

said. "I think you accidently shot off both barrels."

Holiday's eyes moved from his shotgun to Cheney and back again. He lowered the weapon. "Oh, well, in that case, go ahead and take 'em, boys."

A thunderous shout of approval came from the union men as they charged the jailhouse. Then, from above their heads came the sound of a Gatling gun firing into the upstairs windows of the jailhouse. Every man on the street and in the jailhouse fell flat on the ground. The National Guard had arrived.

***

"Where the hell are you, Sheriff?" Governor Tanner shouted into the telephone speaker.

"I'm in Taylorville with a prisoner," Tom said. He hated telephones. It was so hard to understand what the person on the other end was trying to say when you couldn't see them. He hated it even worse that everyone within a block of the general store could hear everything he was saying. Customers had stopped shopping in order to listen in on the conversation.

"There's at least seven people dead and more than two dozen wounded in Pana!" Tanner screamed into the mouthpiece. "Six of the wounded are innocent bystanders. Now, why in the hell would you leave your post to save one man? You had two hundred deputies to help protect him!"

"My deputies were fixin' to help *hang* the man, not *hinder* it!" Tom said loudly, putting emphasis on each word for dramatic effect. "I thought that if I got him out of town, it would calm things down."

"Well, you were wrong." Tanner was beside himself. "I had to send the militia back to Pana to stop the killing spree."

"You oughtn't not have done that," Tom said, though he wasn't sure why. He found himself clutching the receiver to his ear so hard his ear hurt.

"I ordered them to disarm everyone, including your deputies," Tanner said.

"You oughtn't not have done that, Governor," Tom repeated. "T'weren't our fault. T'was the coal company and them scabs that broke the peace."

"Well you just get back to Pana as fast as—" Tanner's voice cut off and Tom hung up the receiver. When he saw that a dozen people who had been gathered around the store counter suddenly went back to their shopping, he vowed right then to never use one of those damnable talking machines again.

***

Over two hundred National Guardsmen supervised the disarming of Pana. By the time Jeb and the Negro strikebreakers started walking back toward the stockade, there were hundreds of weapons lying on the street in a big pile. The deputies, though, refused to give up their arsenal until the sheriff returned. They retreated into the jailhouse. The two dozen coloreds being held in the city jail were released. Bucktooth and Quits joined Garfield and quickly related the story of Big Henry's jailhouse visit and the subsequent gunfight.

"Where do you suppose they took Big Henry?" Bucktooth asked.

"I don't know, but I'm hungry," Quits said. "You suppose Myrtle could cook me up some vittles when we get home?"

When they entered the mine yard, a roll call was being taken. It ended with over thirty Negroes unaccounted for. Jeb joined others reporting the names of a few they had seen on the ground either killed or wounded. A few were believed to have fled the town, a fact that seemed to be verified a few moments later when a contingent of union men approached the mine gate. They produced Ike Alexander, who was bound, gagged and dressed in women's clothes that were much too small for his massive frame.

"Here's one of your brave scabby friends!" a union man shouted. "We caught this coward sneakin' out of town dressed as a woman. He didn't get away, though, 'cause we smelled the nigger on him."

When Ike was brought into the stockade and untied, he tore the dress off and threw it on the ground. He had a gaping wound on his shoulder near his neck.

"They made me put on these damned clothes!" Ike shouted. "Yeah, I was leaving town all right, but not like this. I got caught by a farmer when I was trying to get a couple of eggs out of his hen house. Damned peckerheads nearly pecked me to death."

"I believe Ike," Jeb said. "It's an old war-time lie to claim that a man dresses up as a woman to escape a battle."

"I'm obliged to you, Mistuh Bossman." Ike nodded at Jeb and allowed Buffalo Butts Bertha to lead him over to where she was in charge of a group of women who were taking care of the wounded.

"Where are the rest of our miners?" Jeb shouted through the open gate at the union men.

"Probably halfway to Alabama, I'd 'spect!" the union spokesman shouted back. "Or to hell, where the rest of you scabies will be if you don't get out of town. The United Mine Workers will pay the train fare if any of you want to leave. Otherwise, you can take the consequence." The union man turned and headed back towards town.

The next day, over one hundred Negroes left the stockade before sunrise and boarded the train going south.

20

Tom Downs said little to Rachel when he returned to Pana the day after what the residents were calling "the big trouble." The next morning he didn't think to sharpen his straight edge. He wanted badly to do something normal, but found he couldn't even handle the simple task of shaving. First, he made a mess of the kitchen table when he tried to mix the soap in the ceramic bowl. Then when he patted the lather on his face, he got it all over his best Sunday shirt. His first stroke of the blade on his cheek drew blood that ran down his neck and streaked through the white lather.

"Damn," he said. Holding the razor in front of the mirror, he saw his hand was trembling.

Rachel came up behind him, gently took the blade, and began sharpening it on the long, leather strap hanging from the back of the chair. Tom held a wash rag against his wounded cheek.

"Why are nights so tough when we go through rough times?" Rachel asked. She leaned forward and began shaving the opposite side of his face.

"Too much time to think, I suppose," Tom said.

Because he'd woke up in a cold sweat so many times, he had shared with her his recurring nightmare. In the dream, it was always his father who fired the shot that killed Tom's Uncle Joseph.

"He was a no-good scab, Tom," his father said in the dream, then handed the shotgun to him. "Your brother is a scabby, too."

Tom's brother Matthew stood looking down at their dead uncle, expressionless. When Matthew raised his head, Tom raised the shotgun and emptied the second barrel.

"That was for the good of the many, son," his father said. "Don't never forget that."

After learning of the dream, Rachel said, "But your brother drowned in the river when he was eight." They were sitting on their porch swing the morning that he told her. Children were running around the neighborhood playing kick-the-can.

"He drowned because I let him," Tom said. "We had built a raft, and when Matthew took it out in the water to test it, I threw rocks at him. He slid off the end of the raft. I just stood there and laughed at him while he was screaming for help. I figured he could just swim back to shore. When he went under, he never came back up. I guess an underwater tree branch grabbed hold of his clothes or something."

"Your pa's brother died in the mine from a rock fall," Rachel reminded him.

"Yes, but he was strikebreaking," Tom said. "I was standing on the picket line with Pa when Uncle Joseph went to work that day. Pa cussed at him and told him he'd kill him one day. My pa wouldn't even go to his funeral and he wouldn't let me and Ma go neither."

"Why do the United Mine Workers have to kill the strikebreakers, though?" Rachel asked.

"Cause no one can figure out any other way." Tom nodded toward the children playing in the neighbor's yard. "I guess it's for them."

He sat in his rocking chair for two days after the "big trouble," just staring out the window. The city council had relieved him of his duties pending an investigation of his conduct during the riot. In his misery, he counted the dead over and over. Though he hadn't seen him die, he imagined his childhood friend Frank Cogburn's head exploding in a great gush of brain matter and blood.

Rachel knew better than to do more than bring him food and drink and news of the strike when he asked for it. She stayed near him in the house, though, going about minor cleaning projects she'd always put off.

The mines were working again but with a much reduced labor force. Every train heading south saw Negroes boarding with their families. Most were heading back to Birmingham at the expense of the United Mine Workers. Others paid their own way to Weir, Kansas, to see if they would have better luck at strikebreaking in those coal mines.

"Are conditions so bad in Alabama that the Negroes would take a chance on getting into another mine war in Kansas?" Rachel asked Tom. When he just shook his head and continued staring out the window, she went back into the kitchen to make supper.

It seemed that ever since the massacre of the blacks from the boxcar, her husband had self-doubts. Now he'd made another difficult decision. Even the union men didn't seem to know what to think of the sheriff's conduct during the riot. Some thought the abandonment of his post during the battle was cowardly. Others claimed he had done what was in the best interest of the union. Preventing the lynching of the leader of the blacks kept some public sentiment on Tom's side.

The events in Pana, Illinois, on April tenth were the headlines in every newspaper in the United States. Most of the blame, however, was placed on either the coal operators for refusing compromise or on Governor Tanner for withdrawing the National Guard. All the stories mentioned Sheriff Tom Downs' as a factor to one degree or another in the violence.

Then, on the morning of the third day, Tom Downs' reputation was vindicated from an unexpected source. One of the Negro men heading back to Birmingham told a reporter there had been a planned assassination attempt on the life of the sheriff. The story quickly blossomed into an honest lawman going up against a powerful corporation.

With the pressure off her husband, Rachel insisted he accompany her to Frank Cogburn's graveside service. She'd already prepared for the occasion by donning the black dress with leg o' mutton sleeves she always wore to funerals.

"You need to go, Tom." She laid out his frock coat with the pocket square already neatly in place. He looked at the suit but didn't move from his chair.

"Everyone liked Frank," Rachel said softly. "This sad day may help the community heal the wounds from the divide between union and non-union folks. Please go with me."

As Tom drove the surrey into the cemetery, the funeral procession was just arriving from the Methodist church. A long line of pedestrians was followed by dozens of buggies, many of which were pulled by mules or draft horses.

A much larger graveside service was just dismissing from the Catholic Church area, where Xavier Lecocq was being buried. Only a few of the pro-union crowd left that service to walk over to participate in Frank Cogburn's. As that crowd approached, a half dozen National Guardsmen intercepted them and quickly checked the men for weapons. The soldiers then turned toward Tom.

"I'm still the county sheriff, officer," Tom said when Captain Gibbs approached him.

"The governor's orders are that all weapons in Pana be confiscated," Gibbs said.

The group of union men who gathered immediately behind their sheriff included Holiday Jones, the man who'd humiliated the captain with a good licking several months before.

"The operators tried to have our sheriff assassinated," Holiday said, "or haven't you heard?"

"Disarm this man!" Gibbs barked the order, his jawline quivering. Two soldiers stepped on either side of Tom, and one reached inside his suit coat and withdrew his service revolver.

The union men shouted their disapproval and stepped forward. Tom halted them with a raised hand and they grew quiet.

"I'm here to say goodbye to my longtime friend, Frank Cogburn," Tom said. "I'll not be needing a weapon this day."

Ira Cogburn stepped out of the crowd from the non-union side and walked slowly up to the man who'd once been his son's friend. The sheriff and the former sheriff stood eye to eye. Cogburn raised his hand. Tom shook the hand of the man whom he'd beat during the past November election.

The crowd quietly turned and gathered around the grave, union supporters on one side and non-union on the other. Later, after the casket was lowered into the ground and the mourners began to depart, Rachel took her husband's hand and led him back toward their buggy. When she saw Jeb Turner passing nearby, she moved so they would intercept him.

"Hello, Jeb," Rachel said.

"Rachel." Jeb tipped his hat and looked at Tom.

After a short hesitation, Tom held his hand out and the men shook.

"Where's your mount?" Rachel asked. She sensed that Jeb had something he wanted to say to Tom but was slow to come up with a way to start the conversation.

"I'm afoot today," Jeb said.

Rachel looked at her husband.

"Hop in," Tom said, his face expressionless.

Tom gave Rachel a hand getting up into the back seat of the surrey, then joined Jeb in front. He gave the whip a quick flick. The tasseled snapper clicked just above the sleepy mare's ear, and she pulled the buggy at a slow gait along the grassy lane. Rachel hoped the two would have something to say to one another. Due to the slowness of the mourners exiting the cemetery in front of them, they had plenty of time to think of some sort of conversation. When they finally passed through the cemetery gate and the mare broke into a trot, Rachel took a chance.

"Jeb," she asked, "whatever will happen to that young black girl you saved?"

Since they'd left, Jeb had sat quietly with his head lowered. But he suddenly couldn't seem to get comfortable in the buggy seat. He raised a foot and rested it on the buckboard. Tom glanced over at him, but remained silent.

"I suppose she'll go on back to Birmingham with the others," Jeb said.

"Did you get to know many of the coloreds very well, Jeb?" Rachel asked.

"I suppose so," Jeb said. "Some of 'em are right fine folks."

"Were you friendly with any of those who were kilt?" Rachel asked.

"Sure," Jeb said. "A few, I guess."

"We killed so the killing would stop," Tom said suddenly. "And yes. It was easier to do because they were niggers."

"Do you always start punchin' before you get hit?" Jeb asked. He shook his head to clear the strange notion.

"I don't understand it myself." Tom continued quietly. "All I know is that things are a little better for working men today than they were yesterday. I really don't know what will happen tomorrow, but I believe that without the United Mine Workers of America, we wouldn't have much of a chance, would we?"

"I don't know that, Tom," Jeb said. "I really don't know what tomorrow will bring."

"Well," Tom said, "at least now we'll have a chance to find out." The mare suddenly fought the reins. The sheriff flicked her on an ear with the whip. "This darn draft horse is fine for pullin' a plow," he complained, "but put her behind a carriage, and she just wants to head for the barn."

The three rode the rest of the way home in silence.

21

"The Springside Mine was abandoned last night for lack of workers." Douglas Eubanks announced to those Negroes who still remained in Pana by the first day of June. "No miners are to try and get past the picketers to get back in the mine yard. My mine will absorb those of you who worked the Springside Mine."

"Mistuh Jeb, did they get the mules out?" Garfield asked that evening as the two stood guard duty at the top of the Eubanks mine tipple.

"Why, no Garfield. I suppose they're still down in the mine."

"They's got someone to give 'em feed and water, don't they?"

Jeb hadn't thought about the mules and he was certain that neither had the mine owners. "I'm sure that the Smithson's have taken that loss into account."

Garfield didn't say much the rest of the night. With the escape tunnel that connected the two coal mines flooded from heavy spring rains there was no way to save the animals. The next evening he couldn't seem to stop talking about the mules.

"It's too bad old Swain Whitfield disappeared last December." Garfield told Jeb. "That old fella had plenty of faults for sure but he loved his mules. Why, I remember one time back in 'Bama, they was fixin to shoot a stubborn mule named Haw because it wouldn't do no work. They tried everything. They fed him green apples and dates but nothin' would make ol' Haw pull a boxcar. So the day they was fixin to shoot Haw, Swain thought he'd give that mule one last treat before his demise. He gave Haw a shot of whiskey and a plug of chewin' tobacco. Why you know what happened? That dang mule then and there walked right backwards into the harness. Swain hooked him up and danged if that ol' Haw didn't become the best tobacco chewin', whiskey drinkin' mule in the coal mine. Yes sir, Mistuh Jeb, I can still see that animal walking through them tunnels drippin' tobaccy from his mouth."

The next night Garfield reported to Jeb that he had heard the baying of the mules from the airshaft.

"I'd 'spect they's outta hay by now." Garfield lamented. "I wonder if they'd be able to kick down their stalls and help themselves to some o' them oats and hay that's in the chamber next to them?"

"No, I'd 'spect not." Jeb said. He was getting a little irritated with Garfield's constant jabber about the mules. Then it crossed his mind that the animals were probably out of water as well without someone to open the faucet from the pipes that ran down from the surface. His sleep was restless that night for the haunting baying of the mules in his dreams.

By the third day the long, mournful wail from the mules could be heard echoing through the chambers by those Negroes working closest to the Springside escape tunnel. Every miner that passed the flooded area paused for a quick prayer for the starving animals.

When the next night Garfield didn't report to the mine tipple for guard duty Jeb sent for two replacements. After they arrived he went looking for him. He had a pretty good notion where he'd find the colored man. When he approached the air shaft building he spotted the outline of a man silhouetted against the moon bright-sky.

"That you, Garfield?" he whispered.

Tom Downs stepped from the shadows and leveled a Winchester toward him. The sheriff had a long rope coiled over his shoulder and a mining cap with an unlit oil wick lamp attached.

"What you doing here, Jeb?"

"I might ask the same of you."

His old friend looked more embarrassed than homicidal, so Jeb walked up to him and stood directly in front of the gun barrel. Tom lowered the weapon.

"Bein' you're the law I doubt you're fixin' to do any lynchin' with that rope." Jeb said.

"I was down to the crick coon huntin'."

Jeb had no reason to disbelieve him. Many hunters wore miner's lamps when hunting racoons and carried a rope in case they needed to retrieve a coon that refused to fall from a tree after being shot. Then he noticed a second rope tied around a wood beam was draped down into the air shaft. Without hesitation he reached and took the cap and light from Tom's head.

"What you up to?" Tom asked.

"I'm fixin' to lower myself down this air shaft to that stairwell. Then I'm gonna go give them mules enough hay and water to last a few days."

"You do and I'll shoot you, Jeb Turner." Tom raised his Winchester again.

Jeb took a match from his pocket, lit it with a quick rub on his trousers and held it to the oil wick lamp. When he placed it on his head the flame from the lamp reflected a smoky glow toward Tom's face causing him to block the light with an extended palm.

"Get away from that airshaft!" he yelled.

Jeb took a firm grip on the rope and repelled into the darkness. Twenty feet later his feet touched down onto the wooden stairway. He had only taken a few steps downward when he heard Tom drop behind him.

"Doin' some explorin' there, Sheriff?"

"I'm fixin' to arrest you, Jeb."

Jeb spotted an oil lamp on the wall hanging from a nail. He removed the lamp on his cap and used the flame to light the lantern. Handing it to Tom, he returned the lamp to his cap and continued on down the steps. The sheriff ran off a long series of swear words but held the lamp at arm's length as he followed down the long spiraling stairwell.

When they reached the first level of the mine they had to travel through the narrow tunnel for a half mile until they came to another stairwell. By the time they descended those steps both men were breathing hard and Tom's cursing was becoming less frequent. At this point they saw a lighted lamp hanging on a wall and another about a hundred yards after that.

"Who's down here?" Tom asked. He had left his Winchester so he could descend the rope, so now he drew his service revolver. No sooner was it drawn than a loud bellowing of mules echoed through the tunnel.

Jeb was pretty certain that Garfield was somewhere ahead of them. The rope hanging down the air shaft had been the first clue, but now the lighted lamps seemed to confirm it.

A few minutes later they emerged into the big chamber that housed the cage elevator. From one of the three tunnels came a dim light. Jeb recognized that this was also the source for the sad braying of the mules. Both men ran to the stables where they found Garfield Wallace lying completely still against a wall.

Jeb quickly bent over him and raised his face from the rocky ground. The Negroes eyes opened but his eyeballs rolled counterclockwise as he tried to regain consciousness. Tom took a canteen that was hanging from the stable gate, removed the cork and splattered water onto Garfield's face. After a few minutes he sat up. The miner looked at the two white men then gave his head a hard shake.

"One of them ungrateful mules kicked me with both feet." Garfield said.

"How do you know it was with two feet?" Tom asked.

"Cause I gots hoof marks on both cheeks of my ass." Garfield rubbed his buttocks. "I don't know how a blow down there woulda knocked me out unless my wife is right and that's where my brains is at."

"Your head's bleeding." Jeb said. "Musta kicked you right over the gate and into the wall."

"Head don't hurt but my ass sure does." Garfield tried to get up but fell back down.

"Just stay put for awhile." Jeb said.

"And when you can walk you are both under arrest." Tom said. He still held his gun.

"Well, in the meantime give me a hand feeding these mules." Jeb took a hay hook from the stable gate and held it out to the sheriff.

"I ain't assistin' in preservin' no company property!" Tom shouted.

"Mistuh Sheriff," Garfield looked up. "This here mine war is about done with. I'd 'spect your union boys'll be comin' back down here soon and if'n these critters is dead that'll mean more money the company will spend on mules and less on men."

"Why you riskin' your life for a damned animal?" Tom asked.

"Them mules didn't ask to be caught up in this mine trouble." Garfield said. "I suppose I kinda knows how they feels."

Tom Downs holstered his gun, then stood looking down at the ground. He took the hay hook from Jeb, jabbed it in a bale of hay and threw it into the stable with the mule that had kicked the Negro.

22

"I'm sending the boys back to Birmingham to their auntie's house," Garfield told Jeb two months later when the Pana coal companies announced they had come to an agreement with the United Mine Workers. "Myrtle and I are goin' with the others to work the Carterville mine down in southern Illinois."

"Big Henry's trial is coming up soon," Jeb said. "You don't want to testify for him?"

"I reckon there's enough evidence to keep the judge awake." Garfield said. "Besides, you think they'd listen to a colored man in them lily white courtrooms?"

"No, I guess not," Jeb said. "Besides, they're only charging him with assault. I reckon he'll only get a year or two hard labor."

"Ain't no hard labor in no northern prison gonna damage Big Henry Stevens," Garfield said.

***

"You boys are now working for the St. Louis and

Big Muddy Coal Company," Samuel Brush said to the one-hundred-twenty Negro miners gathered at the Pana train station. He was dressed for riding in a tweed Norfolk jacket with a pair of box pleats over the chest and back. His matching knickerbockers with knee-length stockings and sturdy riding boots made his affluent appearance complete.

"I founded this company in 1893," Brush said, "and two years ago we dug more coal than any company in Illinois. My miners were making more money than any of them had ever dreamed of, but they got greedy. When I bought this company, coal sold for one dollar sixty-three cents per ton. After the panic that year, it dropped to eighty-two cents per ton. We had to drop wages, but the United Mine Workers didn't understand that. They demanded we raise the wages.

"I'm not going to lie to you boys. I brought some Tennessee Negroes to Carterville a year ago but they chickened out, turned their back on me, and joined the union. I offered them the same as I'm offering you, fair wages and a chance to live in the company houses I built a mile north of Carterville. I call the town Dewmaine, but you'll also be hearing about Union City, where the UMW built ramshackle sheds for the coloreds that betrayed me.

"I've been told that you Negroes are well

acquainted with firearms. Therefore, when you get on the train you will be given weapons to defend yourself should it be necessary. Don't worry though. My coal mine is protected by hired gunmen and a Gatling gun. You'll be safe."

Garfield looked at Myrtle and the small number of wives who had chosen to remain with their men rather than return to Alabama with their children.

"This time it's going to work," he reassured his wife.

"Why did you choose Carterville instead of Weir, Kansas?" Myrtle asked.

"Why should we pay our own way to be strike-breakers in Kansas when Brush will take us to Carterville for free and protect us on the way?"

Garfield's confidence in Brush's ability to safe-guard their travel was reaffirmed when the train pulled out of the Pana train station. He and the other Negroes were handed brand new Colt revolvers and a dozen bullets each.

***

Five hours later, the train rolled into a small town called Lauder for a regular station stop. The passengers grew nervous when they sensed a larger than normal contingent of people around the platform.

"You'ems just turn this train around and head

back where you came from!" a voice shouted from outside the train. "Dis here's a union mine."

When they recognized the warning being shouted by a colored man, the miners on the passenger train jumped to look out the windows. The shock they felt when they saw over two hundred black men standing in a wheat field aiming guns at them was quickly replaced by anger.

"What you colored boys doing?" Garfield yelled at them. "We's all black folk in here."

"Don't matter!" the leader yelled. "You ain't United Mine Workers, so you ain't working these here mines!"

"Move your sorry black asses!" Brush shouted out the window as he pointed his revolver at the leader. "We'll run you over if you try to stop this train."

The train lurched and began moving. The gunshots coming from the wheat field were immediate and so intense the men on the train didn't even have time to duck. Two dozen of the men gazing out the windows were struck. The blow from the hail of bullets caused some to be spun to the floor. Others remained standing, a look of shock on their faces. Garfield was one of these. He felt a sting against his right shoulder. When he looked down toward the wound, he saw Myrtle's face looking up into his eyes, her mouth open as she screamed his name. Then he was on his back on the floor of the passenger car, looking up at the ceiling, his wife lying half on top of him, one leg over his as it often was as they slept at night.

***

Garfield awoke in a small room with wallboards running vertically. A light-skinned black man in a suit had his back to him and was bent over what appeared to be a medical bag. When he found what he wanted, the man turned around and smiled at his patient.

"You an Indian?" Garfield asked when he saw the man's round face.

"Half Cherokee, half Negro. I'm Doctor Springs and you are in one of the company houses."

"Where's my wife?" The doctor's somber look horrified Garfield. "Where's Myrtle!?" he shouted.

"She is in the next room, Mr. Wallace."

Dr. Springs didn't try to stop him as he sat up. He helped Garfield to his feet, put an arm under his and led him into the adjacent room. Myrtle's body was lying on a table, her eyes shut. She looked at peace.

"The boys picked out a nice spot in the cemetery for your wife." The doctor put a hand on the grieving husband's shoulder.

"I'll be layin' her to rest back in Bama with her own." Garfield gave a great gasp as his words became reality.

All that night, Garfield sat in a chair at the kitchen table next to his wife. His memories became dreams and his dreams turned into the most wonderful conversations with Myrtle.

"You're just the down rightest, ornery-most, next-to-nothing critter I ever did see," Myrtle told him.

"Why, I'm a ring-tailed bear cat," Garfield said to the spirit. "That's what I am, for sure, I am. Now why don't you just get on up there to Heaven before the good Lord changes his mind about takin' ya?"

"Oh, I already done eyeballed that whole she-bang up yonder," Myrtle said. "I know near ever' tree and gulley."

"So, why you stickin' 'round here for?" Garfield said. "You're just badgerin' me, that's all, ain't it so?"

"You off your feed, husband? You're lookin' a might peeked."

"I got shot, woman. Can't you see?"

"I'm here to tell you to forget about that hole in your shoulder, you ol' coot." Myrtle replied. "It's a long way from your heart, you know."

"Oh, it don't hurt none." Garfield's eyelids fluttered with the lie. "Not one particle."

Garfield had his head on his wife's cold hand and was smiling when he heard the gunshots. Raising his head, he looked at Myrtle's face and tried to make himself believe she was just sleeping. He'd never told her how much he loved looking at her profile when she was sleeping.

"Your wife must have been a wonderful person." Dr. Springs said. He was reclined on an old cot near the fireplace. He rose. Producing a flask and a small tin cup from his coat pocket, he poured a shot of whiskey into the cup and handed it to Garfield.

The hooch burnt Garfield's throat and coated his empty stomach with fire.

"Where's them niggers that kilt my wife?"

"They're picketing the coal mine. You'd better stay away from there. If you open that shoulder wound again you'll bleed to death."

"I'd swing at the end of a rope for just one minute with them scallywags."

"You may swing anyway." The doctor said. "They're saying your colored strikebreakers massacred a whole parcel of white folk up there in Pana."

"When poor people kill its murder," Garfield said. He released his grip on Myrtle's hand and began stroking her forehead. "When rich people kill it's called justice."

"The hurt goes away," Springs said. He placed a hand on Garfield's shoulder as the bereft husband began crying tears onto his wife's cheek. "But not the love, Garfield. Not the love."

"My arms ache, they feel so empty." Garfield

said between sobs. "Why them coloreds down this a way stickin up for the white folk?"

"Well, sir," Doc Springs stuck a finger in his ear and gave it a hard scratching as he gathered his words. "The way I see it, both the union and coloreds in Carterville had strong leaders who were willing to talk. It's my understanding that those in Pana were mostly inclined to fight."

"I'd say that's right possible." Garfield's thoughts were cloudy. He thought of Big Henry's temperament and Tom Down's hate for coloreds as well as strikebreakers. He remembered the dead faces of men he had known for years. He bent over and kissed Myrtle's cold lips that were growing grey and stiff.

Then the front door burst open.

"Garfield!" Ike Alexander shouted. "We were on our way to work, and hundreds of union men turned us back."

"Were the coloreds with 'em?"

"Some were."

"How far to this Union City where the colored unionists live?"

"Not far," Ike said. "Why?"

"Tell the boys to burn the bastards out."

That evening, Union City went up in flames like dried kindling. Only a few women and children were seen as they fled the flimsily built homes and ran for the safety of Carterville. Within minutes, the heat from the buildings became so intense the Pana miners were forced to regroup along the road that led toward the coal mine. Suddenly, from behind them, came gunshots. They turned to see an army of mostly colored union men emerge from a clearing. Being evenly matched, the two sides rushed toward one another, firing as they ran.

As he got closer to the enemy, Garfield wondered if he might already be dead. While bullets kicked up the turf around him, he paused to look back. Men who had been on either side of him had fallen, but he had not been struck. Wishing for a death that would reunite him with his wife, he raced toward the unionists. When he reached their line, one of the enemy pointed his gun just inches from Garfield's chest, but it misfired. The black man turned and ran into the wooded area behind him. He was followed by dozens of others.

"Let the niggers kill each other!" a white union man yelled. With rifles leveled at the strikebreakers, he and several others walked backwards in the direction of Carterville.

Feeling betrayed by his own kind, Garfield had a blood lust he'd never felt before. He ran like a mad man into the wooded area after the black unionists. Other Pana strikebreakers followed. The fighting lasted for hours, and was so spread out throughout the woods, no one was certain if they fired at friend or foe.

By the time the sun came up the next morning, blood had run out of Garfield's shoulder wound and along the side of his body into his boot. The squishy feel of his sock only made the strange world around him even more surreal. Little streaks of yellow sunlight filtered between the brown and green branches of the trees. Spots of scarlet reflected off tree trunks, and here and there black men hung like strange fruit from ropes in the trees.

Garfield found himself separated from the others. He leaned against a big rock, sweating profusely. He had no feeling anywhere on his body as he watched a white-tailed fawn move slowly among the carnage, grazing on green leaves speckled with red that had once been a man's lifeblood.

"Garfield," a familiar voice whispered.

"Yes, Myrtle?"

"Garfield."

"I hear you, Myrtle."

"Garfield."

"I'm comin', Myrtle," Garfield said. "I'll be along directly."

"Look what a mess you made of this forest."

"I didn't mean to, Mother." Garfield fell to his knees and sobbed.

"Garfield," a man's voice echoed softly. It sounded like Mr. Eubanks.

"Yes, sir, boss. I'm listening."

"Your boss needs you, Garfield."

"Yes, sir, boss. I'm coming."

"Why are you going to him, Garfield?" Myrtle asked.

"'Cause my boss needs me."

"But do you need him?" Myrtle answered.

23

The smell of spring rain arrived an hour before the first sprinkles. That gave Jeb plenty of time to smoke, drink whiskey, and remember. The pond that Fanny Cahill had once swam naked in was as still as a mirror, making for a perfect reflection of the blue sky and white clouds. Rumor was that Fanny was leaving town. His imagination began to run wild. First came morbid thoughts. She being held down, raped and beaten. She would have no one to protect her. Not him nor Big Henry. Then he dared to fantasize about taking her up into the Rocky Mountains, away from anyone who would be repulsed by the idea of a white man with a black woman.

When the rain finally arrived, it came slowly and lightly, so Jeb did little more than adjust his hat until it passed. A rainbow tried to take hold in the east, but petered out after only a few minutes. Rachel had always liked rainbows. Once, when she, Jeb and Tom were walking home from school, she had seen a rainbow between the branches of the trees. She squealed like a Comanche and bolted for a clearing. When the boys caught up with her, she was lying on her back in the grass using a hand to trace the colorful spectacle through the sky. Jeb was pretty certain that was the moment both he and Tom fell in love with her. It was little more than a year later that Rachel's umbrella got *accidently* between Jeb's legs when the boys were fighting. From that moment on, she was Tom's girl.

Langford's pond was the one peaceful spot he could enjoy on his off days. For several more hours, he watched the sun set toward the hills and turn the pond gold. When it dropped below the tree line, enough rays filtered through to make the color of the pond pass from a light to a dark green. That's when the horizon seemed to light up like a prairie fire.

Jeb had a good-sized stack of cigarette butts at his feet. It seemed all his life was in that pile. Hard times and good times alike. The whiskey reminded him more of the hard than good. Rachel was with Tom. Fanny would soon be gone. He thought about trying to talk to Fanny. Maybe a conversation would somehow magically turn into the right words and a solution that would allow them to be together.

Jeb was getting yawny when he was startled by the clanging bell of Langford's milk cow approaching from across the pond. The brown jersey eased down to the edge of the water for a long drink. The union boys had got together and bought Langford the cow after his had been assassinated by the *dirty six*. Despite the temporary truce during Frank Cogburn's funeral, there still wasn't much friendliness between the United Mine Workers and those who had sided with the coal company. Jeb thought it had been mighty nice what the union boys did for Langford—as well as for many of the Negroes whose train fare was paid back to Alabama. Sometimes he imagined what it would have been like if he had sided with the United Mine Workers. Maybe then he would've had his childhood friend Tom to share his troubles with.

In the distance, Ora Langford made a yodeling call. Ora was a prize-winning yodeler at the county fair, and also often called square dances. The baggy sack beneath the cow swung from side to side as she ran toward her evening milking. The chiggers would be biting if he stayed in the grass much longer. Jeb's knees cracked when he staggered to his feet and headed toward his pony. It was grazing passively in the little glen where Fanny May Cahill had once swam.

***

Jeb didn't have much more time for visits to the pond for the next few weeks. When the last of the Negro strikebreakers left Pana, most of the company guards were let go. There was so much animosity toward the coal company owners, Jeb was asked to remain on as Howard Smithson's personal bodyguard. Some of the more radical union men were not given their jobs back, causing threats of violence against the Eubanks and Smithson families. Jeb believed that Howard had a good reason for not wanting to hire back the men who had nearly lynched him back in September. Still, those same men who had put a noose around his neck were now saying that if they were given a second opportunity, Howard Smithson would swing.

The unpleasant task of bodyguard was made more difficult when Howard decided to finally marry his longtime sweetheart, Mary Andrick. Tension was in the air on the day of the wedding. The bride was radiant in a white gown, its fitted bodice lined with pearls and the flowing velvet skirt covered in lace.

Jeb didn't know all the guests, since many had come from out of town. They were all aware, however, of the many threats against the groom. Therefore, when the lights went out during the ceremony, there was much screaming and diving to the floor. Jeb pulled his gun from beneath his suit jacket and ducked down next to the bride and groom. Several frightening moments passed until one of the company men announced that the newly-installed electrical lighting system had failed.

Later that evening, the wedded couple boarded the train bound for their honeymoon in Chicago. While he stood on the train platform waiting for the all-aboard, Jeb lit a cigarette.

"Got another one of those, deputy?" Fanny Cahill walked up behind him.

"Ladies don't smoke in public," Jeb said.

"Oh, now I'm a lady?" Fanny moved closer to Jeb than he would've liked. Then she leaned in and whispered near his ear, "That's not what you called me when I stood naked by the pond."

Jeb took a step back. He had thought about this moment and what he would say so many times the planned words were now rolling atop one another in his head.

"Fanny, I, I think you're a, a . . .." Jeb stuttered. "Well, as respectable a sportin' gal as I've ever known."

"You know," Fanny said with a fading smile followed by a slight toss of her head. "I hope in our next life, I'm white and you're black as the ace of spades."

Fanny stepped up on the train platform and entered the passenger car. She was sitting in the back, looking out the window, when he boarded. He walked past her to the white section and sat in the seat facing the Smithsons. For a reason he couldn't fathom, he didn't want to take his eyes off Fanny. He hadn't meant to insult her. Like so many times in his life when he had complicated thoughts, he had become tongue-tied. It was a deficiency he regretted more at this moment than ever before.

The passenger car was nearly empty as the train lurched forward. Jeb expected it might have been because people were aware of the many threats that had been made against Howard Smithson. Still, several dozen well-wishers waved from the train platform to bid goodbye to the happy couple. The Smithsons stood waving to them, and just as they were settling into their seats, a clatter sounded. Howard was the first to dive to the floor, so Jeb grabbed his bride and pushed her down beside him. When Jeb looked up, Fanny Cahill watched him with her hand over her mouth, laughing.

Then he noticed dry rice on the floorboards next to the open window. For the last time in their lives, the eyes of Jeb and Fanny met for just a moment. He joined her in the laugh.

***

It was a new century the day Big Henry Stevens walked out of the Chester, Illinois, state penitentiary a free man. He was met at the gate by Garfield Wallace.

"I'm sure proud to say howdy to you," Big Henry

said as the two old friends shook hands.

"And I'll say it right back to you." Garfield couldn't help himself from staring at Big Henry's knobby red knuckles.

"Fightin' in lockup is the only entertainment I've had this past year," Big Henry explained without being asked.

Then, without a word, they walked along the street to the train station, all the while being stared at by the white citizenry. Once they were aboard and sitting in the colored section, they felt free to speak. As usual, it was Garfield doing most of the talking.

"I married Myrtle's sister, Emily," Garfield said. "After her husband died in the Wilmington massacre last year, she had two boys to fend for. Just made sense we'd marry. I wanted to write and tell you but didn't know if there'd be someone to read it to you."

"I learned a little readin' from a preachin' man who was locked up with me," Big Henry said. "Have you heard from Jeb Turner?"

"Jeb married Rachel Downs after her husband drownt in the Kaskaskia River," Garfield said.

"Tom Downs drowned?" Big Henry asked.

"He sure enough did. He was fishin', and they say a crazy old lady started screamin' that her daughter was drowning. Downs jumped into the water. They say he bobbed for that gal for near on twenty minutes. He must have wore hisself out, 'cause finally one time he just didn't come back up."

"Why'd you say the lady was crazy?" Big Henry asked.

"Because the woman's daughter drownt two years ago," Garfield said. "They say the mama just goes to the river bridge every few weeks and screams that her daughter is drowning."

"Oh, my Lord." Big Henry said quietly.

"But you knows what's even stranger than that, Big Henry?" Garfield leaned his face closer to his friend's. "It was a little colored gal Tom Downs lost his life tryin' to save."

Big Henry and Garfield sat quietly for a few moments listening to the churning of the train wheels.

"Anyway," Garfield finally continued, "after Carterville, the United Mine Workers all across Illinois got the wages they wanted and an eight-hour work day. They also have a union fella servin' as a checkweighman who makes sure miners don't get shorted for what they loads."

"Where is Carterville?" Big Henry asked.

"Down south yonder a ways."

"Remind me to stay clear of that place. Why'd those coloreds down there side with the union?"

"I'd 'spect they just ran down a different road than we did." Garfield looked out of the corner of his eye to see how Big Henry took that comment.

"Maybe we'd a took that road ourselves if the union boys had talked to us instead a killin' us." Big Henry said. He shifted uneasily in his seat. "I had a lot of time to think in the pen."

"There's more time than money in this world. That's a fact for sure," Garfield said, thinking of what little time he'd had with Myrtle. "I suppose, truth be told, there weren't never no trouble in Carterville 'til us Pana boys came along."

"Maybe so." Big Henry nodded. "But angel winged we'd a been if Tom Downs would a had his way."

"I sure do reckon he was a might touched in the head when it came to scabs and colored folk." Garfield stared out the window for several minutes. Finally, without looking at his friend, he spoke softly and slowly. "I joined the United Mine Workers, Big Henry," he said. "I want you to come home with me. I gots a job in a mine only a few miles from Springfield."

"Why not in Springfield?" Big Henry asked. "They have plenty of mines."

"Most won't hire coloreds there yet," Garfield said.

Big Henry's jawline quivered.

The other Negroes on the train ducked down below the windows.

"I really hates to tell you this right now, Big

Henry," Garfield said as he lowered himself in his seat, "but we can't be seen for a few minutes."

"Why for?" Big Henry asked as he ducked down beside his friend.

"Because the trains a passin' through Virden in a minute," Garfield said. "They don't allow coloreds in their town.

Big Henry raised up to where he could look out the window, and was just in time to see a big sign with a few simple words he was familiar with: NIGGER: DON'T LET THE SUN GO DOWN ON YOU!

The powerful black man raised up in his seat and looked proudly out the window. Garfield sat up beside his friend and smiled.

Big Henry Stevens was back.

EPILOGUE

The Negro woman who sat in the backseat of the Ford sedan was sixty-seven years old in 1949. People who didn't know her thought she was in her late eighties. Her body, which had once captivated every man she met, was now thin from malnutrition and disease. She stooped when she walked with the aid of her cane, the result of countless beatings at the hands of many men. Her once magnificent face was as dry and wrinkled as a raisin left too long in the sun.

She had once thought there was nothing that would've induced her to return to the town of Pana, Illinois. She had been content to sit on her porch in Springfield and watch the birds and the squirrels and sometimes her many grand-nieces and nephews. Then the letter had come from Eleanor Burhorn, a teacher in Pana who was writing a paper for her master's degree about the Pana coal miner's strike of 1898 and 1899.

Miss Burhorn asked her ever so nicely to come to Pana for an interview and to show her where many of the events of those terrible days had occurred. Burhorn implored her to help, stating she could find no other Negroes who'd been there. Nor, she said, was there any written record of the black experience during those eleven horrible months when over one thousand of their men, women and children lived in Pana.

"Auntie," her nephew said after he read the letter, "you must meet with this lady. Who else can give voice to what our people suffered during this time?"

She listened to her nephew. In his struggle to obtain a ministerial degree he had overcome almost as many obstacles during his life as had she. She finally agreed to let him drive her the hour and a half to Pana, though she insisted on riding in the backseat of the sedan.

"Were you ever in love, Auntie?" he asked over his shoulder as he drove.

"I suppose maybe, once, long ago."

"Have you ever seen him again?"

"Every night in my dreams. I see him with his shirt off beside a beautiful pond. I see him on a train with me, laughing with me. I reckon that God gives us such sweet dreams so we can see light during nightmares."

"Where is he from, Auntie?"

"From another world, child."

As they cruised past corn fields at forty-five miles an hour, she told him part of the story and became increasingly anxious. "How do we know this Burhorn woman won't twist my words to fit what white folk's want to hear?" she asked. "How can I make her understand how we were treated?"

"She's powerful anxious to meet you." Her nephew insisted. "You are a mighty important lady, Auntie. Your story is as fascinating as any adventure book I've ever read."

"You make me feel mighty prideful, child. But I recollect it weren't nothing like that."

"Do you believe in God, Auntie?"

"No," she said, staring out the window. "I tried religion once. It didn't take. I'd 'spect the world began when I was born and it'll die when I'm gone."

She saw a familiar air shaft chimney where the Springside mine had once stood. Surrounding it was now a tall mound of dirt. Far ahead she recognized the train station. They entered the city limits. A sign in big black letters caught her attention.

"Stop the car!" she shouted. "Turn around. We're going home."

"But, Aunt Fanny, we've come all this way," her nephew said. "How are they going to understand what Negroes went through? You're the only one left who can make them understand."

A tear found its way into the crevice of one of the many wrinkles on Fanny May Cahill's face. "All they have to do is read the sign," she said. "Now turn this flivver around."

Her nephew did as he was told. As he drove back toward Springfield, he glanced through his rearview mirror once more at the large sign that read:

NO COLOREDS ALLOWED IN PANA AFTER SUNDOWN

END

The Sayings of Henry Stevens
By Carl Sandburg (Springfield, Illinois, 1917)

If you get enough money you can buy anything except. . . you got to die.

I don't like meatheads shootin' off their mouths always wrasslin' 'n wranglin'.

The cost of things to live on has gone too high.

They ought to be brung down where they's more equal like with other things.

One summer potatoes was peddled around Springfield here for fifty cents a bushel; another summer I paid four dollars a bushel. Tell me why this is. We got to work to eat.

And the scripture says: "Muzzle not the ox that treadeth out the corn."

Human is human. Human may be wrong but its human all the same.

There's time when a scab ought to have his head knocked off his shoulders.

But first we ought to talk to him like a brother.

I pay a dollar a month to the coal miners' union to help the street car strikers.

It costs me $25 if they ketch me ridin' on a car. That's all right.

Las' Monday night I busted somethin' in my left arm.

I walked, mind you, I walked a mile and a half

down to the doctor's office.

It kep' on swellin' an' when I got home
my wife had to put salt and vinegar on to get
my sleeve loose.

They always did say Springfield is a wickeder
town for women than Chicago.

I see 'em on the streets. It always was an' I
guess always will be.

Fifty per cent of the men that gets married
makes' a mistake. Why is that?

You're a white man an' I'm a Negro. Your
nationality don't make no difference.

If I kill you everybody says: "Henry Stevens, a
negro, killed a white man."

I got a little Indian blood in me but that
wouldn't count.

Springfield is Abraham Lincoln's town.

There's only eight mines out of twenty in
Sangamon County

Where the white miners let a Negro work.

If I buy a house right next to the Peabody
mine that won't do no good.

Only white men digs coal there.

I got to walk a mile, two miles, further where
the black man can dig coal.

The United Mine Workers is one of the best
or-gan- IZ-a-tions there is.

United means union, and union means united.

But they's mines runnin' twenty-five years and

the white man never lets the Negro in.

I remember when we was tryin' to organize we met in barns an' holes. We met in the jungles.

I used to go to all the meetin's them days. Now we meet downtown in a hall.

Now we's recognized by everybody
fur one of the most powerful or-gan-IZ-a-tions in the United States.

I don't go to meetin's nowadays but if they's a cause to strike for I'll strike.

I'd live in the fields on hard corn for a just cause.

Yes, for a just cause I'd live in the fields on hard corn.

ABOUT THE AUTHORS

Kevin Corley   Douglas E. King

Sundown Town is Kevin Corley's third novel on the history of coal mining in Christian County, Illinois. After retiring from a career as an educator, Corley turned to his love of writing as a way to retell the stories he had shared with history students in his classroom. Since to write this novel he would have to speculate on what the African American experience had been in 1898-99 he asked Doug King to co-author with him.

King brought a wealth of knowledge and understanding that enhanced the development of many of the characters. His professional career spanned almost thirty years in information technology. He served the Springfield community as a board member of the United Way and was a founder and president of the Springfield & Central Illinois African American History Museum. He is currently retired and living in Springfield with his wife Pamela. The couple have been married since 1971.